Leah, Mother of Valor

Angelique Conger

Leah, Mother of Valor

Women of the Covenant, Volume 6

Angelique Conger

Published by Southwest of Zion Publishing, 2026.

Copyright

Book Cover by Dar Albert

This is a work of fiction. Similarities to real people, places, or events are entirely coincidental.

LEAH, MOTHER OF VALOR

First edition. January 29, 2026.

ISBN: 978-1946550842

Written by Angelique Conger.

Table of Contents

Scars

Sickness left me weak and lying on my sleeping pallet the day Rachel entered our lives. Mother and a healer had cared for me, mopping my face with cool damp cloths, as the illness raged within me. Mother leaned across her stomach, swollen with my unborn baby sister, to reach my face.

"You will stop hurting soon," she said. "Eila gave me her most powerful herbs to stop the burning."

She dipped her cloth in the bowl sitting near my sleeping pallet and squeezed the excess water out. The rushing of the water returning to the bowl made my head hurt even more.

I put my hand over my eyes and moaned.

"Move your hand, Leah. I cannot set the cloth on your head."

I removed my hand and fell into the darkness brought by the cooling cloth. I moaned. "Hurts, Mama. Hurts."

"I know, Baby, it hurts. You will heal, Jehovah willing. Eila has done everything she can for you now."

She sucked in a grunt and held her breath long enough I wondered if she still sat beside me. "I suspect you will have a sister or brother before the night ends. Pray for me, as I pray for you."

"Yes, Mama."

I allowed the darkness to take me into sleep.

During the night, Rachel pressed out of Mama's body. Only the thickness of the wall separated me from Mother. I lay moaning from the fiery heat in my body as she screamed through the agony of childbirth.

Mother, all her maids, and Eila focused on helping my sister to birth. No one came to soothe the burning of my face with cool, damp cloths. In that time, the burning illness left red blisters on my face and body.

Eila gave Mother a lotion to spread on my blisters after Rachel's birth. Although it soothed the burning pain, it did not prevent the scars that marred my face. Even as a small child, not yet two, those days burned into my memory as deeply as the scars on my face. After that, I never called my mother Mama. She was always Mother.

As I grew older, Father searched for a husband for me. He brought a young man home to meet me.

"Does not Leah have beautiful eyes?" he asked one man.

The young man stared at me, seeing only the scars on my face. "The eyes are beautiful," he replied, "but ..." He ran from the house saying nothing more and never returned.

Other men came to visit, having heard of my beautiful eyes. But none could see any beauty of soul or spirit beyond my scarred skin. No young men. No old men.

I spent hours in my early womanhood years gazing into my polished bronze mirror, smoothing lotion into the scars on my face and wondering how a man would ever want me, hoping Father's words describing the beauty of my eyes would entice a man.

I could not blame my beautiful little sister for the scars. I suspect I would still have these scars even if she had not chosen that day to make her entrance into our world.

Rachel struggled to hide her slim, lithe body from others even in the modest dresses Mother insisted we wear. Even as a little girl, I remember men watching her move through Harran toward the well or the market as she walked gracefully between Mother and me.

As we matured, men struggled to keep their eyes off us. Their eyes followed me until they saw my face. I learned to cover my face with my hair or a tichel to protect me from stares and hateful comments. Rachel seemed oblivious to the stares focused on her or me, and never noticed the ugly remarks whispered behind hands.

One day at dinner, Father surprised us with an announcement. "Your brothers tell me they have other responsibilities with their own herds. They can no longer take my sheep to the well for water."

Our married brothers never enjoyed herding Father's sheep. Over the years, they often pushed the responsibility off onto our herders, until robbers attacked and he lost some. After that, Father insisted they join our herders.

"How will you water our sheep?" Mother asked.

"Leah and Rachel will take turns going with the herders each day to give them the water they need."

"Us?" Rachel cried. "The sheep stink."

"You," Father responded. "Someone from the family must go to ensure the sheep get enough water."

"How will we protect the sheep from robbers?" I asked.

"If you are there, our herders will protect you and the flock. Without someone from our family there, other herders will push our sheep away before they get enough to drink," Father said. "Our herders are honest, but they should not be required to fight for our sheep unless a family member is there."

"Can one of our brothers not come water them? They will gain from your flocks more than Leah and me. You should expect them to help," Rachel said. "How can you expect us to fight off the other herders? We are women."

"My herders will fight for you. No, do not ask them to go alone. I have spoken," Father said. "Rachel, you and Leah will take turns going to the well each day. Work out who goes first between yourselves."

Father had rocked up the spring and covered it with a round rock, thin at the edges, and heavy enough that it required more than one man to lift it. He allowed our neighbors, who also raised sheep, to water their flocks there. In our desert home of Harran, our well ensured the animals had enough water. They uncovered the spring once a day. Although Father owned the well, the others would drive our herders away without one of the family there.

I could count on Rachel whining every time it was her turn. She would often whine to me, "Leah. Take my turn to water the sheep. I have other things to do. I dislike their smell."

Many times, I took her turn, and she never repaid me. She repaid me only when I did not feel well.

I never understood why Rachel argued about leading the sheep to the well. Men always looked at her. They often urged her to take her turn to bring her sheep forward to drink ahead of the other flocks. They never did that for me.

That morning, as usual, Rachel begged me to take her turn to water the sheep. "Why must I take the sheep to be watered?" she had asked, stamping her foot against the wooden slats making up the porch outside our kitchen.

I shrugged. "It is your turn. It is my turn to get water from the well. Then we will deep clean the kitchen."

Her foot twitched again. "What will I do if Father brings a man to our home to discuss marriage to one of us?"

Her suspicions were not without reason. Father brought men into our home more frequently in the last months.

I heard him arguing with mother only nights before. "There must be some man who will marry Leah. The scars on her face chase away the eligible men I bring. They only look at Rachel and refuse to consider Leah."

"Leah is gentle, patient, and kind. Cannot your men visitors see that?" Mother retorted.

"All they see are her scars."

I had hurried past their chamber, unwilling to hear more. Because of me, Father could not find a husband for Rachel. Many of our friends were married with children.

I refused to let their rejections hurt me, for most did not worship Jehovah. I did not understand why Father would even entertain these men. He had taught us to seek only those who did.

"It is your turn today, Rachel. You know it is," I said when she begged me to water the sheep for her yet again.

She stamped her foot again on the worn wooden slats. "Why must I lead the sheep to be watered?"

I shrugged. Although I preferred to go as the herders treated me a little better than the other men, I said, "It is your turn. You know Father insists we both go."

She rolled her eyes upward, staring into the sky. "Father prefers you over me because your eyes are beautiful."

My eyes! Do you not see the scars?

She tugged on her beautiful long braid, the colors of dark and light brown twisted through it. She thought it ugly. Silly sister.

"Father will find a man for you before he finds one for me." Her wail grated on my nerves.

Hardly.

"You are the beautiful one, Rachel. Your slim, lithe shape entices men. The eyes of the herders never leave you when you go to the well. Do you not see?"

She lifted her foot to stomp again, but set it quietly on the ground. "Men look at eyes first, not the body shrouded in layers of clothing. And they look your way. Every time you go to the well."

At the scars on my face.

She stamped her foot this time. "How will I find an eligible man at the well?"

"Do you see men with Father today?" My gaze turned toward the front of our home. I lifted my hands. "I do not. Father will find each of us an eligible man. He will find one for you after he finds one for me, as is the custom. As yet, I have no man. Why should he find one for you?" I bit my lip.

Would he ever find a man who would accept my scarred face?

"Just because you are the oldest," she cried.

"You know it is our way. It would disgrace Father if you married before me."

"It is custom, not law. Why can he not find men for both of us?" A sheep nudged against her leg, bleating. "Fine. I will go with you to the well."

She turned and marched toward the well, with the sheep and their herders following her.

How could I have known she would meet Jacob at the well? If I had known, I would have traded her this time.

Man from the Well

I desired a man to marry as much as Rachel did. I heard whispers as I pulled water from the well that morning, whispers that we would never marry if Father had to find a man for me before Rachel could marry. At seventeen, many already considered me too old for marriage. If Father did not find a man for me, I would cause us both to become unmarried spinsters. I ducked my head and hurried home, but the pain lingered. Would Rachel never marry because of my scars?

Father often brought men home to visit, hoping to find a man worthy and willing to marry his daughters. I often heard some of them arguing with him. I remembered their hurtful words as I crossed the grassy space between our family well and the kitchen where mother and our maids were doing a deep clean, carrying my urn of water that morning after Rachel asked me to take her turn watering the sheep. Their words still stung.

"You know I must marry my oldest daughter first," Father had told the men each time before they left.

None of those men wanted to marry me. One or two had wanted to marry my sister, but not me. If they had, they would have returned to marry me. Rachel's exasperation with me grew with each visit. She hid it well, but I heard her complaints through our adjoining sleeping chamber wall. She had kicked her side of the wall a few times after Father's last visitor left without taking time for dinner.

The blame was not hers. I would not want to wait for an older, uglier sister to find a man before I could marry, either.

Cold water sloshed onto my feet from the urn. My last steps into the kitchen were squelchy and cold. I set the urn on the rocks beside the fire and pulled the pot toward me. With greater care, I poured the cold water into it. I did not want to put the fire out. Mother's displeasure was not something I wanted to experience. She would not be happy to see me with wet, squishy feet.

When I heard no reprimand, I gazed around the kitchen. "Where is Mother?"

"Gone," Zilpah, my maidservant, said. Father had assigned her as my maidservant when we were both ten. I longed for her smooth, dark-tanned skin. Even if she had scars, they would not show like on my pink skin.

I joined Zilpah in cleaning the wall beside the cooking fire, a greasy, smoky mess.

None of us missed Rachel's squeal coming from Father's office. "Father, I met a handsome man at the well."

Good for Rachel. She always meets men.

"Why has she not come to help us?" Shiri, a maid with sparkling eyes, asked as she emptied a cupboard of dishes.

Without allowing my boiling emotions to spill over, I said, "She met a man."

Soon, Mother returned, and Father and a group of his guards marched past the open kitchen door.

I glanced at Mother with my eyebrows raised.

She shrugged her narrow shoulders. "He is going to meet Rachel's man. We will learn more when he returns. We have no time to wonder now. The kitchen must be cleaned, especially if we are to have a visitor."

The maids itched to gossip about this man, but could not with Mother in the kitchen.

"I will share with you when Laban tells me. No need to gossip about it now," she said. Mother's no-nonsense attitude kept their mouths shut.

"Yes, Mother," I said, and rinsed out my cloth before scrubbing more on the wall. "How clean must we get this wall?" It seemed silly to scrub it much since it would be nasty again by the next evening.

"Clean," Mother said.

I sighed. My hands were red already, but I continued to scrub beside Zilpah. We had almost finished when Father and his guards clattered past the kitchen door. I wanted to peek at the stranger when they came past, but I was too busy with the wall.

I will meet him later. Perhaps I can show him to his chamber.

"I will go meet this stranger," Mother said, dropping her cleaning cloth in the water. She glanced at Shiri and Bilhah, who was Rachel's maidservant. "Clean the cold closet while I am gone."

Zilpah glanced at me. I shook my head. "Not us. Not now."

"How handsome do you think this man really is?" Shiri asked. "To Rachel, every man is handsome."

"She is young," Ada, our plump cook, said. "We have work to do."

"He could be handsome," Zilpah murmured.

"He could," I said with a shrug. *It will not matter.*

We finished cleaning our wall and joined the maids emptying the cold closet. I retrieved a cloth from the basket near the fire and tied it around my mouth to block the reek of spoiled food. Most of the food we removed continued to be edible, but some had rotted. We set these in a pail to carry out for the animals.

When we had the closet empty, I poured some of the hot water into a container with cold water and added soap. We each grabbed rags and washed the shelves of the cold closet.

Before Mother returned, we had the closet cleaned and returned most of the food.

When Mother joined us once more, Ada asked," Why is Rachel not here yet? Should she not be here helping?"

"Yes, where is Rachel?" Mother asked. "Laban introduced me to Rebekah's son."

"Rebekah?" I asked. "Do you mean Father's sister, Rebekah? He must have traveled far. He will want a bath."

"Rachel should have been here long ago," Mother said, ignoring my questions. "I would send her to settle this son of Rebekah into his chamber. Since she is not here," her eyes roamed across the kitchen, "Bilhah. Go to Laban's study and tell him you are there to show Rebekah's son to his chamber. Give him the last one on the left, the one Gera occupied before his marriage."

The chamber where my brother lived? More than overnight*? A handsome man would stay here with us? I guess he would as Rebekah's son. We have a responsibility to care for family. But why not send me? I am the oldest sister.*

Before I could open my mouth to ask, Bilhah sashayed out of the kitchen.

"Mother? Why did you not send me?" I asked.

"You are dressed in cleaning clothes, not prepared to meet a man who came from Canaan to find a bride. You will meet him when he joins us for the evening meal."

I bit the inside of my mouth, struggling to keep my words inside. Zilpah wanted to shout out in my defense, but I caught her eye and shook my head. "Do not," I silently mouthed.

Mother's nose wiggled at the stench of rotten food and stared at me.

"I am taking the pail of rotten food out to the animals now." I snatched the bucket of stinky food and slipped past her before she could complain any more.

Mother liked her home clean and filled with a lovely fragrance. Like Rachel, she did not enjoy these chores, and her disgust emerged in bitterness, a sentiment she had expressed most often as long as I could remember. I hoped never to express my distaste to cause pain to my family. I loved my mother, but I sometimes feared her. I suspect Rachel and our maids feared her as well.

When I returned, Mother had left once more, and the maids continued to clean the kitchen.

Mother returned to the kitchen before Rachel, who eventually moped into the kitchen. When she did, I looked up and smiled. "You joined us?" I asked, keeping my voice syrupy sweet.

I knew she wanted to stomp her foot, but Mother's frown prevented it. "I took the sheep to the well." She removed dishes from the shelf and dropped a rag into a bucket of hot water to wash underneath them.

"And you met a handsome man." I dropped my rag into my bucket of water, leaving it there. "I heard you tell Father. Since then, I have waited for you to join us in the kitchen. I knew you were back."

"I had other things to do." She flipped her braid over her shoulder and scoured the shelf.

I reached into the hot water and found my rag, squeezed the water from it, and returned to my cleaning.

"Other things to do?" Mother asked. "Like dancing in your best dress?"

"I hoped to help Father get him settled," Rachel murmured.

"I sent Bilhah to show him to his chamber," Mother said. "You were unavailable, too busy dancing in your own."

And I took slop out to the animals. Mother could have allowed me to show our guest to his chamber. I allowed my breath to come out in a soft sigh, hoping no one heard.

"What is this man's name?" Zilpah asked, stretching her back.

"Jacob," Rachel said.

"A strong name," Shiri said.

We worked together, removing the grime from the fire. Around me, the others gossiped and laughed. I withdrew into my thoughts.

Perhaps this new man, this Jacob, will show interest in me. Perhaps he has a kind heart. Will he?

I doubt he will after seeing Rachel first. He will do little more than glance my way. Will I ever find a man willing to overlook my scarred face?

"Where are you, Leah?" Zilpah murmured, touching my arm.

I shook away my thoughts. "Thinking."

"Shiri asked what the strange man looked like," Zilpah whispered. "You did not join the questions. Are you well?"

I nodded. I looked towards the others. "Yes, tell us what he is like."

"I heard his voice, deep and kind," Shiri said.

Rachel let her hand rest on the table she washed. "He is taller than any of our herders. I suspect he is taller than Father, and he is the biggest man in Harran. Jacob cannot hide his muscles beneath his clothing."

Things Rachel would notice.

"His eyes?" I asked. "What color are his eyes?" *And are they kind?*

Rachel closed her eyes. I knew it to be a pretence. She knew well the color of his eyes. Without opening them, she spoke in a slow, whispery voice. "Blue. Blue with a fringe of dark eyelashes." She sighed. "His brown hair and beard are unkempt and dirty. I suspect it is from his travels."

"He will clean and brush those," I said. Rebekah's son would not be unkempt, not in his uncle's home.

Bilhah stepped into the kitchen as Rachel spoke. "His eyes are deep blue," she added. "And so kind. And he is strong."

Kind eyes. There is hope for me.

"He is a handsome man with a rugged face," Rachel said, frowning at Bilhah.

"A handsome man in our home," Shiri said. "How did he find us?"

"Why would he come all the way from Canaan to Harran?" Bilhah asked.

"Did you not ask him?" Zilpah asked.

"I directed him to his chamber. He looked tired. He will want a bath." Bilhah glanced at the pot of heating water. "Good. There will be more hot water for him."

More? Did menservants take water to him? They must have while I carried out the slop.

Jacob

We finished the kitchen, leaving the fragrance of food simmering on the edge of the fire that had enticed us as we worked. Our hands wrinkled from the water. Our backs ached from the effort. But the kitchen sparkled.

Mother tasked Shiri with baking bread for the evening meal, while Mother, Rachel, and I went to rest before changing for dinner.

After resting for a short time, I rose to find a dress to wear to dinner. I shook my head. *What dress will help him look at me?*

Zilpah pushed into my chamber. "Your mother sent me to help you dress."

"She does not trust me to dress myself after all these years?" I asked, allowing frustration to slide into my voice.

She set her fists on her hips. "I have helped you dress since we were ten. And a man is here for the evening meal. Avagail sent Bilhah to Rachel and called Alma to help her. This man must be special."

I breathed out a sigh. "He is special. He is Father's sister's son. I do not know his reason for coming so far from Canaan, but he is here in Harran now."

"Perhaps he came to find a wife. You should wear your most beautiful dress." She walked to my trunk and searched for a dress. "This blue dress will work. The blue makes your eyes dance."

"Dance?" Skepticism shrouded my voice. "My eyes dance?"

"They will dance in the candlelight in this dress. You do not realize how beautiful your eyes are. You are a beautiful young woman."

"Hah!" I snorted. "Everyone knows my scars make me ugly. No man wants to marry a scarred woman."

"You are beautiful inside, and your eyes overcome the scars on your face." She touched a scar. "They fade. They will not be noticeable one day."

"One day, but not today." *Jehovah had allowed the illness and the* scarring. *I would not complain again, not aloud.*

Zilpah dressed me with care and gentleness. She brushed my hair until it shone, letting the soft curls fall across my back and shoulders. "You have beautiful hair, too, Mistress Leah."

I nodded. "Mmm." I stared in the mirror and sighed. My eyes were beautiful. *I can only have beautiful eyes and spirit, and perhaps beautiful hair. Will a man ever want me?*

I shrugged as I stood, prepared for dinner. How would this Jacob treat me?

As I entered the sitting area, the stranger, Jacob, stood. Bilhah and Rachel were correct. He was a handsome man. He stood taller than Father, though not as broad, and his dark eyelashes outlined the deep blue eyes that seemed to bore through me. No wonder the women were all agog over him.

"Jacob, this is my older daughter, Leah," Father said.

Jacob took my hand and bowed over it, and I ducked my head. "Leah, it is good to meet you."

"I have heard much about you, Jacob."

"Two beautiful daughters, Laban. You are blessed."

"I am. I would rather not leave them for their brothers to care for. I seek a husband for them."

Jacob swallowed. "One man for both?"

"If I must. Many men have more than one wife."

Jacob ducked his head. "I have seen that. My grandfather had a wife and a concubine. They caused him much trouble."

Father tipped back his head and guffawed. "Women will do that. But a man must marry his daughters to honorable men."

"Yes, sir. He must."

Mother entered, and Rachel followed behind her. Jacob's eyes followed Rachel. He had seen me, but he had eyes only for her. It did not surprise me.

Father and Mother led us into the eating area. Jacob took Rachel's arm, tucking it into his right elbow. I prepared to follow behind them, but he took my hand with his other hand and walked with me as well.

His mother had taught him well.

If only he had eyes for me.

I thought Father had spent hours with Jacob since Rachel watered the sheep, but it seems he had not, for he questioned Jacob about his home and family during the evening meal.

"How is my sister now?" Father asked.

"Mother and Father love each other. She has been happy with Esau and me, her only children. But it has been difficult for her since we grew older. We needed wives, and none of the women in Canaan worshiped Jehovah. Mother tried to send us here ten years ago, but Father always had reasons to keep us at home."

"Our daughters were not old enough to marry ten years ago," Mother said.

Jacob looked at us. "No. I see that, but sometime sooner would have been better for Esau."

"What happened?" Father asked, leaning on the table.

Jacob slumped. "Even though Mother made us promise we would not find wives among the Canaanites, Esau found two wives to marry among the Hittites."

I sucked in a soft breath.

Jacob stared at his plate. "It broke Mother's heart. She insisted I leave before I found a wife from among the Hittites or the Philistine women. Father agreed."

Jacob swallowed then lifted his head. "It was hard on her. She married Isaac to be with a man who worships Jehovah. She never expected to have her son marry Canaanites."

I averted my gaze from him. No reason for me to act needy.

Rachel sat lost in her thoughts, a dreamy expression on her face. Jacob turned to her. "Do you often take the sheep to the well?"

Rachel did not hear him, even though she stared at him. She did not respond.

I reached behind Jacob and nudged her shoulder. "Rachel, did you hear the question Jacob asked?"

She shook herself. "Question?"

Everyone chuckled. Her face reddened as she tittered with us. I could see she did not know why we laughed and pulled her tichel across her face.

Jacob spoke again. "I asked if you often take your flocks to the well."

"Oh." Her tichel dangled from her fingers. "Father gave Leah and me the assignment of taking the sheep to the well. Today was my turn."

"And I had to convince you to go," I teased. "You wanted me to take your turn." I wished I had worn my tichel. I would pull it across my face as she had, teasing Jacob.

Everyone chortled again. I smiled at Rachel, hoping she would let me take her next turns.

"You must miss your family," she said.

Jacob rubbed his mouth. "I miss my parents. I even miss Esau and his strutting ways. As twins, we were close."

Pain filled his face, but he smoothed it before others could notice. *Were close?* I wanted to ask.

"You must miss your twin," Mother said. She could show consideration and kindness when necessary.

"We have been close since before our births, but the rivalry between us is strong." He pressed his lips together. "Mother tells me I held Esau's heel during our birth. I suppose I wanted to be the first one born, but he was in the way."

"Babies have little choice in that," Mother said with a frown.

"Perhaps," Jacob said, turning from Rachel to Mother. "I know little about babies. Mother had only Esau and me. We have loved each other and fought together since our birth."

Rachel and I were near in age and close. But we, like many sisters, had our challenges. Mostly, Rachel wanted to marry as soon as possible, and I was in her way.

The meal ended, and Mother led us into the sitting area, where everyone took comfortable seats. Rachel and I sat at opposite ends of the long seat. Jacob sat between us. I tried not to shiver as he sat next to me.

"And your father, Isaac?" Father asked. "How is he doing?"

"Father has been ill, but he is still active in the business of raising sheep and goats and selling their wool. Our wool is still considered the best in the land. I pray Jehovah protects him."

"And did you help with the animals?" Father asked.

"I have always loved and cared for the animals. They have been my friends for many years. While I am here, may I take your sheep to their pasture and to the well? There is no need for your beautiful daughters to risk themselves everyday taking your flocks to the well."

My heart raced. *Beautiful?* Then he glanced at Rachel. My heart returned to its normal speed.

"At risk?" Rachel gasped. "Risk of what?"

"Men wait near wells to abduct lone women. I want neither of your daughters taken." He looked at Rachel, then at me. "I can take the sheep to the well," Jacob told Father. "It is not safe to send your daughters."

"They go to ensure our flocks get the water they deserve. If they do not go, the men will chase away my herders."

"They will not chase your herders away with me there," Jacob said.

Father nodded. "I do not want the other herders thinking they can take our share of water."

"I will go with Rachel and Leah until you are certain I can handle the herders," Jacob said, glancing towards each of us.

I looked forward to our time alone with the sheep.

I went with Jacob the next morning to water our flocks. I had not been alone with a man before, except my brothers. We were not alone then either. The sheep and their herders were with us, but Jacob walked with me at the head of the herd. We allowed the ram and ewe that always led the flock to come between us.

"You do not complain about watering the flocks?" Jacob finally asked.

"I do not mind. It takes me away from the chores Mother finds for me to do at home. She thinks we should be kept busy."

Jacob kicked a rock down the trail. "Father kept us busy. But when we were young, Esau and I found different tasks."

"You said you enjoyed working with the animals." I glanced over at him, then kicked the same rock he had kicked. "What did Esau do?"

Jacob frowned and kicked the rock a little further. "Esau joined the hunters. He liked to hunt for food for the family. He was not satisfied with eating only mutton and goats. He loved to eat venison and meat from other wild animals."

"He likes to hunt and kill them?" My stomach churned.

He glanced at me. "Does that bother you?"

I came upon the rock we had kicked and kicked it along the path. It bounced off the plants on the side of the trail. "I suppose it does not. We all need to eat. But he enjoys killing innocent animals?"

Jacob shrugged. "I guess the animals are innocent. Jehovah placed them on the earth for the use of man. If we do not eat them, the lions or crocodiles will."

I shuddered. "Yes. That will happen. But it is hard to think of them."

"Do you not eat mutton? We had mutton stew last night." He kicked the rock.

I stared at the ewe trotting beside me. "I do, but I do not like it. The animals are my friends."

"That is the problem with being with our animals so closely. We grow to love them."

"Yes. I will be sad to lose these two." I glanced at the ewe and ram that ran between us.

"Perhaps you will not know."

"It will sadden me."

We arrived at the well. Some of the other herders had not arrived.

"It does not look like everyone is here," Jacob said, glancing around the clearing.

"No," I looked around at those who were there. "Two herds are not here yet. Father decreed we not remove the rock until everyone is here. In the past, water was lost because the water flowed while waiting for those who had not yet arrived."

"That makes sense," Jacob said. "We can wait for the others."

Soon the bleating of flocks warned us that the other herders had arrived. I nodded to Jacob. "They are all here now."

"Who moves the stone?"

"I never have. It is too heavy. The herders move it."

"That stone is heavy. I do not doubt that you do not move it. I will go move it." Jacob strode to the well and rolled the stone from the well. He signaled me to bring the flocks. I stepped forward, and the sheep followed me. I stepped aside and watched them drink.

"They will try to drink too much if you let them," I said.

"Sheep are the same everywhere," Jacob said with a chuckle.

We watched them until they had drunk enough, then I called the sheep away. Our herders and I moved back to wait for the others to water their sheep. Jacob stayed next to the stone, speaking to the other herders and watching their sheep as they drank.

The men laughed and talked together. Jacob's easy ways endeared him to them, becoming their friend. He exuded friendliness and understood these men. I could never understand them. I was happy to allow him to take the flocks to the well, although I enjoyed walking there with him.

When he had ensured all the flocks had received water, the flocks separated, each following the herder who led them. Jacob returned the stone to the top of the well and stepped down the path to lead our sheep toward our pasture.

Iben stepped to Jacob's side. "I will show you the way to our pastures."

Jacob nodded and turned to me. "Will you be safe getting home?"

"I always walk home alone from here. I will be safe."

"Do you have a weapon?"

"My sheep crook." I waved it. "And my belt knife." My arms and legs tingled.

"Good. I would not want you injured or taken. Go right home."

I brought my arm to my chest in salute. "Yes, sir."

Jacob laughed. "I want you to be safe."

I caught my breath and held it briefly. "I have done this for years, since my brothers married and took their own sheep to the pasture."

Jacob brought his fist to his chest. "Remember to watch for strangers."

I laughed. "As I always have."

Excitement

I enjoyed my turn taking the flocks to the well with Jacob. I hoped he would consider me to be his wife. We talked about many things, especially his life in Canaan. It sounded lovely to me to live in tents and move often. I would not be required to live with Father and Mother any more, as large families separated into several smaller tents.

Much as I loved my parents, I hoped to move away from them. I would be happy to live near Jacob's mother. She sounded kind, and best of all, I would not be required to live in her home. I feared Mother and Father would require Jacob and his new wife, whether he chose Rachel or me, to live in their home. They have a large home, but the walls are thin. I would not want everyone who lives in the house to hear what goes on behind closed doors. What if we fought? They did not need to hear our discussions, nor did they need to hear us as we loved each other.

I certainly did not want to hear those things from Rachel and her husband, whether it was Jacob or another man. I wanted to live in a home of my own, as Mother had moved into her own home when she married. As I walked to and from the well where we watered the flocks, I watched for homes near ours where I could live with a husband.

I found one I liked. Zilpah and I went there one afternoon, looking around from the outside.

"No one has lived here for years," she said.

I lifted a drying limb of an overgrown bush. "No. I think the old couple left to live elsewhere."

"Sad that no one lives here now. The bushes are overgrown. They stopped blooming long ago." She pointed to a stunted, dried blossom. "They did not bloom this year as much as I remember."

I waved at the sagging, peeling shutters. "The house will need repair as well. The shutters sag. We cannot go inside, but Jacob can make the repairs. He tightened the stairs so they no longer squeak when we climb them."

"Jacob? Do you hope he will marry you?"

I swallowed the lump rising in my throat. "No. But I can dream."

The house called to me. I wanted to go inside, but it belonged to another, and it would be wrong to enter it. I tried to remember what had happened to the couple who had lived there when we were small. I did not remember why they had left the house empty.

My parents stifled me, insisting I follow their rules and work beside Mother, even when I had other preferred tasks. I still loved them, but because of their overbearing persistence, I refused to ask Mother about the house. She would learn of my desire to leave her home. And, when others learned of my dream, they would tease me. I struggled with my confidence enough already.

The house filled my dreams every night. In them, I trimmed the flowers and cleaned the inside, making it mine. I woke each morning hoping Jacob would invite me to marry him and take me there. If not him, perhaps Esau would ride into Harran and sweep me off my feet, inviting me to return to Canaan with him.

Dreams.

Then, after two weeks of taking the flocks to the well, Jacob once again suggested to Father that he could take the flocks to the well without Rachel's or my help.

"The men know I serve you and your flocks. They respect me, and your animals love me as I love them. I fear for your daughters. They walk home alone from the well, and strangers lurk near there. I fear Rachel and Leah will not stay safe. I would not want you to have to chase those strangers to retrieve your daughter."

Father bowed his head in thought. I had not seen strangers. I frowned and glanced at Rachel, who also frowned. We enjoyed going to the well with the flocks now.

Father looked at me, then at Rachel. "I would not want to chase after men to rescue my daughters, nor would I want to pay a ransom."

Ah, that *is the reason. He does not want to pay a ransom for his daughters. He would do it for his sons.*

"Jacob can handle the flocks and the herders of other herds. Jacob, congratulations. You now have total responsibility for my animals." Father looked at Rachel and me. "You two have other duties at home. You can work on those during the time you would have gone with Jacob to the well."

"Cooking and cleaning," Rachel mumbled so low I did not believe others heard.

"More time to sew and weave," Mother said. "You two are old enough to prepare for a marriage."

I glanced at Jacob. He kept his face still as he continued to eat. *He said he had come to find a wife. Which of us would he choose? Good thing Father has only two daughters.*

Father had provided looms for us when we were younger. If Mother did not keep us busy cleaning, she kept us in the weaving space working on weaving fabrics for our homes.

I wove a blue wedding blanket in the next two weeks, hoping to spread it across the marriage pallet, as Rachel wove a red blanket. We both hoped Jacob would choose us.

Then one morning, Rachel breezed into the weaving space with a smile bigger than I had seen on her face in many years. "Why the smile?" I asked.

She shrugged. "I am happy. Is there a problem with my smiling?"

"No," I drug out the word as I tried to understand my feelings surrounding her grin. "I rarely see you smile when you enter the weaving space."

Rachel lifted a shoulder. "I am happy. I feel like smiling."

My stomach churned. Something had happened. She knew something — something I did not want to know.

I wove the final three rows of my blue and white blanket and removed it from the loom. I folded it with care, hoping I could use it soon. I carried it to my chamber and put it in the trunk with the other items I had prepared earlier.

As I fingered my other wedding treasures, I considered what else I would need to use in a new home, perhaps the home I so often passed. I had most of the things I would need for a home already.

I sighed. *Will I ever be able to use these? Will* any *man agree to marry me? Will Jacob? Not now. Rachel has heard something.*

I considered what I needed to weave next. Perhaps towels. I would not weave beautiful fabric for a wedding dress and tichel yet. It may curse my hopes for a husband.

That evening, as dinner ended, Father cleared his throat. "I have something to announce before we leave." He gazed around the table, staring at the three women sitting there. "Jacob has asked to marry Rachel."

"Me?" Rachel cried.

She was pretending. She heard something about this earlier. I struggled to keep a smile on my face.

Father gazed at Rachel before continuing. "Jacob has no bride price. He agreed to work for me for the next seven years instead."

My gasp joined Rachel's. I knew Father would demand an enormous price, but seven years of work?

Her lip quivered, but she maintained her smile.

"Are you willing to marry Jacob?" Father asked Rachel.

We were Father's daughters. We had no choice in whom we would marry, or when. He had the responsibility of finding a man for us, and he could set the bride price.

"Yes, Father," Rachel said, her face glowing once more. Jacob reached his hand across the table and took Rachel's hand.

Father scowled at them. "We will conduct the betrothal this Sabbath at the end of the Sabbath service. You two may sit together now and walk together in the evenings. But you must remember, this is a betrothal, not a marriage." His look became stern. You will have none of the rights of marriage until after the seven years. You may not touch each other in unacceptable ways."

Rachel will struggle to wait seven years, but for Father to expect them to be chaste will be a challenge for them both. I would not want to have the same limitations.

I gripped her hand in sympathy. She turned and smiled at me. I saw tears shimmering in her eyes. I would cry as well.

With my hopes dashed, I complained of a headache when the family adjourned to the sitting area and returned to my chamber. I could not face her joy. Not then. My heart was breaking.

Later that evening, I heard Rachel enter her chamber. I needed to show kindness and congratulate her. I sucked in a deep breath and tapped on her door. When she called, "Come," I entered.

"Congratulations," I said. "You won Jacob."

"Was it a competition?" Rachel asked, allowing her fingers to brush her brown blanket as she sat on her sleeping pallet.

"How can you think it was anything but a competition?" I asked and set my fists on my hips. "Jacob came here seeking a wife. Father has two daughters, you and me. Jacob would marry one of us." I sighed. "I hoped he would choose me although I knew it to be a dream. You are the beautiful sister."

Rachel brushed her hair back across her shoulder. "I wish ... but it is not possible."

"What do you wish?" I leaned forward, the hurt softening in my heart.

"I wish Esau and Jacob had come together earlier. Then I could have Jacob, and you could have Esau."

I snorted. "And Jacob and Esau would have fought over you. You are the beautiful sister. Esau would not want me."

"No, Leah!" Rachel leapt up. "You are beautiful. Esau would have loved you."

"With these scars?" I brushed my fingertips across my face. "I see them in the mirror every day and have done for most of my life."

"But they are fading —"

Before Rachel could say more, I lifted my hand to stop her argument. "You are not the first to suggest they are fading. Zilpah said the same thing. I see the scars. I know they are there. And every man Father brings here hoping to marry me off, sees my scars."

"You have beautiful eyes and a beautiful soul."

"Bah!" I barked. "No man seeking a wife recognizes beautiful eyes or a beautiful soul. He wants a beautiful woman without scars."

Rachel's arms surrounded me. "I am sorry."

"For what?" I sniffed. "It is not your fault my face is scarred and ugly. They will fade, some time in the future. Perhaps Jehovah will send a man who will see past them."

My tears fell on her shoulder, though I did not want her to know the depths of my grief. What could she do?

I kept myself aloof in the days before the Sabbath. I did not trust myself to keep my grief to myself yet. I knew I would come to terms with this in time. But not yet.

I sat at the end of the line on our family row beside Mother at the next Sabbath observance, not yet willing to cheer Rachel on. I ignored all the comments whispered by those in the congregation.

Our brothers Gera, Shelomiy, and Chayim sat with their families behind us, acting as a buffer between us and the others. I concentrated on the backs of the heads in front of me.

Daniy, the leader of our little group of believers, led us in our worship and spoke of obedience to Jehovah's commands. At the end, he asked if anyone had needs or blessings to share, as he often did. Three men stood, asking us to pray for their families. One man announced that his family would leave Harran within the month to live with a distant family. Two women stood, sharing the news of their coming babies.

Then Father stood. I wanted to hide from everyone. Instead, I sat up straighter and stared at a point behind Father's head.

"I am here to announce the betrothal of my daughter, Rachel, to Jacob, the son of my long-lost sister. I have agreed to allow them to wed."

Daniy called Jacob and Rachel to the front, but I stopped listening. My thoughts turned to the house down the lane from ours. *Would Father purchase it and allow me to live in it with a servant? I would never marry. If kind, generous Jacob would not have me, how can I expect another man who loves Jehovah to desire me as a wife?*

Father stood once more. "We have agreed to a bride price of seven years' labor. He brought no gold nor jewels to purchase a wife as the servant of Abraham sent when he came for Rebekah. My daughter is as valuable to me as Rebekah was to our father."

Gasps and whispers filled the sanctuary. Daniy called them to silence. Although the whispering stopped, the place filled with tension.

That is why he demands seven years.

"And you agreed to this?" Daniy asked Jacob.

Jacob bowed his head. "I have nothing to give but my time and hands. I willingly give them for this beautiful woman."

Rachel agreed to be betrothed to Jacob, and Daniy completed the betrothal rite. I tried to pay attention, but in my disappointment, my thoughts flew elsewhere. I wanted to be the one participating in a betrothal. After all, I was the oldest.

Preparations

I did what I could to be cheerful for Rachel and supportive of her seven-year wait. I would not enjoy it if Father required me to wait so long. What was Father thinking? Did he not want to lose Rachel to Jacob? Was he afraid Jacob would take her far away to Canaan as Isaac had taken Rebekah? Or was it greed?

Whatever the reason, Rachel's frustration swelled, filling the space around her. Father had given her permission to walk with Jacob outside, as long as Bilhah chaperoned them.

"Why must Bilhah always follow us everywhere we go?" she complained one day as we wove together in the weaving chamber.

"Perhaps Father does not trust Jacob." I said, a question filling my statement. *Or he does not trust you.*

"He trusts Jacob. Who would not? He does not trust me. Why can we not marry before Jacob completes his commitment to work? Jacob is honorable. He would not leave before his covenanted time."

I suspected her frustration came from her desire to have the rights of marriage now that they were betrothed. Many others lived as married couples during the betrothal period. But Father refused Jacob and Rachel that privilege.

In the evenings, Jacob shared the story of his disagreement with his twin, Esau, and his flight from home. He often spoke of his desire to return to his parents and brother. As much as he desired to return home after his and Rachel's marriage, he waited to hear from his mother before he could consider returning. She had promised to send a message when Esau no longer desired his life.

Rachel and Jacob adjusted to the restriction over the years, spending as much time as possible with each other. While Jacob served Father with the flocks and in the fields, Rachel spent her days preparing household items for her new home.

She planned on sharing a home with Jacob that was not within Father's home. Even though Jacob did not have a mother and father nearby for them to live with, our parents would not expect them to live in their home. I envied them.

"I will offer a sacrifice to thank Jehovah for my safety and for Rachel," Jacob said one evening near the end of the first year of their betrothal.

"Do you have the authority?" Father asked, his jaw dropping a bit.

"My father, Isaac, had the right given him from his father and Jehovah. As a young man, I served with him since I was young."

"You helped your father?" Mother asked, bringing her hand up to her chest. "Did Esau?"

"We both helped at first." Jacob chewed on his beard. "After a time, Esau found other things to do. Before I left Mamre, Father blessed me and bestowed on me the right to perform sacrifices."

"Did he also give that right to Esau?" I asked.

"He may have, but Esau lost the right by marrying Canaanite women."

I bowed my head and chewed on my lip. *Even if Esau had come, he may not have had the same blessings as Jacob. Perhaps he would have if he* had come *earlier.*

Mother put Rachel, me, and our female servants to work preparing food for the meal that would follow. We cleaned and cooked for a week. Mother set the men servants to work setting up tables and benches in a field for the others of our small group of Jehovah worshipers. She sent messages to the other women in our group of worshipers, inviting them to participate in providing food for the meal.

I had hoped Father would find me a husband before the end of the first year of Jacob's service. It did not happen. I did not know then that Father had already determined that he could not give me to a man who worshiped an idol god. He could not face the possibility of having one of my children given to a god as a sacrifice.

I wish he had shared. I would have understood his motives better.

On the day of the sacrifice, Jacob walked ahead of Rachel.

"He desires to stay clean in body and soul before performing the sacrifice," Rachel told us.

Jacob sat beside Father during the Sabbath service that day, rather than Rachel. At the end, when Daniy called for us to announce needs or blessings, Jacob stood.

"It has been a year since I agreed to work seven years to pay the bride price for Rachel. I have built an altar and will sacrifice a perfect ram in gratitude for Jehovah's blessings today after this meeting. All are welcome to join us afterwards to participate in the sacrifice and for the meal that will follow. I understand Avigail and other women have prepared food to accompany the part of the ram that will be ours to eat afterward."

When everyone had gathered, Jacob led his ram, which followed him without being tied, up the ramp to the altar.

Jacob spoke to us. "At some future day, Jehovah will clothe himself in a body like ours. Those with whom he will live will cruelly take his life. As God, he will take upon himself all our sins, our ills, and our sorrows. This ram, and every other sacrifice, represents Him."

He lifted the ram onto the altar and continued the sacred rite.

Nyssa, one of our maids, had told us of attending a sacrifice to Libnah that had horrified her. The mother of the chosen child had screamed until long after the priest had taken its life.

I feared Jacob's sacrifice would repulse me as Nyssa's story had. However, a feeling of warmth and calm surrounded me. The ram looked into Jacob's eyes, never crying nor complaining. Although it gave its life, I found it a beautiful experience for the ram and those who observed.

"Consider your blessings and the requests you desire from Jehovah," Jacob suggested.

"Give me a husband and a family," I prayed. Although I feared the grief of still not having a husband would overwhelm me, a sense of completeness filled me.

After that, I no longer worried about Father finding a husband for me. Jehovah would resolve that problem. I did not know how it would happen. I only knew it would. Perhaps Esau would come to Harran and choose to marry me. It no longer mattered. I knew I would have a husband. I could wait for Jehovah.

Each year, on the anniversary of their betrothal, Jacob performed a sacrifice. Those who worshiped Jehovah joined us to observe the sacred rite each year. We looked forward to the event that marked each year until Rachel and Jacob would be married. Many hoped it would continue in the years after.

In those years, on many nights I dreamed of caring for my home. I directed maidservants, helped clean the kitchen and other spaces in the house, and wove blankets and rugs. I never dreamed of the man who would be my husband. I trusted Jehovah to provide me with a husband.

Like Rachel, I prepared items I would need for a home. After weaving towels, sheets, and rugs, I went with Rachel and our maids to dig clay and made pots, urns, and eating dishes for our home.

"Why do you work so hard to prepare for a home?" Rachel asked once. "Do you expect a man to come from Mamre for you?"

Her giggle hurt.

"Father will find a husband for me. Jehovah has promised me." I bowed my head and offered a silent prayer. *Please.*

In the sixth year, I wove a soft fabric, which I dyed a deep blue, which complemented my dark gray eyes. I planned to sew a new dress and a long tichel for my wedding day. I did not know when it would happen. I only knew it would come.

Rachel was often mercurial in the days following Father's injunction that they would not wed until he had received his full seven years of work. Some days she could not stop smiling as she worked to prepare for her home. On other days, she moped and moaned about her seven-year wait, complaining that Father had forced them to wait. She wanted children.

So did I.

In the sixth year, Father often argued with Jacob. "Live with us in our home. You plan to leave for Mamre when you can. Why take another home?"

"It is my right to head my household. I deserve a home. Rachel deserves the home she has dreamed of all these years."

They looked at homes throughout Harran.

I would miss Rachel. She had been part of my life since my earliest memories. I had been less than two on the day Mother left my side to give birth to Rachel.

"Jacob has concerns about going home to Mamre," Rachel told Mother and me as we worked at our looms one day near the end of the seventh year. "He does not know if Esau has forgiven him of his infractions against him yet."

"That makes me happy," Mother said. "I am not ready to have you move so far from us."

"I will not be far from you. We have found a home," Rachel said.

"Oh?" I asked. "Which home?"

"The one down the lane. The one owned by the couple who left Harran about ten years ago."

I suppressed my squeak of surprise. It sounded like the house I had dreamed about since Jacob had arrived.

"The home owned by Sufy and Gaitha before they left?" Mother asked.

"Yes, that home," Rachel said with a giggle.

My home. They are moving into the home I have dreamed of for more than six years. How can they do that? I swallowed. *They did not know my dream. Jehovah will make it right.*

"Has Jacob talked with Sufy and Gaitha's family about it?" Mother asked.

"He has tried to find the owners, but since they and everyone in their family left, no one is left to purchase it from. Jacob is going to the leadership of Harran. He believes they will sell it to him."

"Does he have coins to purchase it?" I asked.

Rachel's smile lit the space. "Father allowed him to take care of the young lambs and goats whose mothers refused to feed them or whose mothers died early in the time Jacob started working to pay his bride price."

"Your father recognized Jacob's need to earn a few coins in order to support you after you marry," Mother said. "What has he done with those lambs?"

"He has cared for them as he cared for the others," Rachel said. "Few mothers died or refused to care for their young each year. However, those first lambs and goats have now become parents. Jacob has a small flock, and those animals have thick wool. He has sold it for many coins. He has enough to purchase the home that once belonged to Sufy and Gaitha."

I slumped in my chair. Jacob would purchase the home I had dreamed of living in with my husband for almost seven years. I would not be given the opportunity to clean it up and make it mine. It would be Rachel's home.

I bit the inside of my lip, pushing the tears to fall within me rather than across my face.

"Congratulations to you and Jacob," I said. "You will be happy there."

Rachel's excitement increased as the days passed, bringing us closer to the end of the seven years. Jacob purchased the house I wanted. He and other men cleared the way so Mother, Rachel, the women servants, and I could go clear out the dust and dirt that had settled on the floors and shelves. I joined them, knowing it would never be my home.

Rachel's excitement and her many requirements and complaints caused turmoil in the household. All the women leapt to her requests for help with clothing, packing, and other needs for her wedding. Mother tasked the servant men to take Rachel's baskets and trunks of homemaking items to her new house. Then Mother and I joined her there to set the rugs, cushions, and other household goods where she wanted.

I disagreed about where she put other items, but she would make it her home, not me. I listened to her happy chirping and worked to be happy for her.

As we walked home two days before the wedding, Rachel put her arm around my waist. "Thank you for helping me as much as you have. I know how hard this must be for you."

Hard? These past years have been painful. I should be the one to marry. I am the oldest. I do not deny you Jacob, but where is my man? I trust Jehovah. He said I would marry.

"It has been difficult," I said, forcing a smile. "I am happy for you. Jacob is a good man. Father will find a good man for me."

She squeezed me tighter before releasing me from her embrace. "Father will find you a man. You are a beautiful woman."

I snorted. "Perhaps he will find me a blind man."

Rachel and mother tipped their heads back and chortled. I joined them. *It would take a blind man to choose to marry me.*

"Your father will find a man for you, Leah," Mother said. "Some man will fall into your arms, captivated by your beautiful gray eyes."

I coughed. They could not see my pain.

"Your man will come. Be patient," Mother said, hugging me around the waist from the other side.

"Perhaps I should accept that I will be alone all my life and stop hoping," I murmured.

"No!" Rachel and Mother cried together.

"Your father will resolve this," Mother added.

Jehovah is on my side. I trust him more than I trust Father.

A Surprising Day

Father called me to his office on the day of Rachel and Jacob's wedding day.

"Do you have a dress and tichel prepared for your marriage?" he asked.

I had completed it months earlier. "Yes. Have you found a husband for me?"

"I have. You must be married before Rachel. You know the customs of our land. The older daughter must be married before the younger. Jacob has demanded that I give him his wife. I have delayed as long as I can."

"But he has worked the seven years for Rachel as you covenanted," I said. "He has paid her bride price. You would not require him to wait while you find me a husband when you have tried these many years and failed."

"No, Leah," Father said. "Jacob will wait only one more week."

"But we are preparing for the wedding feast tomorrow! How will he be required to wait another week?"

"You will marry Jacob," Father said in a flat voice. "You will —"

"Me! Jacob has worked to pay Rachel's bride price. She has waited as long as he has." I struggled to show my respect for my father. "She will be as angry with me as Jacob will."

He hushed me. "Leah, keep your voice down. This is between you and me. No one else is to know."

"Know? Know what?"

"You will marry Jacob at the feast tonight."

I sucked in a breath and lowered my voice. But the anguish remained. "But Rachel —" *Rachel will hate me for taking her husband. Jacob will hate me. He desires Rachel, not me!*

"— will have her turn. But you will be first. Before I introduce you after the feast tonight, you are to dress in your wedding finery. Drape your tichel across your face. Never move it, never allow Jacob to remove it until morning."

Jacob will not think I am Rachel. He knows the way she moves, the way she talks. Even with my tichel, he will know I am not her.

"Jacob will want to kiss me, will want to kiss Rachel."

Kiss! He would want to kiss her. He has kissed Rachel. He will know her kiss. It will give me away.

I did not like Father's plan, but could not dispute with Father. Custom decreed that the oldest daughter must be married first. Jacob was the only available man who worshiped Jehovah. Who else would I marry? Like Rebekah before me, I had no other choice. I bowed my head in resignation.

"Neither Rachel nor Jacob will be happy, but I will do it."

"You have no choice." Father swept his hand flatly in front of him. "I have decreed it. I am your father. You know our customs. You will not be at the feast, as is our custom. Jacob will not try to feed you. You will be brought to him at the end of the feast and married. It will be dark. He will not question, for I will tell him it is our law and custom that a husband cannot see the wife before he has consummated the marriage. He is not to know it is you until then."

I knew the ways of our land. Men feasted and drank while women waited and celebrated separately. I suspected Mother would shorten this celebration for the women to keep the news of a changed bride from Jacob. What would we do?

"Jacob will hate me."

"He cannot hate you. You will be his wife."

I bowed my head in thought. Jehovah had promised me a man. I never expected it to be Jacob.

"What about Rachel? How will you keep her away from Jacob? She will not accept this quietly." *Rachel will scream her grief and try to alert Jacob to the deception.* "How will you keep Jacob from knowing?"

"Jacob moved to his home yesterday. He will enjoy the feast, perhaps imbibe too much wine to notice he has the wrong woman until morning."

"And Rachel? How will you keep her from running to Jacob?" I fidgeted in my chair. I never expected to take Rachel's husband as my own.

"Rachel is my daughter," Father ground out the words through clenched teeth. "She will obey me, as you will. She will do as I tell her. Jacob will not hear Rachel's screams of anger if she disagrees. She will be gagged and tied to her bed if she tries to run to Jacob. She will not defy my wishes."

"She will be angry with me. We love each other. This will end that."

"She has no choice. You have no choice. She will accept this. It will be as I demand."

"She will see it as a betrayal. I would."

Father lifted his fist. "You will marry Jacob tonight. You have no choice. Rachel will marry him next week if he agrees to work another seven years."

My eyes widened. "Another seven years? He has already worked seven years to pay Rachel's bride price."

"He paid your bride price. If he still wants to marry Rachel, he will work another seven years. I will allow them to wed next week, after you and he have been married long enough for it to be lawful for him to take another wife."

I sucked in a deep breath. *I have hoped for a man like Jacob since the day he declared his love for Rachel. I did not expect this. How would this night have been different if Esau had come with his brother to find a wife? I would never know.*

Father sent me to my chamber. "Your mother knows the plan. She will not expect you to help with the feast. You are to stay there until I call for you. I give you Zilpah as your maidservant to serve you all your days. She will come to you when it is time to dress for the wedding."

"Give me Zilpah? How can that be?"

"Her mother gave her to me. I give her to you."

How can one own a person?

I walked to the door, then turned. "What of my wedding blanket and other beautiful things I made for my home?"

Father stroked his beard as he considered my question. "Does it matter tonight?"

"It matters to me! I spent many hours weaving my blanket, dreaming of the night I would sleep beneath it with my new husband."

He stroked his beard without speaking.

"Rachel's blanket is on the sleeping pallet. Not mine. My blanket is blue. Hers is red," I argued.

"Jacob will not know or care."

"I will care!"

Father harrumphed. "I will send Zilpah to exchange the blanket after the feast has started. Jacob will not know the difference. Men will bring your other things tomorrow."

"And when we arrive at his home? Will he not notice?" I fought to keep my voice calm.

"Jacob will not notice. He will be too interested in consummating the wedding. Trust me. I know men who have waited seven years for their brides."

An excited shudder shook my body. I stilled it. "I dislike deceiving such a good man."

"It is not your deceit. It is mine. I will accept his anger. Once it is done, there is nothing Jacob can do. You will be his wife."

"Yes, Father." I opened the door and returned to my chamber. I could do nothing else.

I opened the door to my chamber and stared at the familiar surroundings. This would be the last afternoon I would call this chamber mine. What would I do while I waited?

Someone had set empty baskets and trunks on the floor. I could pack my belongings to be brought to me later. I opened a trunk and pulled my clothing off hooks, and refolded and tucked them into the basket.

I had not filled the trunk before Zilpah opened the door enough to slip into my chamber. "Your father sent me to help you pack. Where is your wedding blanket?"

I opened a different trunk and removed the blanket and gave it to Zilpah.

"I have had many surprises today. I did not expect to help you prepare to leave this house as a woman about to be married. Nor did I expect your father to give me to you as your maidservant."

"Does it cause you grief?" I asked.

"No," Zilpah said. "I would rather be your maidservant than Rachel's. She has a temper."

"Rachel," I exclaimed in mock surprise. "Does she have a temper?"

"You do not see how she treats the maids when we are alone. Your mother sometimes treats us the same way. You treat us much kinder. I am more grateful Laban did not leave me here to serve Avigail."

"I try to treat you as I would like to be treated if I had been given as a servant to others," I said. I lifted my blue wedding dress and tichel from the trunk and hung them on a hook. "I will wear this tonight."

"Excellent," Zilpah said. "I will help you dress when it is time. For now, however, rest. You will have a long night and need your rest."

I lay on my sleeping pallet and watched her move through my chamber, removing my belongings and setting them in the baskets and trunks. Before long, my eyes closed and I slept.

The sun had set, and the light darkened when Zilpah entered with an urn of warm water. "It is time for you to prepare for your wedding."

Zilpah helped me wash and dress, taking care with each step. "You want to be beautiful for your new husband."

"Until he sees my face," I said.

"Your scars are fading. He will not see them in the dark." Zilpah brushed my hair.

"It is not the scars that cause me concern. Jacob believes he will marry Rachel tonight, not Leah. I fear his anger in the morning when he sees he did not get the woman he expected, working seven long years to pay Rachel's bride price." I glanced at her reflection in my polished brass mirror.

She frowned. "That could be a problem."

"It will be a problem."

She brushed through the length of my hair and lifted the brush. "This is not your choice. Your father insists." She brushed again with more vigor.

"I know. You know. Mother knows. Father knows. Even Rachel will know and not be happy. But Jacob does not know. He will not be happy. He loves Rachel, not me." I grimaced.

Her eyes narrowed. "He will not be happy, but he will get used to the idea."

I sighed. "I hope he does. Would he consider getting rid of me?"

The brush halted once more, this time half-way down the length of my hair. "Can he do that?"

"I do not know what he can do. I pray he will accept me and that his anger will not cause him to mistreat me." I chewed the inside of my lip, and moisture filled my eyes.

"Do not cry. You do not want him to see tears on your face," Zilpah chided.

"He will not see them." I winced. "I am to keep my tichel over my face until I am with him in the morning."

"Until it is too late?"

I nodded.

After a pause, she resumed brushing my hair. "Jacob is a good man. He will accept you. It may take some time, but he will accept you."

I closed my eyes as tears leaked from them. "I hope you are right."

Marriage

We waited a long time before Mother jerked my door open. "Leah, are you ready?" she asked.

"I have been ready for a long time," I said.

"Zilpah, brush her hair and help me drape her tichel over her," Mother ordered.

Zilpah lifted the brush and ran it through my curls once more. "It is beautiful," she whispered.

The two women then draped the tichel that matched my blue wedding dress over my head. Mother slipped a bracelet onto my arm.

"You must be beautiful for Jacob," she murmured.

I grunted, and Mother glared at me. "You are beautiful, Leah, my firstborn daughter. Do not allow anyone to tell you otherwise."

"Then why must we deceive Jacob to get a man to marry me?"

Mother ran her finger across my face. "Your scars do not define your beauty."

"You are not a man forced to marry the older sister."

Mother growled and mumbled under her breath as she adjusted my tichel. When she had satisfied herself that Jacob would see no part of my face in the darkness, she nodded and hugged me. "This is your special day, Leah. Jacob is a kind man. He will understand what your father has done. I pray he treats you well."

"I never wanted to share a man with my sister," I murmured.

"Nor did I want to help you deceive your husband before your marriage day. But it must be so. No other man will have you, and according to Harran Laws, you must be wed before Rachel."

"Law or custom?" I asked.

"Custom? Law? What does it matter? Your father insists on it. Come. They wait for you." She opened my door and led me down the stairs.

As we passed Rachel's chamber, I heard a soft sob. My heart broke. I did not desire to cause her pain. *I would not be here if Father had not required it of me, sister. I never wanted to take your husband.*

What can I do? If I try to rush in and change places with Rachel, Mother will beat me and drag me away. Even if I succeeded, Father would beat me tomorrow. I am lost. Jacob and Rachel will hate me, and I am stuck as an unwanted second wife. Always. Oh, Jehovah, you know best, but did I have another choice? I must obey Father and Mother.

Mother led me down the stairs and into the garden where the men feasted.

Father performed the marriage rite. It did not last long. I suspect Father did not want to cause Jacob to suspect treachery. As he had ordered me before, I did not speak my agreement, only nodded my head and hummed.

Jacob attempted to lift the tichel to kiss me, but Father reminded him of the custom that he could not until he had sanctified and consummated the marriage.

Jacob groaned, but let my tichel slip from between his fingers. "I will wait."

"She is shy," Mother said. "Do not remove the tichel until morning."

I could smell wine on Jacob's breath. Even still, he chuckled. "Rachel is not shy."

"She is about this. Please be kind and do not remove her tichel," Father said.

Jacob shook his head. "I will." He took my hand. "We have waited seven years for this. Shall we go home?"

I nodded, and we turned to walk down the path to his — our home.

I had dreamed of going to this home with my husband. I let thoughts of Rachel slip away, allowing me to enjoy this man.

Someone had lit candles for us. They had burned low, but still gave enough light for us to see to climb the stairs to the sleeping chamber.

I swallowed as he opened the door. *Would he expose Father's deceit before consummating the marriage?*

I glanced at the sleeping pallet. Someone had spread my blue wedding blanket across it. Jacob did not notice the difference.

"I will be gentle," he whispered and blew out the candle.

I did not know becoming a wife could be so wondrous. I did not desire to misrepresent myself to my new husband. But I had no choice. My father had demanded this.

Jacob lay next to me after our loving, his arms surrounding me, and slept. I lay marveling at the love he showed me. Would he continue to treat me as well after he discovered my father's deceit?

I woke before Jacob and pulled my tichel over my face as he stirred beside me. I wanted him to love me one more time before recognizing Father's deception. He rolled over and pulled me close.

"Rachel," he murmured. "Come to me."

I allowed him to pull me close.

He murmured loving words, and I responded by moving close and kissing him. I understood now the joys of marriage.

Jacob closed his eyes as I kissed him. My tichel brushed against his face.

"You are my wife now. You no longer need that tichel."

Before I could catch hold of the tichel to hold it across my face, Jacob pulled it off.

I stared at him, waiting for his response. Would his love overcome the deceit?

"Leah?" He tilted his head to the side and pursed his lips.

I struggled to maintain eye contact with him.

"How did this happen? Where is Rachel?" He tapped his finger on my bare shoulder.

I swallowed. "Father."

"Your father said you could not speak nor show your face because of the customs of your land. I believed him." Jacob's voice was filled with tension, although he did not shout at me.

"He instructed me to keep my face hidden and warned me to stay quiet," I whispered. I hesitated, then added, "He threatened me ..."

"Laban threatened you."

I closed my eyes. "He insisted this must happen. No other man will have me. Not ... Not with these." I ran my fingers across my face.

"You are a beautiful woman, Leah. Your father did not need to trick me."

I opened my eyes wide and stared into his. "You would have married me if he had asked?"

"Not last night. I worked seven years to marry Rachel. It is Rachel I love." His face tightened around his eyes.

"He would have beaten me."

At that, Jacob sat up and pulled on his robe.

"I cannot have your father threatening my wife."

I rolled my lips inward and reached toward his back, then pulled my hand back. "You are angry he threatened me?"

"You are my wife, although you are not the woman I bargained for." He shoved his feet into his sandals. "I must speak to Laban. I will return."

He stalked from the chamber. I listened to his feet pound down the stairs. *Now what? Will he turn me out after speaking with Father? What should I do?*

I rose from the sleeping pallet and looked for a dress to wear. I had no desire to put my wedding dress back on, but I had no other clothing.

Zilpah pushed the door partway open and peeked in. "Are you well?"

I put my hands over my face and bowed my head. "I do not know. What will Jacob do now that he has uncovered Father's falsehoods?" I glanced at my wedding dress, lying in a heap on the floor. "I need something to wear."

"Your trunks and baskets were delivered early this morning. I brought this one for you. Will it do?" She held up a blue dress.

I sagged onto a stool. "Thank you. That dress is perfect."

"I will help you dress," Zilpah said, closing the door. "How long do you think Jacob will be?"

I pushed my hair off my face. "How long will it take Father to smooth Jacob's anger? He feels cheated." I glanced at Zilpah as she pulled the dress over my head. "As he should. Father deceived him. He is angry that Father threatened me, his wife." I shook my head. "My greatest fear is that he will go to the judges of Harran and complain. He can demand that the marriage not be valid and require that it be dissolved."

Zilpah gasped. "Jacob would not do that! He is a good man. He would not slander you and Laban like that."

Tears pooled at the bottom of my eyes. One leaked out. "He could express his anger toward Laban. I would. He worked seven years for Rachel and woke up with Leah."

"He will not do that. He will not discredit you. If he did, you will never find a man who will take you."

"I have not found a man yet who loves Jehovah and wants me." My tears spilled.

Zilpah pulled her linen cloth from the pocket hanging from her shoulder and handed it to me. "You cannot cry. He does not need to see you with a blotchy red face."

"No," I said, dabbing away the tears. "It is bad enough that I have these ugly scars."

"Your scars are almost gone." She stared around the chamber and found the water-filled urn. She took another linen cloth from her pocket and dipped it in the water. "Use this. It will help take away the red splotches."

I traded cloths with her and washed my face.

"Sit here. I will brush your hair." Zilpah indicated the stool beside the dressing table.

I sat while she brushed my hair. The movement of the brush soothed me.

When she finished, Zilpah retrieved my sandals and brought them to me. I slid my feet into them and stood.

"Is there food?"

"There is. Shall we go get you some food? Jacob should be hungry when he returns."

Rachel's Wedding

Jacob returned after we waited a long time in the kitchen.

He slumped into the chair across the table from me and rubbed his head.

"Are you hungry?" I asked.

He nodded, saying nothing, only pressing the sides of his head in circular movements.

I rose and stepped behind him, pushing gentle fingers beneath his to massage his head. Jacob dropped his hands and moaned.

"This day should not be stressful," he mumbled. "It should be a day filled with loving and joy, not anger and confusion."

"My father?" I asked.

His head nodded beneath my fingers.

"What will you do?"

"What can I do? Your father demands I work for him another seven years to marry Rachel." His muffled voice sounded from behind his hands.

I gasped. "Must you wait the full seven years again?"

He shook his head. "No."

"Do you want to share with me?"

"Do you have food for us first?"

"I do." I moved to the cooking fire and lifted the food Zilpah had helped me prepare. I set it on the table in front of us and served him.

Jacob took a bite, then stared at me. "Did you cook this?"

I ducked my head. "I did, with Zilpah's help. Mother insisted we learn to cook. Does it taste good?"

He swallowed his food. "It does. You learned well. It tastes much like my mother would cook."

My face warmed. "Thank you."

After he ate a few more bites, I lifted my head and dared to ask the question burning within me. "What will you do about me?"

"I told you earlier. You are my wife." He set his spoon on the table.

"You will not go before the judge to have our marriage dissolved?"

He blanched. "Why would I do such a terrible thing to you?"

I shrugged. "You have reason."

"Perhaps, but I will not do such a thing. Laban insists you and I spend this week together as husband and wife."

"This week? And then?" My stomach turned upside down.

"And then, Laban promised I can marry Rachel."

"You will have two wives?" I asked. Other men had more than one wife. I never expected to be Jacob's wife, let alone to have my sister married to my husband.

"My grandfather, Abraham, had two wives. I sought direction from Jehovah. He confirms the rightness of this. I had not planned to marry two women." He lifted his head and gazed into my eyes. "But your Father changed my plans. Now I must work another seven years."

"When will you return to work for Father?"

Jacob lifted his spoon and dipped it into the food. "In two weeks. One week for us, and one more week to spend with Rachel."

And what will I do while he enjoys Rachel?

"Do not worry about Rachel now," Jacob said, seeming to hear my thoughts. "We need to get to know each other better now." He took my hand and led me up the stairs to the sleeping chamber.

During the next week, he treated me with the same tenderness he had the night before when he thought I was Rachel. We spent time alone together, with only Zilpah in the house to help cook and support us. She stayed out of our way. Rather than wait for Zilpah's help, Jacob helped me dress.

I cared for Jacob deeply before our week ended.

"I thank you for your kindness," I told him the morning before he was to go that evening to marry Rachel.

A bark of laughter escaped his lips. "You are my wife. How else should I have treated you?"

"You could have shown your anger." I brushed my fingers across my throat.

"Other men may have, but I could not. My mother taught me to treat women respectfully. I agreed to marry you that night."

"But you did not know it was me. You expected it to be Rachel."

He nodded. "But it was you. Jehovah will bless us for our obedience."

"What do you want me to do now?"

His eyebrows crunched together. "Do?"

"Would you like me to move to another chamber? You planned to share this one with Rachel." I bit the inside of my lip. I had delayed moving my things out.

Jacob glanced around, considering the space in the house. "This is a big house. You are the first wife. Rachel can have another chamber."

First wife! I have considered myself to be second all week. I am the first wife.

"Should I move her possessions into another chamber then?" I internally itemized which were hers and which were mine.

"Rachel would like that."

"Have you talked to her?" My lower lip slipped out in an unconscious pout.

Jacob kissed it. "I have not spoken to Rachel since before I married you. You know I love her, but I honor you as my first wife. Trust me to care for you as I will care for her."

I swallowed the jealousy that squirmed through me. Jacob cared for me. He would always love Rachel, but he would treat me well, regardless of my father's deception. I blew out the pain.

"I will move her possessions to the chamber across and down at the end of the hall. Will that be acceptable?"

Jacob thought about it. "That should be far enough away for you women. Neither of you will want to know what is happening in the other's chamber."

I leaned forward and kissed him.

"You are truly aware of our needs."

"Grandfather Abraham gave each wife a tent. We live in this house. We will make it work."

After loving me one more time as his only wife, Jacob lay down to rest, knowing his night would be long. I went into Rachel's chamber and found her red marriage blanket spread across her sleeping pallet.

I looked at Zilpah, who shrugged. "I moved her marriage blanket here when I brought yours," she said. "You would not want her blanket in your chamber."

Together, we moved Rachel's possessions from my chamber, making no noise or waking Jacob, so we could set up her new chamber. It did not take long to move her possessions and place them as she had earlier put them in the chamber that became mine.

Zilpah and I moved through the house, placing some of my possessions in place of Rachel's. Some I left in the trunks and baskets, knowing Jacob would want to return to his homeland. We did not need to use all the household items when we could keep some for later, when we had our own tents.

We put some of Rachel's possessions in the trunks and baskets that came from our parents' home to Jacob's home, which would become Rachel's and mine. When we completed the task, I sat at the table drinking juice. Jacob came into the kitchen.

"You have been busy," he said.

I stood to get a cup for him and poured him the juice before I sat next to him.

"I prepared for Rachel to join us."

"You are a good woman, Leah. Few women would willingly open their homes to another."

"I have no choice. You and Rachel chose this house to live in. Father wedged me into your home, although I have dreamed of living here since shortly after you came to Harran. I did not expect to live here with you, although I dreamed of living here with a husband."

"You did not dream of marrying me?" Jacob teased.

"Not after you declared your love for Rachel. I knew you desired her. I hoped a man would want me, even with this face."

"Your face?" Jacob jerked back as though I had slapped him. "What is wrong with your face?"

"The scars that cover my face. You see them." My hands leapt to cover the scars.

Jacob leaned forward and tugged my hands away and traced the scars. "I no longer see these. Your beauty shines through your eyes and your actions. Those other men were wrong to refuse you. I will honor you as my wife through all eternity."

"After Rachel. You love her," I said.

"I do. I will always love Rachel. But you are my first wife, and I will always care for you." He leaned forward and kissed me. "Shall we go upstairs?"

I glanced out the window. The sun shone above the house. "Do we have time?"

"We do." He pushed his chair back and took my hand. "Come with me."

My heart sang. Jacob loved me and would love me in his way for all eternity.

Later, I helped him wash and dress to prepare for his wedding.

Jacob kissed me before he left. "I will return."

"I will be here when you return, but I will stay out of your way so you and Rachel can spend time together. She deserves a week alone with you, as I had a week."

He kissed me again, a long kiss. "Few women would understand."

"Father foisted me onto you. You would not have married me if he had not. I am grateful for your consideration."

"I have grown to care for you. After Rachel's week, the three of us will become a family."

I nodded. I would miss him as he dedicated his next week to Rachel. He strode out the door, whistling softly. I allowed a few tears to trickle down my cheek, then I looked around for something to do for a week.

Tomorrow, I would get my loom and weave while I waited for him. Father would send a man to help me move it. Not today. Father would not have time for me while he celebrated Rachel's marriage.

How long would it take? The men feasted before our wedding, but I did not hear the noise of men celebrating. Perhaps they celebrated more quietly.

I retrieved my mending basket and moved to our sitting area. Zilpah joined me, and we worked together, planning to visit until time to sleep. She left to get a tray of meat and cheeses for us to eat, then lit a small candle to light our work. I thought we would be asleep long before Jacob and Rachel arrived.

I did not want to cause Rachel problems. After all, she had given up her dreams because of me, although not willingly. I would not choose this, but Father gave us no choice.

I yawned. It had been a busy day, and I wanted to leave the house dark as it was when Jacob brought me here. Zilpah lit candles to light the way to Rachel's chamber before we expected Jacob to return with her. I finished my last seam and pushed the needle into the needle keeper when I heard the door open.

Zilpah stared at me, then blew out the candle. We sat in silence as Jacob led Rachel past the sitting area and up the stairs.

"Where will we go?" Rachel asked as they climbed upward.

"We go to your chamber," Jacob said. "Leah and Zilpah have prepared it for you."

"My chamber?" Confusion filled her voice. "Not yours?"

"You would not want to sleep in the same chamber as Leah. You have a chamber of your own."

"And do you have a chamber?" she asked.

"I will sleep —"

They had reached the top of the stairs, and we could no longer hear their voices.

"She did not see us," Zilpah whispered.

"No. We should —"

The door opened once more. "Zilpah, are you here?" Bilhah asked.

"We are here," Zilpah said.

Bilhah felt her way among the furnishings as she moved into the sitting area. "I hoped to find you. Laban gave me to Rachel as her maidservant. Can you show me where we will sleep and where Rachel is?"

"Come with me," Zilpah said. "I will show you the way." She took the candle from the wall and turned to me. "Will you need me to relight the candle?"

"Yes, please. I can find my way up the stairs in the dark, but I will want a candle in my chamber."

The second candle wick flamed, brightening the sitting area until the two maids left.

I sighed and picked up the candle they left for me and went up the stairs, making no noise. Rachel did not need to be reminded of my presence yet. This would be a long week for me, as I was certain the past week had been for her.

I still stood staring at the sleeping pallet. "It will only be a week, and then he will return to me."

Zilpah entered after showing Bilhah to her chamber and glanced toward the chamber where Jacob made Rachel his wife. She then gathered my sleeping robe into her hands.

"Jehovah has been kind to me. Do you remember telling me to trust Him?" I murmured.

She nodded and held out my robe.

"I did not expect Father's deceit to become a gift," I said as I dropped my dress to my feet. "Now I have a man who cares for me, one who does not see the scars on my face."

Zilpah helped me dress in the sleeping robe, and I moved to the stool in front of my dressing table.

"I missed doing this," she said. "Jehovah is a mighty God. You are blessed."

"Jacob brushed my hair last week. He said my hair is as beautiful as my eyes." I sucked in a shuddering breath. "He will return to me."

"He will come back to you. He cares for you. Trust Jacob as you trust Jehovah."

After Zilpah brushed my hair, I sat in the chair near the window. She turned down the covers of my sleeping pallet.

"I will sit here for a bit. Go on to sleep. I will be fine," I said.

She nodded, looking as if she wanted to embrace me.

Instead of accepting her concern, I turned to stare out the window.

"Goodnight, then. I will return as usual in the morning."

I lifted a hand, wanting to accept her embrace, but the door closed, and I did not want to disturb Rachel.

Sharing

Father sent both my loom and Rachel's to our home when I asked for mine.

"Rachel will need her loom in the days after Jacob returns to work. Perhaps she will need to weave clothing for her child," he said when I returned to his home to ask for my loom.

I glanced away. *No thought of a child for me yet?* I ducked my head.

"Perhaps. We will both need to weave, even with all the things we made in the last seven years," I said. "One of us will be with child before long, and we have not yet woven blankets or fabric for little ones."

"Yes," Mother said, watching from the door as I gathered my baskets of yarn and the threads we had spun. "One of you will soon have a child, and I will be a grandmother again."

"You are a good grandmother. Our brother's children love you. Ours will too."

"The day comes too soon. Was it not just yesterday you were laid in my arms?"

"It seems so," I said, "but I have lived twenty-four years now." I lifted a basket of thread.

"And finally safely married," Father said. "Leave those. My man will carry them to your home."

I set the baskets near the door. "Yes, to a man who I want to care for me," I murmured. "Will they bring our looms soon?" I said louder.

"How can he not care for you?" Mother said.

I shrugged and said nothing.

"My men will bring your looms within the hour. Can you wait that long?"

I nodded. "I can wait. The maids and I will ensure we have space for both looms." I lifted a basket of thread in each hand. "I can carry these with me."

"Must you leave?" Mother asked. "I have missed you this last week, and now both of my daughters are gone."

"I must ensure we have space for both looms in the weaving chamber. I will return later." I kissed mother on the cheek and gave my father a quick embrace before returning to my home.

My home. What a lovely thought! *Yes, I share it with Rachel, but we no longer live in Mother's home.*

When the men arrived with the looms, I reminded them to move them in as quietly as possible.

"Remember, Jacob and Rachel celebrate their marriage," I whispered.

The men sniggered, but said nothing and worked to make as little noise as possible as they set the looms in the chamber. I heard their laughter as they strode past the window of my new weaving chamber.

I shook my head and set to work. I knew one of us would have a child in the coming months. I decided to weave a sage green blanket for Jacob's first child, whether that child was Rachel's or mine. It gave me something to do, something to think of besides what was happening in Rachel's chamber.

At the end of Rachel's week, long after Jacob had left to care for Father's flocks, she wandered down the stairs looking for food.

"No one brought us food this morning," she said, a whine filling her voice.

"Your week with Jacob is finished," I said. "It is time to become part of this household. We will need to divide up our duties as wives and the responsibilities for our home."

Bilhah dished up a bowl of grains from a pot at the edge of the fire and brought it to Rachel.

"It should be me who has the most responsibility," Rachel said. "Jacob and I chose this house. It would have been mine, except Father forced Jacob to marry you."

I swallowed the bile that leapt into my throat. Did she blame me? "I dreamed of living in this house since Jacob asked Father to marry you. It could have been mine if a man had married me in the seven years Jacob worked to earn you. But no man did, and I am the first wife, married to Jacob before you. I can claim total responsibility and insist you do all I say."

Her mouth dropped open, and she spluttered, unable to form words.

"However, I will not. We are sisters. I know Jacob loves you. I will do all I can to encourage him to love me as well. I will not treat you as an inferior wife. We can be equal. Do you have any ideas about how we can divide up the responsibilities?"

We sat together for almost an hour, working to divide the responsibilities between us and our maids, Zilpah and Bilhah. We would share the cleaning and laundry responsibilities since we shared a husband. It took time, but we worked out a division of responsibilities that would be fair to both of us.

While Rachel worked on her tasks, I completed the task I had begun earlier, then went to the weaving chamber to work.

I had almost completed the small, soft, sage green blanket on the loom, hoping to need it for a baby soon. I suspected one of us would have a child. I hoped it would be me, but if not, I would have a gift for Rachel.

I ran the shuttle through the last rows as Rachel entered the weaving chamber.

"That is a beautiful blanket. I did not know there was a chamber for weaving in this house," she said, sitting on the stool in front of her loom. "When did Father send these over?"

"I went to Father the morning after you married Jacob. I needed something to keep me busy. I can only mend and clean for a short time before I go wild." I pulled my shuttle off the end and started it back across the blanket for the last time.

She looked away to stare at the baskets of threads and yarns I had set neatly on the shelves. "Did you bring our baskets of yarn and threads over as well?"

I nodded as I finished the row. "Father sent these over with his men. They chortled when they got back outside because I demanded they work without noise and not disturb you and Jacob. They said you were too busy to notice."

"We heard nothing. They were extra quiet, or we were busy ..." Crimson crept up her pale cheeks.

I tied the final knot and began to take the blanket off the loom.

"I thank you for the quiet," Rachel said, looking over my shoulder, "but you never said who that blanket is for. It is not big enough for your sleeping pallet."

I finished the last steps and held up the blanket. "I made a baby blanket. With two wives, Jacob should have a child soon. He said Jehovah promised his grandfather, Abraham, a large family. One of us should become with child soon."

Rachel sighed. "One of us should."

I could see the desire to be the first spread across her face before she smoothed it. "May we both have a child," she added.

I held up the blanket and shook it straight. "Two at once would be wonderful. One from each of us," I said. "Jacob is a twin. Perhaps we will have twins."

"Your blanket is beautiful. A child will use it within the year." She bent to examine the threads in the basket.

"Within the year," I agreed. "What will you weave first?"

"A baby blanket, I think. Mother says you never have enough blankets."

"Or bottom wrappers," I said with a giggle.

"No. Never enough of those."

Rachel found the colors of yarn she wanted to use while I folded the blanket and nestled it in an empty basket. *How many more would I weave before I carried a child?*

Rather than setting the wefts for another blanket, however, I strung lighter threads. We would need bottom wrappers. I would begin by weaving a length of fabric for them.

We worked on our weaving, talking with each other as we had as young girls before we vied for our one man.

"I love the window in this room," Rachel said as the sun moved across the room. "You set the looms to receive the best light."

"Thank you. I worked to have strong light. Sunlight is best when weaving."

Rachel nodded. "And we can watch for Jacob's return."

I planned for that, but did not want to admit it. "Can we?" I stood and stretched, then walked to the window. "He should come this way soon."

"I hope Father treated him well," Rachel said.

I ducked my head. "Jacob has done much for Father. He should treat Jacob better."

"He found a way to extract another seven years of free labor from our husband. He has not treated him fairly."

"That should change," I said, turning away from the window. "I hope it does before long."

Rachel leapt from her stool and raced toward the kitchen door.

I glanced out the window in time to see Jacob's back. I followed her into the kitchen, hoping to spend time alone with him. It *was* my turn.

I entered in time to see him kissing Rachel. I would need to be faster the next day.

"Do you have a kiss for me?" I asked, aware of the whine that threatened to enter my voice.

Jacob turned and kissed me. "How was your first day together as sister wives?" he asked.

"Good," Rachel said, taking his hand and pulling him toward her. "Come, I will help you get clean for dinner." She turned to Bilhah. "Is there hot water in my chamber as I requested?"

"Yes, mistress," Bilhah murmured.

Rachel led Jacob up the stairs. As they reached the top step, he looked over his shoulder and grinned with a shrug. He did not look very unhappy about the situation. I was, but I refused to show my jealousy.

Instead, I turned toward Zilpah and Bilhah. "Is the meal almost prepared?"

We worked together to finish preparing the meal and setting the table.

Tomorrow, Rachel will be here, *and I will be with Jacob. I will not have this happen every day. One more thing to work out.*

With Child

In the next days, Rachel slipped out of the weaving chamber or from the sitting area, where we mended clothing, before I could get to the kitchen to greet Jacob first. She turned to grin at me as she led Jacob up the stairs for time alone with him. He spent that time with her, and after eating and some time together with me in the sitting area, he led Rachel upstairs to sleep.

I boiled, but how could I complain? I knew he loved Rachel and had asked her to marry him. I was the unwanted wife. How could I encourage him to love me as well?

I bit back the hateful words that threatened to spill past my lips, even during the day when we were alone. Rachel would whine to Jacob if I said anything unkind. I could not bring myself to object. Certainly, Jacob would see my compassion and grace. Surely, he would learn to love me.

After three weeks, I met Jacob at the gate as he returned home. Exhaustion filled his face. When he saw me, he grinned. "Hello Leah. How is my first wife today?"

"I hoped we could spend some time together. I know you love Rachel, but she is having her womanly time. Can you spend the next few nights with me?"

Jacob put his arm around my waist and pulled me close. "I will do that. I have neglected you."

"You love Rachel. I understand that. I hoped you would learn to love me as well."

"I ... I care for you." He pulled at the top of his tunic. "I hope I learn to love you as I love Rachel."

"That is all I ask. I know Father abused your kindness and forced me on you, but I hoped you would find a little love for me."

He stopped and gazed into my eyes. "You are an exceptional woman. I care for you. I admit, my love for you is not the same as my love for Rachel. I will spend more time with you. My love will grow."

He walked me into the house with his arm around me. I felt loved for the first time since he had married Rachel.

Rachel frowned as we walked through the door. Jacob kissed her, then went upstairs with me. I fought the urge to turn and poke my tongue out at her.

I helped Jacob wash the dust from his body and face. He took me in his arms and kissed me. My heart thumped so loudly I thought he could hear it.

After dinner, we sat together in the sitting area, sharing stories of the day. We stayed there with Rachel longer than they had stayed with me. I shoved away my resentment, for he would sleep with me that night.

Rachel frowned when Jacob kissed her cheek, took my hand, and bid her goodnight.

"Leah tells me you suffer from the womanly time. I will sleep with her tonight."

Rachel spluttered. She had hidden it from him the night before. Now he knew she would not have a child in the next nine months.

He followed me up the stairs, touching my back, supporting me. As the door closed, he took me in his arms and kissed me. I enjoyed our loving that night, pretending he loved me and only me.

Jacob spent four more nights with me before returning to Rachel's sleeping pallet. I did not mind. I would not have womanly bleeding for nine more months. He had given me a child in the first week of our marriage.

Over the next weeks, I did not share my condition with either Jacob or Rachel. Zilpah knew. She helped wash our clothing. We folded my clean clothing together one afternoon in my chamber.

"You have had no bloody clothes in the wash since you married Jacob," she said. "Do you have something to share?"

"I do not want to share yet, but yes. I am with child. I will wait a while longer before sharing with the others. Perhaps Jacob will notice."

Zilpah grunted. "Perhaps." She folded a dress and set it in a chest.

"You do not think he will notice?"

Her hair swished back and forth. "Jacob is too intent on what happens to Rachel." She glanced up to see my trembling chin. "I am sorry, Leah. We both know he loves her."

"I hope he will love me more when I present him with a son." I folded the length of fabric I wove earlier to make bottom cloths.

"You think this will be a son?" She shook a robe and folded it.

I lifted my shoulder. "I pray to Jehovah it will be. My son will have the birthright."

"Jacob will have to love you after the birth of this child."

"I pray he does."

A month later, Rachel suffered again. Once more, Jacob slept with me while she did.

We enjoyed the next nights together. I did all I could to help Jacob love me more. I listened to his complaints about the way Father treated him. "Your father has more sheep now than he did when I arrived. I have helped him increase his flocks as I care for his lambs better than the herders. Jehovah is blessing your father."

"May Jehovah bless you as he has blessed Father," I said.

"He will when it is time. I bring home more sheep each time the ewes have lambs."

"Will we ever be able to leave Harran? I would like to meet your mother and father."

Jacob kissed me. "We will return to Canaan someday. I must work for your father for another seven years. By then, Esau should accept us."

Perhaps if we had had more than five nights together in a row, our relationship would have improved. I do not know, for we did not. After every five days when Rachel's womanly curse ended, Jacob returned to her sleeping pallet.

On the third night, three months after he married me, Jacob surprised me as he ran his hand across my stomach. "Have you suffered from the woman's moon time since we married?"

I lay with my eyes closed, loving his gentle touch. "No. Not since before we married."

"It has been almost three months." His hand stilled on my stomach.

"And?" I did not dare open my eyes.

"Your stomach bulges. Do you have something to tell me?"

I opened my eyes. "Do you think I should?"

"Is this child mine?"

I sat up and pulled my knees under my chin. "How can you ask? You watched my father try to give me to any man who would take me for seven years. He had to trick you into marrying me. No one sees past the scars on my face."

"I no longer see your scars. You are my beautiful wife, and will be the mother of my firstborn child."

"Do you think I am beautiful?" I tried not to allow him to see how much I wanted to hear those words.

"You have lovely eyes."

I sagged. "You see only my eyes?"

"No. I see a beautiful woman with our child growing within her. Are you well? Do you need to rest? Are we safe?"

I shook my head. "I am healthy. I do not need to rest. I am well enough to be with you for months."

"Father spoke of insisting that Mother rest when he learned she carried us." His hand rested on my knee.

"When did she know she carried two babies?" I asked. The warmth of his hand calmed my frustration.

"She dreamed of us fighting within her. After several nights of these dreams, she prayed for understanding. Jehovah told her we would strive against each other for most of our lives. That is why I left home and came here."

"I thought you came to seek a wife?"

Jacob rested his chin on my bent knee. "I did, but Mother helped me gain the birthright blessing that day. That night, Mother heard news of Esau's threats to take my life so he could have the birthright back. Father called me to him before sending me away and confirmed the blessing he had given me earlier that day. Esau had married Hittite women and lost the birthright already. Mother did not want me to make the same mistake."

My jaw dropped. "Hittite women? He married more than one?"

I knew that. He told us soon after arriving in Harran, but I had forgotten.

"Two friends on the same day." He swallowed. "At least, I waited a week before taking a second wife, and my wives are sisters."

"Does that make it better?"

"Some. What makes it right is that both of mine love and honor Jehovah." He leaned forward and kissed me.

"And Esau's wives do not?" I asked.

"They are Hittites. They converted to believing in Jehovah, but I fear they will return to the religion of their fathers." He kissed my chin.

"What is bad about those religions?" I lifted my chin and closed my eyes.

"Their idol gods demand sacrifices ..." He kissed me once more.

"Jehovah requires sacrifices."

"Not sacrifices of our children."

My eyes popped open and I stared at Jacob. "Children? I could never worship a god who expected that."

"Nor could I." Jacob's insistent mouth took mine in his. "We will speak of this later."

"Did you know Elkenah and Libnah demand children as sacrifices?" I asked the other women in the house the next morning as we cleaned.

"Do you not remember Nyssa's stories of the screaming mother? Have you not heard the shrieking mothers?" Zilpah asked. Her eyes opened wide. "Many here in Harran worship these gods. How have you not heard the cries in the temple squares on feast days? Mothers shriek as their children are taken from them by the priests. I can hear them from far away."

"They sacrifice children here?" My heart pounded at the thought, and I grabbed the back of a chair to balance me.

"They do. When Jacob sacrificed to Jehovah, I breathed a prayer of gratitude that He did not expect a child," Bilhah said. "The wailing of mothers during sacrifices to Libnah brings me to tears, and I never enter the temple grounds to watch."

Rachel turned, a tablecloth hanging from her hands. "Did Jacob not tell you why his grandfather, Abram, and Sarai left Ur?"

I stared at her. "No. I did not know they lived there."

"His father, our great-grandfather Terah, gave him to the priests of Elkenah to be sacrificed," she said. "Abram escaped only when Jehovah sent an angel to save him and destroy the temple. They left Ur soon after and never returned."

I closed my mouth with a pop. "But the priests never tried here? Is that why Abraham sent a servant to take Rebekah to Canaan?"

She gazed at me for a short time before nodding. "They never tried, but he was warned to leave. Abraham will not return to Harran. Would you?"

I swallowed the bile filling my mouth. *I cannot understand why my parents continue to live here. They taught us to worship Jehovah. Do they really?* I remember the idol figurines scattered around Mother's house. *Does Mother worship these idols or have them there to protect us from the prying eyes of visitors?*

Would the people of Harran want to sacrifice us to their gods if they learned we worship Jehovah? I wanted to leave, But Jacob had agreed to work for seven more years.

I heard of women who fought nausea in the early months they carried a child. However, Jehovah blessed me. I did not suffer that ailment while bearing my first child. Because of that, only Jacob and Zilpah knew in the first months.

In the few nights we spent together, we spoke of many things. Perhaps to help prepare me for the birth of my child, Jacob shared with me how he helped the ewes birth their lambs.

"The ewes are silly creatures," he said. "They think they must find a place to be alone when they give birth, especially when a paid herder is with them."

"And if you are there, one who loves them?"

"They will stay closer to the flock, seeking my assistance."

"They do not know the wolves and lions will hunt the lambs, drawn by the blood?"

"You would think so," Jacob said, shaking his head. He kissed my face and ran his hands across my swelling body. "But they are not like women. They do not seek another to help them. They find a place far away and do it alone."

I shivered with delight. "Poor animals. They should know you are there to help them and stay close."

"When I am there, they stay closer. Few of them seek shelter in a bush or ravine. That is why I must be with them while they lamb." He ran his finger along my arm.

"When will they begin to lamb?" I asked. Every second with this man warmed my soul. Every second he spent with Rachel, I longed to be with him.

"The days warm. I expect to receive word any day. The herders have all been given instructions to come get me when the first ewe shows signs of wanting to wander away."

"The sheep are blessed to have you."

"And I am blessed to have you," Jacob said, kissing me.

How I desired those kisses every night. How I yearned to have him with me more than on those days Rachel could not. But he loved her, not me. He was kind and gentle, but his first love would always be Rachel.

About a week later, as Rachel waited for Jacob's return and Bilhah and Zilpah prepared the evening meal, a herder stopped by the house and rapped at the kitchen door, leaving a message with Bilhah. "Jacob sent word that he will not return home tonight, and maybe not for a few more nights. The ewes are dropping their lambs, and he thinks he is needed."

"Tell Jacob I will miss him," Rachel called from inside.

"Yes, mistress," the herder said. "I will tell him."

I entered as the herder shared his message and Bilhah closed the door. I rubbed my back. Sitting at the loom had become more difficult as the child within me grew. "Did I hear Jacob?"

"No," Zilpah said, shaking her head. "A herder brought a message."

"The ewes are lambing," Rachel said, straightening her dress and lifting her head. "He must stay with them until all the lambs are born safely."

I sat in my chair and put my hands on the table. "He told me they would soon be lambing. I expected him to have been gone last week. The ewes are late." Zilpah dished food onto a plate and brought it to me.

"Babies come when they are ready," Bilhah said. "That is what my mama told me when I was still with her." She carried a plate to Rachel.

I set my elbow on the table beside my plate and leaned on it. "Does she help with the birthing of babies?"

Bilhah drew herself tall. "She does. I helped her to help mothers give birth to many of our neighborhood children before she gave me to your father as a maidservant."

Confusion filled Rachel's face, as though she had not heard before that Bilhah's mother had been forced to give her away. "Why would she do that?" she asked. "Could she not care for her children? I would not give my children away."

Bilhah bit her lower lip. "I pray you never need to give your children to others. When my father left her, she could no longer care for so many children. She gave me to your father, and my brothers to other men. When she left me, she had only my younger sister. I do not know if she kept her or gave her to another."

Rachel nodded and began to eat.

"Did she train you to help in childbirth?" I asked. It would help to have someone who knew about birthing babies living with us.

Bilhah turned her gaze toward me. "Yes. I can help if no problems arise. I was only ten when Mama left me. Do you know someone who needs midwife care?"

Rachel lifted her head and stared at me as though she had not seen me for a long time.

"Perhaps," I murmured and continued to eat.

"You have changed," Rachel said. "What about you is different? You did not argue with me when I wanted you to take the flocks to the well, even though you knew it was my turn. You always gave in to me. But you are ... even gentler now. What has happened?"

"Can you not tell?" I asked, my hand cradling the child within me.

"No! You are not! Tell me you are not with child," she cried.

"I can tell you I am not, but it will not change the truth," I said. "My child will be born in about five months."

"So soon!" She counted back on her fingers. Her face lost color. "You became with child during that first week as a new bride."

She must have tried to prevent this by keeping Jacob to herself. Jehovah had other plans. "Yes."

"Does Jacob know?" she demanded.

"How can I keep it from him? I am always available when you are not. I spend a few nights with him each month. He noticed early, probably because of his experience with the sheep."

Her eyes filled with tears. She wiped them away with her napkin. "I wanted the first child," she whispered.

"Jehovah blessed me in my grief."

"Your grief?" Rachel shouted. "What grief? You spent time loving *my husband* before I could. How could you grieve?"

I lifted my head and stared into her face. "He spends most of his time with you. He gives me only the little time you allow me. There is no love between Jacob and me. What greater grief could a wife have?"

She sucked in a breath, preparing to shout more at me, then dropped her head. "A wife who has no children."

Reuben

Rachel tried to be kind to me in the next months, but sometimes her jealousy slipped through. She tried to keep Jacob away from me, but he could not stay away. I carried his child. His excitement increased each day.

Mother and Father were excited when I went to see them.

"Why did you not tell me sooner?" Mother scolded. "I could have made more things for your child."

"I have been weaving and sewing since Rachel's marriage. I have blankets, bottom wrappers, and clothing prepared."

"You never have enough," Mother said. "I will make more for you."

Father beamed at me as never before. Until then, he had never shown pride in me. I was always the girl with a scarred face, the one no man would have. He always preferred his sons over his daughters, and Rachel before me.

"I did the right thing, insisting Jacob marry you," he boasted.

It is never right to force a man to marry a woman.

In the next months, my body enlarged more than I considered possible, partly because I had not been around women who carried a child within them. Mother laughed when I complained about my shape.

"You look lovely. Your child will be healthy."

I prayed it would be so.

Jacob treated me kinder as the day of my delivery drew closer. He stayed with me most nights. On the morning of Reuben's birth, he kissed me softly and left the chamber, unaware of the cramping pains that shot through my body. I had lain still, pretending to sleep, not wanting to cause problems between him and Father.

Soon after he left, the cramping pain increased. Zilpah came in to help me dress and found me curled in a ball against the pain.

"Are you ill?" she asked.

I could almost speak. "My ... stomach ... The ... babe ..."

She touched my stomach. "Is your child coming? I have never been near a woman when her child is coming."

"Nor have I." *But this hurts. I need help. Oh, Jehovah, bless me.*

"I will get Bilhah," she said and ran out.

I remember little more. Bilhah came soon after, followed by Zilpah.

Rolling, cramping pain engulfed me. When it stopped, and I could breathe once more, Zilpah wiped my brow with a cool damp cloth.

Eventually, another woman asked me to stand. I could not move on my own, so they helped me to stand. The pain caused me to squat.

"Push!" someone cried.

Then Jacob sat on the stool I held on to. "You can do this, Leah," he encouraged. "You are strong and beautiful."

Beautiful, looking like this?

But another pain swallowed me. All I could do was bear down, trying to push the pain out.

Somehow, it ended. The pressure and pain ended.

"You have a son," a voice said.

A son. I have a son for Jacob. Now he can love me.

I had little time to rest, for another cramping pain tore through me. "I thought this was over!" I cried.

"Not yet," the woman's voice murmured. "We have to get the afterbirth out. Push once more. Then it will end."

I pushed.

Something slipped between my legs.

I panted.

Jacob lifted me into his arms, even though I was a bloody mess, and carried me to the sleeping pallet, where an older woman washed the mess from my body.

"I am Eila," she said. "I helped your mother give birth to you and Rachel."

"Eila?" I asked. "Where is Bilhah?"

"My daughter Bilhah?" she said. "She is here. We helped you together. You did well, and you have a beautiful son to show for it."

"A son? I have a son?" I struggled to believe the words. *A son for me? A birthright son?*

"Yes, my dear Leah," Jacob murmured from the chair beside me. "We have a son."

Zilpah set the squalling babe into my arms, wrapped in a blanket I had made.

"He is hungry," Eila said.

"How do I feed him?" I frowned at my ignorance.

She showed me how to offer him my breast. Soon his cries stopped, and I felt a satisfying tug.

Jacob lay on the pallet beside us and wrapped an arm around the babe and me. "We have a son."

I glanced into his eyes and saw the love I craved. I would do this again to have him look at me like that. I did something Rachel had not. I gave Jacob a son.

"A beautiful son," I said.

Eila, Bilhah, and Zilpah left the chamber to give us time alone.

When the babe released and lay asleep in my arms, we unwrapped the child, examining and counting his little fingers and toes.

"He is perfect," I breathed.

"As is his mother," Jacob said.

"Am I perfect?" I gazed into Jacob's eyes.

"A perfect mother. A perfect wife. I thank Jehovah for you."

I will accept that.

"I love you, Jacob."

"And I love you, Leah."

Tears leaked onto my pillow. *Jacob loves me. We have a son. All the pain was worth it.*

I gazed at my sleeping child until Jacob suggested I sleep. "You had a rough delivery. Sleep while you can. I will watch our child. He will be safe."

I nodded and closed my eyes, accepting the darkness of sleep.

The fragrance of soup and warm bread woke me.

"I brought soup for you and Jacob," Rachel said.

I pushed myself up on the sleeping pallet, groaning. "Where is my baby?"

"He is here, in the basket, as you planned," Jacob said from the other side of the pallet. He helped me sit and kissed me. "How are you doing?"

"Sore. Not as tired as before." I glanced toward the basket where my child slept. "How is my Reuben?"

"Reuben?" Jacob and Rachel said almost together.

"Yes. I chose to name him Reuben last week after much study. I was certain I would have a son, and 'Behold, a son' feels right."

Reuben fussed. Zilpah lifted him from the basket and changed his bottom wrapper before bringing him to me. "He is hungry, I think, Mama."

"I think so as well." I took him and bared my breast to feed him. It took almost no time for him to remember how to latch on and begin to suckle.

My gurgling stomach echoed through the space.

"I knew you would be hungry," Rachel said. "I will dish up some soup for you."

"I cannot eat hot soup over Reuben," I said. "I will spill it on him."

"I will dip some bread in the soup for you," Jacob said, sitting in a chair next to me.

"You brought the soup up?" I gazed at Rachel. "And did not spill it?"

"Why does everyone think I would spill?" Rachel cried. "I have carried hot soup up the stairs before."

"You must admit it is unusual for you," I said.

Rachel spluttered, and I laughed with Jacob and Zilpah. Rachel spluttered again, then joined us.

"The soup is tasty," Jacob said, dipping his spoon into his bowl for another taste.

"Is it?" I asked.

Jacob dunked a corner of a hunk of bread into the soup and brought it to my mouth, holding his other hand beneath it to prevent it from dripping on little Reuben. I bit it off and chewed.

"Delicious," I said. "Did you make this, Rachel?"

"We started it last night after you went to sleep," Rachel said. "I put it over the fire this morning so you would have food to eat after the birth of your child ... Reuben."

"Thank you," I said, as Jacob held the bread over for me to eat. Reuben's little fingers surrounded mine. Love filled me. I did not expect my love for him to overwhelm me so fast, even though I had loved him since I knew he would be born to me.

I finished the bread and started on another mouthful before Reuben pulled away.

"Do not forget to pat his back and get his burps out," Bilhah said from the other side of the chamber.

I untangled Reuben's fingers from mine and moved him to my shoulder and patted his back. He burped as I moved him, and again after patting him. I ran my hand across his soft, fuzzy head.

"Good boy, Reuben," I murmured and moved him to my other breast. He grabbed on and suckled once more.

"You are doing well," Bilhah said, stepping closer. "To stay healthy, you will need to massage your stomach."

"But it hurts," I moaned. "It hurts more when he eats."

"It will hurt more if the last bits of blood are not pushed out of you. It will make you sick if you do not push it all out."

I moaned again.

"Your little one, Reuben, did I hear?"

I nodded.

"Reuben will help to push it out as he eats. That is why you are getting small cramps while he eats. It will help you heal."

I spent the next days close to my chamber with Reuben, getting to know each other. Jacob came to us each evening after working with the flocks and spent the night with us. I loved the fragrance of the animals, and Rueben loved his papa.

After eight days, the bleeding from his birth ended, and I slowly rejoined the family, taking my child with me as I eased back into doing chores with the others.

Jacob stayed with me at night for a few more nights, then came every other night, then every third night, until he stopped coming to my chamber, except during the monthly time of Rachel's womanly bleeding. I had hoped he would spend more time with Reuben and me, but I knew his love for Rachel would overcome his desire to be with us. Reuben was still a babe, after all.

Jehovah's Will

After I left my chamber with Reuben, I slowly returned to my chores. It took time for me to learn how to work, especially when Reuben cried for attention or needed food.

Mother came often to visit, holding my baby and loving him. Rachel turned her back, not wanting us to see her grief. Although she spent more time with Jacob than me, and it had been only a little more than a year since their marriage, her barren womb caused her pain.

One day after Reuben and I left our chamber to help in the house, Mother came early to visit. Reuben lay on a blanket on the floor, squalling for me to pick him up.

Mother knelt on the floor next to my fussing child. "Is my little grandson hungry?" she cooed. She picked him up. "Oh, Leah. Where are your bottom wrappers? Reuben is soaking."

I handed her a dry wrapper and stood back while she changed him.

Reuben stopped crying as she took the wet and soiled cloth off his bottom. "Do you like that?" she asked little Reuben. "I need to cover you before you fountain on me." She covered him and tied the wrapper.

My baby stopped fussing when his grandmother lifted him into her arms.

"Reuben wants me to hold him all the time," I said with a little wail.

"He is tiny. It is important for him to feel you close," Mother said. She took the blanket from the floor and tied it around me.

"Here, Reuben will be happier if he is close to you," she said, tucking him between the blanket and me, and tied it again. "You can use both hands and still continue to do your chores."

Reuben snuggled into the blanket, and after a short time, slept. It took me some time to feel comfortable that he would stay safely next to me and not fall. I put my hand on his back or beneath him until it became as comfortable for me as it was for him.

When Reuben was a little more than three months old, Jacob offered a sacrifice, thanking Jehovah for the birth of his son. I sat in the front row with Reuben. Mother sat on one side and Rachel sat on the other. Jacob took Reuben after the rite to offer a prayer and to give him a public name.

"We name him Reuben," Jacob said.

"Why that name?" Mother whispered. "Everyone can see you have a son."

I swallowed my pain at her question and answered in a low voice. "Because Jehovah has looked upon my affliction and given me a son."

"I see no afflictions in your life. Jacob married you, even with your scarred face. You have a beautiful home. And now the first son." Mother waved her hand toward our home.

"What more could you desire?" Rachel asked softly.

I fought back the scream I wanted to use and whispered, "Jacob has eyes only for you, Rachel. Perhaps he will see me now I have given him a son."

I will not share the sorrow *of watching my husband leave my side to spend the night with my sister, even though I knew it would happen.*

"You have Reuben. Surely he loves you more now?" Mother murmured.

"How can I be certain of that when he spends most nights with Rachel?" I sighed.

Mother's eyebrows rose, then turned her attention to Jacob and his rite.

Father caused this. I am grateful that Reuben *loves me. I would also have liked to have had a husband who loves me.*

Soft words whispered in my ear. '*Jacob will learn to love you. You are with him because it is my will.*'

Thy will, Jehovah?

'*Yes.*'

I considered the thought. I prayed about it. Why would Jehovah want me to marry Jacob? But I could not doubt the words I received. They were certain. Jehovah willed Jacob to marry me.

I will wait for his love. Thank you for giving me a husband and a child.

I felt a gentle embrace. *Jehovah loves me. Reuben loves me. That is enough for now. When doubts fill me again, as they so often do, I will remember this day.*

I basked in the attention given to me that day, although I shuddered when women commented about Jacob's love for me.

"I am blessed," I said.

One woman added, "Jacob is blessed to have two beautiful wives and a handsome son."

All I could do was nod and duck my head.

But then the woman turned to Rachel. "Should we expect Jacob to celebrate your son soon?"

Rachel bowed her head. "I do not know when Jehovah will bless me with a child."

The woman tutted and left to visit others.

I set my hand on the back of Rachel's hand. "You will have a son. Jehovah loves you. He will send you a son."

"When?" she asked, her voice roughened by tears.

"I do not know, but Jehovah does."

Jacob spent most nights with Rachel. It saddened me, but I knew they desired a son.

We returned to our routine of Jacob sleeping with Rachel except on those nights during her womanly struggle. On those nights, he stayed with me and Reuben. Reuben loved his papa and cooed and smiled at him.

Two months after the sacrifice, I felt another child settle in me. I would have another child to comfort me as I had hoped. Perhaps Jacob would learn to love me with this child.

Once more, I said nothing to anyone, but kept the news to myself. But Jacob knew.

"You have news for me?" he asked one night less than three months after I conceived, as we prepared for bed when he came to spend the night with me.

"News?"

"You glow. Do you have another child within you?"

"Glow?" My face warmed. "The glow of embarrassment or nausea?"

He kissed me. "You carry my child again."

"It is early."

"But you know. You carry another child. Will it be a son?" He kissed me again.

I leaned back from his lips. "How can I know? What will Jehovah send us?"

He pulled me close and kissed me again. I loved the tickle of his beard. I could almost believe he loved me. "Jehovah promised me many sons. This will be another son."

"Then why ask?" I teased.

"I wanted you to tell me."

"I am not ready to share with others. It is early, and Reuben is young. Can you imagine what Mother and Rachel will say?"

"Rachel will be sad." Jacob leaned back and frowned. "I do not know why Jehovah continues to close her womb."

"It will come," I said. "Jehovah loves you. If you are to have many sons, she will have to do her part."

He grinned and kissed me. "I am grateful you are doing your part."

The next morning, nausea prevented me from leaving my chamber. The sickness caused me to stay in bed for a few weeks. Zilpah took Reuben with her, allowing me to rest, until my stomach settled enough to allow me to once again join the family.

Soon after, when Reuben was about seven months old, while the three of us sat in the sitting area talking about daily events, Reuben crawled over to Jacob. I watched as Jacob continued to share about his day.

"The lambs will come soon," Jacob said. "I will stay out with ... Hello, Reuben. What is this?"

The baby had clutched onto his papa's long robe and pulled himself to his feet.

"Reuben!" I cried. "You waited to stand for your papa!"

"This is the first time?" Jacob asked. "What a big boy you are!" He picked Reuben up and spun him around, exclaiming about him.

My cheeks hurt from grinning. Jacob loved Reuben, and Reuben loved Jacob.

When Jacob set Reuben on the floor and returned to his seat, the little boy crawled back to his papa and pulled up onto his feet. He stood and patted his papa's knee, babbling at him, and bouncing on his toes.

Jacob bent to pull the boy onto his lap, and continued speaking.

"How can you continue to work so hard for our father when he does so little for us?" Rachel asked.

"Jehovah will provide," Jacob said, bouncing Reuben on his lap. "We have just over five years until my servitude is completed. He allows me a few of the flock to support our family." His face fell. "But not enough."

I leaned forward to brush lint from Reuben's knees. "What can we do?"

"Trust Jehovah to soften your father's heart," Jacob said. "Our family is growing. We will need more to feed us. I am grateful for your vegetable garden."

"I feared we would not have enough," Rachel said.

"Do not fear. With your garden and the occasional sheep, we will be fine until my time is complete. Jehovah provides."

Jehovah provided. We always had sufficient for our needs, though we were never extravagant.

Reuben weaned early, coinciding with Jacob's annual thank sacrifice to mark the end of his ninth year of serving Laban. We celebrated double then, celebrating the end of nine years working for Laban and Reuben's weaning. Jacob carried his little son on his shoulders through the group of those celebrating, enjoying the compliments and congratulations from the men and women who worshiped Jehovah with us.

"He is a big boy," Mother said. "He has grown fast."

I smiled. "He is. Jehovah has blessed me."

We watched Reuben holding his father's hand as they walked among the other men. Warmth filled me. Jehovah loved me.

Bargain

Mother and Father visited more often than any of us liked, and insisted that Rachel, Jacob, Reuben, and I go visit them. It was never pleasant for any of us. Father always took over the conversation. He treated Jacob as a hired man, rather than the son of his sister and the husband of his daughters. It frustrated me, but what could I do? He was my father, and I was taught to honor and obey him.

"You have done well with my flocks, Jacob," Father said one night when we shared dinner at his home, about seven months after I knew I carried a second child. "It is as if the numbers grow because of your care."

"I love the animals, and they know it," Jacob said. He glanced at Rachel, Reuben, and then me. "As I love my family."

Jacob touched Rachel's arm, and she blossomed. She smiled at everyone, even me. I had not seen her smile in months.

"You have done well with the flocks," Father continued. "But not so well with your family."

"My family?" Jacob asked. "Leah has given me a son and carries another child. Our family is growing. We have been a family for less than three years."

Father's stare rested on Rachel. "But you have not given me grandchildren from Rachel. She is still slim. No child has stretched her body. Why?"

Rachel gasped from the other side of Jacob. I bit my lip and stared at my lap, not wanting to cause more sorrow for my sister. I heard our mother's sharp breath.

"We have done our part," Jacob said. He took Rachel's hand. "Jehovah has not yet blessed Rachel with a child. We pray He will bless our union with children soon. Jehovah caused my mother and my father's mother to wait many years before allowing them to have children. Rachel's time will come."

"Will it? You say you love Rachel. You must love Leah, for she has two children."

"I do," Jacob said. "I love both of my wives. For now, Jehovah is blessing Leah with children. For that I give Him thanks, as you should."

I lifted my head in time to see Father blanch. Unaccustomed to having his hired men, or the husband of his daughters, speak back to him, he swallowed. "I will add my prayers to yours. Surely Jehovah will hear and answer my prayers for Rachel."

Do not pray for Rachel. You are not worthy to ask.

A sadness filled me for my father. *Will Jehovah hear his prayers? He commanded all to lift their voices in prayer to Him. Even the wicked.*

"Yes, Father, pray for Rachel, as I pray for her," I said. "She deserves children."

Jacob nodded at my side. "And Jehovah will bless her with children when it is time." He took my hand in his. "For now, it is Leah's time to give me sons."

I smiled at him. Rachel closed her eyes and bowed her head. *May she know how much we all love her and desire good things for her.*

Jacob spoke up. "My family will do better if you allow me to have a few more sheep from the flocks. Some days ..." he cleared his throat. "Some days we have little meat on our table."

I swallowed. What would Father say or do?

"You do not have enough meat to eat?" he asked. "You may take the old ewes and rams."

"But they live long. They continue to give us warm wool," Jacob answered.

I held my breath. Father needed to allow Jacob more to support us.

"You may have the wool from those older sheep. My daughters can spin and weave. They can sell what they do not need."

We already do that. We need more.

"My wives have done that since the beginning. Still, we sometimes suffer."

Father huffed out his breath. "You have the orphaned lambs and those whose mothers refuse them. What more can I give you?"

"I have helped your flocks grow," Jacob said. "Give me, I pray, one of each fifty, that I may have sufficient to care for my family."

Father's head shook back and forth. "No. You will take all my gains. I will give you one of each five hundred. That should help your family."

"No," Jacob said. "Give me one of every seventy-five. We need more."

The two men bargained like this until Jacob agreed to accept one of every 250 sheep as his own. The tension had grown until my chest hurt.

"But it is to be a onetime gift. Do not come to me asking for more," Father said. He folded his arms across his chest and leaned back.

Jacob leaned across the table to take Father's hand. "Done. I will not come back for more. There is enough for me to care for my family."

"Do not take the best. Those are mine," Father warned.

"No. Only the older, weaker ones."

I shuddered. How could we survive if we received only the old and weak?

As we walked home together, Rachel voiced my concerns to Jacob. "How will we live if you take only the old and the weak? And one of 250? That is not enough for us. Does Father have that many sheep?"

Jacob adjusted the sleeping Reuben on his shoulder, then pulled her hand into the bend of his elbow. "Indeed, he does. When did you last visit the flocks?"

She spluttered. "Not since you took over the watering. Are there many more?"

Jacob laughed softly. "You should come watch me take them out some morning."

"Reuben would love to do that," I said. "Can we come with you soon?"

"All of you are welcome to watch us leave or return home. I do not suggest you join me during watering time, however."

"Why?" Rachel asked. "We did it alone before you came to our rescue."

"That was before our flocks grew, and before the local men became interested in taking a few for themselves. We are forced to fight them off too often."

I gasped. "Yet you never speak of it?"

"It is part of my responsibility to your father. In a few more years —"

"Not many more than four," Rachel said.

"Yes, in not many more than four years, I can be free of Laban. But he has been good to me. I have a growing family." He adjusted his grip on Reuben and opened the door to our house. "And will soon have a small flock of my own." He held the door open for us to enter.

Rachel entered first, although it was my right to enter first. I did not argue with her. "A small flock of old and weak animals."

"Perhaps," Jacob said with a grin. "But with Jehovah's help, they can be healed." He signaled for me to enter.

"How many will you get?" I asked as I passed him. "Father thinks he gives you few animals. I saw him gloat."

"Ah, that is true," Jacob said. "But he seldom visits his flocks. He has many more than he thinks. We have built a larger paddock for them twice in the last three years."

Rachel giggled. "Father is giving you more than he expects, then?"

"Yes."

I woke Reuben early the next morning. "Do you want to go with Papa and me to look at the sheep this morning?" I whispered.

"Sheep?" he said, his little voice groggy with sleep. Then he jumped from his sleeping pallet. "Go with Papa? See sheep?"

I helped him pull off his nightclothes. "Yes. Papa says we may go with him to see the sheep this morning. But you have to stay with me when we reach the paddocks. Papa will be busy, and you are too small to go with him. The rams and ewes are bigger than you. I would lose you."

His eyes widened as he nodded, his face solemn. "Stay with Mama."

I pulled a tunic over his head and tied it at his waist. "You look like your papa. It will not be long before you are big enough to go with him to tend your grandfather's flocks."

The child threw his shoulders back and stretched tall. "I big. Go with Papa."

"Not yet, my dear Reuben," Jacob said, entering the chamber. "You must be at least as tall as the lambs before I can take you. But you and your mother can watch me lead the sheep away as I take them to the well this morning."

Reuben clapped his hands. Jacob bent to help the boy with his sandals. "You must have a covering on your feet," he said. "The sharp stones hurt."

I slipped my feet into my sandals. "I do not want my feet hurt by the stones."

Reuben bounced toward the stairs. I followed behind him. The weight of our second child slowed my steps. Rachel met us at the top of the stairs, yawning.

"Such a horrible hour to be up," she complained.

"The flocks await," Jacob said.

He walked behind her, balancing me down the stairs and into the kitchen.

We had warned Zilpah and Bilhah of our intentions to go with Jacob, and they had prepared food for us to carry with us to the paddocks. Reuben chattered in his baby talk as we walked down the path to his grandfather's house, around the side, and to the paddocks.

"You have increased the number of flocks," Rachel gasped.

Jacob grinned. "I told you."

"More than double, triple what we had when you came," I said, equally amazed at the number of animals in the paddock.

"Keep Reuben safely back," Jacob said. "I will go bring them out."

He strode to the paddocks and opened one gate, entering to allow the sheep to surround him with loving cries. He opened the gate and led them out, telling them to wait. Other herders stood with each flock as Jacob brought another from the next paddock until all were milling about, sounding their need to move on in soft baas.

At last, Jacob moved to the front of the first flock. He called to them, and like when Rachel and I took them to the well, an older ewe and ram hurried to join him. Then, with a word, he led them down the well-worn path past Reuben, Rachel, and me toward the well.

I lost track of the number of animals in the vast flock, but many times more ran past than in the days when I led them to the well with the help of herders.

The sheep followed behind, hurrying to do as Jacob had asked. None lagged. None wandered away. It took many long minutes for them all to trot past us. As they passed, Reuben clapped his hands and cheered.

After they had all passed, Rachel and I walked home with Reuben.

"Father has many more sheep than I expected," Rachel said.

I lifted Reuben into my arms. "Many more than we ever took to the well. Father should be happy to share a few with Jacob."

"When is Father ever happy to share?"

I murmured my agreement.

"When he is causing others to share." Rachel's voice turned bitter.

"He is always good at that," I agreed, unwilling to match her tone. I held my little son close, happy that Father had forced this on me.

Another Child

Two months later, we worked together in the garden, harvesting vegetables for our table. Bilhah and Zilpah carried the squashes and other hard vegetables to the storage area beneath the house where they would keep without spoiling in the coolness. We placed the others into baskets for storage. Our garden had produced well for us that year, and we did not fear the cool of winter. We would not starve, especially since Jacob had sheep he could slaughter for us to eat. The fragrance of the earth mixed with the vegetables. This usually comforted me. But on that day, it turned my stomach, causing me discomfort.

A tightness wrapped across my stomach occasionally as we worked. I tried to ignore it, as we needed to harvest the last of the vegetables before the cold. My hand strayed to my stomach once or twice as the tightness hardened. Bilhah glanced at me when this happened, but I shook my head, warning her to silence.

I appreciated Zilpah's careful attention to Reuben, who wanted to find his papa and the sheep again. I could not chase after the child. Not that day.

Only Rachel seemed oblivious to me and my small groans when the pressure became too much. I waddled behind her, holding Reuben's hand after we picked the last of the vegetables. Zilpah carried them to the storage space. I huffed out a small breath, happy to have that chore completed. A larger chore awaited my attention, and it would not be patient much longer.

I struggled up the stairs, stopping frequently to breathe. Reuben waited with me while I rested.

Zilpah entered soon after Reuben's little snores filled the chamber. She found me sitting on my dressing stool, rubbing my stomach, and panting. She hurried to my side and touched my shoulder. "Are you well?"

"As well as any woman about to bring a child into the world," I said when the cramp that tore through me relented.

"I suspected today is the day," Zilpah said. "I will get Bilhah."

"Not yet," I said. "Let her rest a bit after our morning's efforts."

She sat with me, her eyes widening each time I stopped everything to breathe deeply and rub my stomach.

"You should probably get Bilhah now," I said when the cramps came closer together.

She turned and raced out my door. I heard her footsteps pounding on the stairs. "But do not wake Reuben."

"Mama?" He stood in the doorway, rubbing sleepy eyes.

"Yes, Reuben?"

He came and set his hand on my enormous stomach. "Brother come?"

"Yes, Reuben. Your brother is coming. When Zilpah returns, go with her. She will give you a snack and take you for a walk. When you come back, you can meet your new brother." *Or sister.* I did not know the child would be a boy.

"Brother, come," Reuben called in his little boy voice.

I would soon have two children if I survived the pain of its birth.

Steps pounded on the stairs. Bilhah or Zilpah?

Bilhah knocked on my door and hurried in, carrying her basket of supplies. "I expected you would need me today. I put on a pot of clean water. Zilpah will bring it soon. How are you doing?"

I glanced at Reuben. "This babe desires to enter the world soon." I grabbed my stomach and groaned.

Zilpah entered during that cramp. She took Reuben by the hand and brought him to me as it eased. "Kiss Mama. We will get a snack and go for a walk."

I nodded my gratitude to her. "Go with Zilpah, Reuben."

The door closed behind them as another cramp rippled across my stomach.

"I will help you prepare to bring this child into this world," Bilhah said. "I do not think you will wait much longer for its entry."

"His entry."

"Yes, his entry." Bilhah stripped my clothing from me and helped prepare me for the birth.

It did not take long. Bilhah did not have time to call for help from her mama. My little son slipped from within my body faster and easier than Reuben had.

As I lay on my sleeping pallet, panting in exhaustion, feet pounded up the stairs once more. "Who forgot to tell me about my son's birth?" Jacob called.

Bilhah glanced at me. "Not my responsibility. He kept me too busy."

She shrugged. "He knows now."

The door opened and Jacob entered.

"Did you wash your hands?" Bilhah demanded. "Or do you still have the stench and filth of the animals on you?"

Jacob muttered something I did not hear, and my door opened and shut once more, followed by his feet pounding down the stairs.

"He could have washed here," Bilhah said. "But he needs to control his voice." She handed me the wrapped bundle of my young babe. "You have a son."

"Jacob will be proud," I murmured.

"Yes. He will." Bilhah busied herself with cleaning the floor.

Jacob opened the door a second time, this time with greater care. "Is my son here?"

"He is," Bilhah said. nodding toward me and our child. "He feeds."

"It is a son!" Jacob shouted.

Bilhah and I warned him with a shush.

He sat on the stool next to my sleeping pallet and gazed at our child. "What will you name this one?"

"Simeon."

"A fine name for a son," he said. He bent to kiss my forehead and touch the babe's fingers that stretched to cup my breast. "A fine son."

"Where is Reuben?" I asked.

"I will ask Zilpah to bring him up. I am going out now," Bilhah said, gathering something wrapped in a rag into her hands.

"And ask Rachel to come meet her nephew," Jacob added.

"Thank you for your help," I said.

"My pleasure," she murmured and closed the door behind her.

Bilhah had lit candles to drive the darkness from the chamber. Jacob brought one closer to examine Simeon's face. "A fine, healthy boy," he said. "You have given me another son." He leaned over and kissed me. "You are a blessing in my life."

But not yet your love. I smiled at him, willing him to add the words. He did not.

Zilpah tapped on the door.

Jacob called, "Come," and she and Reuben entered.

"Bilhah says you have a brother for Reuben," Zilpah said.

I lifted the blanket from the babe's face. "Yes. Reuben, you have a brother."

Reuben stood on his tiptoes and peeped into the baby's face. "My brother?" he asked.

"Yes, your brother," Jacob said, pulling him onto his lap.

"Not play." My little son's face twisted.

"You can play with him soon. He will grow fast like you did," I said, patting his leg.

The door opened once more, and Rachel entered. I glanced up to see her wipe the jealousy from her face. I smiled. "Come see your nephew."

She joined us and offered congratulations and kind comments about his wrinkled, handsome looks. "What will you name this child?" she asked.

"Simeon."

She scrunched her eyebrows together, her forehead wrinkling. "Simeon? Why Simeon?"

"Because Jehovah heard my husband hates me, and still He gave me another son." I glanced at Jacob and bit my lip.

"I do not hate you," Jacob murmured.

"Perhaps not," I said. "But you love Rachel, not me."

"I care for you. You are the mother of my children," he answered.

But you will not speak of love to me when Rachel is near. Your love for her is always stronger. I know that. I accepted that when we wed. But I would have you speak occasionally of loving me.

"Jacob cannot help but love the mother of his children," Rachel said. "Simeon is a lovely boy. He will keep Reuben company."

I shrugged. "When he grows. For now, he is too small." I turned toward Jacob. "I understand. You have always loved Rachel. Perhaps you can love me a little more someday."

"I do," Jacob said, focusing on me. "I love our children and you." He glanced at Rachel with a little shake of his head.

Jacob spent most of the next few days with me and the children. I imagined this was how it would have been if he had loved me rather than Rachel. But deep in my soul, I knew it would not happen.

Concubine

One day, as I sat on a chair, straightening the contents of a high cupboard, Rachel squatted to clean a low cupboard. The maidservants worked elsewhere, leaving us alone to work. We had not worked without them for many months.

I sighed. "You are still so lithe and beautiful."

She glanced up at me. "I long to have your ample body and the children that go with it."

Our eyes met. "I would have your womb filled with a child, as well."

She stood without groaning or complaint and stepped over to hug me. "I forget your love sometimes in my sorrow. You understand me."

How would I behave if I were a childless wife? Would I struggle with jealousy and bitterness?

I returned her hug. "I do not want to know how I would act if I were the childless wife. I would have enjoyed extending our sisterhood as we shared childbirth and raised our children together."

"Instead, I suffer intense grief and pain of barrenness." Rachel stepped back from the embrace. "If only ..."

"If only we could have enjoyed having children together," I said as she stooped to her cupboard once more. "Jehovah knows why we have not."

I am grateful I am the wife given children.

"It seems to be a pattern among the family of Abraham," Rachel murmured.

"Pattern?" I stopped moving the dishes and set my hands in my lap.

"He asked Sarah to wait close to seventy years before she gave birth to Isaac."

I nodded, remembering the stories Father told of Isaac's servant coming to take his sister, Rebekah, as Isaac's wife. "Did she not give her handmaid to Abraham?"

She nodded. "She did. Hagar gave them Ishmael before Isaac came to their family. Rebekah did not have children for many years of her marriage to Isaac, either."

"Did she consider giving her handmaid to Isaac?" I asked.

"No." Rachel sounded sad about that. "Instead, she waited and gave birth to twins, Esau and Jacob."

"And Father gave Jacob two wives. Jacob had no choice."

Is it a pattern? Am I like Hagar, the handmaid given to the husband for children? No, I am the first wife. Yes, the unexpected wife, but I am Jacob's wife, his first wife.

"Father caused many problems," she said with a snort.

Was she warning me that she would follow Sarah?

Two Sabbaths later, we attended the Sabbath service together as a family. As usual, Jacob settled me and our sons in our seats, then sat next to Rachel on my other side with our maidservants near us. Zilpah helped with the two boys.

I enjoyed the meeting and the sermon. At the end, when everyone expected to leave, Daniy, our teacher, asked if anyone had problems or announcements, as he did every Sabbath.

Rachel stood. Jacob held her hand and whispered something to her. She shook her head, dropped his hand, and stepped to the front. "I have an announcement."

People in the room stopped fidgeting and looked forward once more, their attention focused on Rachel.

"You may remember Sarah, Abraham's wife, waited many years to conceive her only child, Isaac. To give Abraham a child, Sarah gave him her maidservant, Hagar, who gave them a son."

Rachel gestured to Bilhah and waited for her to move forward to join her. Bilhah slumped as she walked forward, head down and hands clenching and unclenching.

What is Rachel doing? Is she giving Bilhah to Jacob? How could she when she is already jealous of me?

I stared in wonder as Rachel continued.

She signaled to Jacob to stand beside her and Bilhah. I gasped.

Jacob straightened his shoulders and glanced at me with a look of sorrow filling his face. He smoothed the sorrow away, then stood and walked up to join Rachel.

She took his hand in one of hers and clasped Bilhah's hand in her other hand. She gazed into Jacob's eyes, almost willing him to understand.

"As of today, I give my handmaid, Bilhah, to Jacob. Her children will be mine," she said after taking a deep breath. "Jacob, I give you my maidservant. Will you take her as your concubine?"

Jacob swallowed, then nodded. "I will."

She turned to Bilhah and lifted her hand. "And will you, Bilhah, give yourself to Jacob as his concubine, and mother of my children?"

Bilhah sucked in a deep breath and slowly released it. "I will."

I gulped. *Another woman* vying *for Jacob's time and affection. How would we all handle it?*

Rachel put Bilhah's hand in Jacob's. "I present Jacob and Bilhah."

I bit my lip and watched Jacob take Bilhah's hand and walk with her down the aisle and out the door. I stared at their backs. *How would this affect our lives?* Rachel returned to sit in her seat, leaving a seat between us where Jacob had sat, shuddering. Compassion filled me, even though Rachel had done this to herself. But she sat too far away for me to reach.

Daniy led us in closing prayers, and the congregation stood to leave. Reuben helped me stand, and I made my way through the hands reaching out to touch me in a daze.

Rachel followed my sons and me home, arriving soon after I did. She ran up to her room, closing the door with a little bang. I directed our new nursemaid, Amina, to give the boys food, then climbed the stairs to rest in my chamber.

"Did you know Rachel would do that?" Zilpah asked as she helped take my slippers off.

"I wondered after what she said last week. But I did not expect it. Rachel struggles with envy now. How much will it increase after Bilhah gives Jacob a child?" I sat heavily on the sleeping pallet.

"Do you believe Bilhah will conceive soon?" Surprise filled Zilpah's voice.

"Jehovah will do what He will do. I suspect Bilhah will be found with child soon." I dropped my Sabbath dress to the floor. She picked it up and draped it over a hook, removed a simple dress, and slipped it over my head.

"Get some rest. I will help Amina with the boys."

"No, I will go spend the afternoon with them. Reuben will have questions. I should be there to answer them."

Zilpah nodded, then whispered, "You will not do this to me?"

I glanced at the children's toys in the corner. "Why would I?"

She left, closing the door behind her.

Is Rachel sobbing on her bed? How will she handle this? Time will tell. Jehovah, bless Rachel. Bless us all.

I followed Zilpah down the stairs and met my sons in the kitchen. Zilpah gave me a snack, then she and Amina left me alone with my children.

"What happened?" Reuben asked. "Why did Auntie Bilhah go with Father?"

I swallowed the lump filling my throat. I had expected this question, but had not yet constructed an answer. After I pondered for a few moments, I said, "Auntie Rachel is sad that she has no sons like you to love. She gave Auntie Bilhah to your father, hoping she could give Auntie Rachel children to love."

"She can love me," Reuben said. "I love her."

"I know you do, son," I said, pulling him onto my lap. "Auntie Rachel struggles. Keep loving her."

For the next three days, everyone was subdued to give Rachel support. Although she gave Bilhah to Jacob, she cried much of the time Jacob spent with her maidservant. Those of us in the house did our best to help her through her difficult time.

Changes

Three days after Jacob left with Bilhah, I stood at the window, watching the soft light of morning. I heard low voices outside. I listened, trying to hear their words. I could distinguish Jacob's low, rumbling voice. The other must be Bilhah. They had returned.

I smiled. Jacob had returned. I missed him, even though he had only been gone three days. He gave Rachel and me seven days each when we married him. I supposed three was appropriate for a concubine.

I sighed. Rachel's jealousy of my sons had complicated things in our household. Bilhah's status had changed. We could not treat her the same. She would require a chamber on the same floor as Rachel, my boys, and me. I had moved my sons to a chamber in the middle of the long hall, giving me privacy. Bilhah would need similar privacy. She could not sleep in the chambers below the kitchen among the maids. It would not be proper for Jacob to go there to be with her.

Which chamber shall I assign her? We have empty chambers available on this floor. Perhaps the chamber across from the boys? It sat midway between mine and Rachel's. Yes, that would do.

I went to my closet and chose a dress, which I pulled over my head, then picked up my nightdress that lay in a puddle on the floor. *Zilpah will complain that I did not wait for her to help me dress. But she does not know I am awake already.*

I sank into my chair to rest, amazed I felt the weight of another babe so soon.

The kitchen door bumped closed with a soft thud. Jacob would be off to care for the animals once more.

I need to talk to *Bilhah. She must know where to move her things, and I need to inform her of her change in status.*

I sat a little longer, watching my husband walk across the compound toward Father's sheepfold. Whatever Rachel did, she could not take this joy from me. I loved watching Jacob walk toward the paddocks each morning.

A short time later, I heard footsteps on the stairs. Zilpah and Bilhah spoke in soft voices. I stood and moved toward my door, hoping to intercept them and tell them which chamber I had given to Bilhah. Then I heard Rachel's shout and moved faster.

She had forced this. Did she not recognize the change in her maidservant's status?

I pushed the door open to see Bilhah standing straight, clutching a basket of her belongings and facing my angry sister halfway down the hall. "Jacob instructed me to move into this chamber, since my position has changed."

Poor Rachel had not anticipated this. She hesitated, her breathing raspy, and her nostrils flared. Flinging her arms wide, she shouted. "He wants you here? So near to me? Does he not know the woman of the house makes those assignments?"

I stepped closer to them. "What is going on?"

"Jacob assigned Bilhah to this chamber without asking me!" Rachel said in a roar as she turned to me in surprise.

"It is my right as first wife to make chamber assignments," I said, staring at Rachel until she dropped her eyes.

"Jacob told me to take this chamber," Bilhah said, ducking her head and closing her eyes.

I looked at the open door, then at the other doors in the hall. "This chamber makes sense, since it is a distance from yours, Rachel, and mine. We cannot expect Jacob to go to the maid's quarters to be with his concubine. You changed Bilhah's status. Jacob is correct.

This chamber is suitable for her. In fact, I chose this chamber for her before she came up to occupy it."

Rachel stuttered something, then turned on her heel and returned to her chamber, not quite slamming her door behind her.

I shook my head at the sound of her door, then turned to Bilhah. "Do you need anything?"

"Not that I know of. I brought my possessions." She pointed to the other baskets in the doorway. "Zilpah helped me."

I nodded. "When you finish, perhaps you would join me in the sitting area. I have mending to do and could use your help."

Bilhah eyed Rachel's closed door. "If Rachel ..."

"Rachel has Nita to serve as her new maidservant. Your position in the house has changed. While we mend, we can discuss the differences. Now, you and Zilpah put your belongings away, then come find me in the sitting area."

I returned to my chamber to brush my hair. Zilpah could braid it for me later.

As I sat mending, I considered the changes to our household, as I had since Rachel surprised everyone with her announcement. My body was growing again, reminding me of Bilhah's most important duty since coming to our home. I would need her again to help me give birth to this child.

Continue as the healer in our home, I ticked.

Rachel and I no longer helped with washing our clothing. As Jacob's concubine, Bilhah should not be required to join in cleaning the clothing. A second change.

What else? Nausea reminded me of the obvious. We would have to find time for her to be with Jacob. I had taken the week during Rachel's womanly time. We would have to confront Rachel about this one. Bilhah deserved to have regular time to be with our husband. I had heard of women whose womanly moon time coincided when living in the same home. Thankfully, that had never happened to me.

Bilhah would know if that would be a problem for her. Another point to discuss with her.

Should I offer her space in the weaving chamber? Rachel will never agree to that. I suspect I would like to see her response to that. But, no. It would not be fair to Rachel or Bilhah.

Another point to discuss, or not. *Does Bilhah even know how to weave?*

Meals. Other maids could cook, unless Bilhah had a favorite meal she wanted to prepare.

Dishes? No. The other maids would clean up after meals while Bilhah joined us as a family in the sitting area. *Rachel may walk out, but if Bilhah is to have her children, she is part of our family and deserves to know what is happening in Jacob's life as Rachel and I do.*

Another point then. She is to join us after the evening meal.

As I reviewed the points, Bilhah came in, took the top article of clothing needing mending, and sat in a nearby chair. We sat mending in comfortable silence until I sucked in a deep breath and spoke.

"This is a big change for you. Did you expect all these changes?"

Bilhah's head jerked up. "No. I thought only of trying not to consider what would happen that first night." She shifted her feet and held Reuben's tunic up, hiding her face.

I giggled softly. "I remember when Father surprised me with the information that I would be the woman Jacob married that night. All I could think of was the wedding night. Mother never shared anything about *that* with me."

I suspect she never thought I would find a man who would marry me.

"You? Really?"

"I believe every virtuous woman struggles with the marriage night." We giggled together for a moment. "You are a normal woman. Do not consider yourself to be different about that."

"That is helpful to know." She set the tunic on her lap. "You said we have things to discuss ... about my changed status?"

I shifted in my seat. "I was thinking about it as you came in. How do you think things will change for you?"

"My living space has changed. I expected Rachel to be unhappy, though not as angry as she was. She did not think any more about how this would change our lives than I did."

I grunted. "She often forgets to think things through."

"I want to continue as the healer. Who else can help deliver your children?" She glanced at my stomach and grinned.

Does she know yet that I am with child again?

"My thoughts are the same. You have a gift. You do not want to give it up, and I," I touched my stomach where the new babe lay hidden, "*will* need your services again."

She leaned forward, her hand hovering over my stomach, then sat back. "Thank you. I do not want to give up the opportunity to heal others."

"And I could not take that away from you. Do you have any other thoughts?" I leaned back and returned to my mending, giving Bilhah time to consider the issue.

"Dishes and washing clothing?" she murmured, picking up Reuben's tunic once more.

"No. That will change. No more of that. We have other maidservants who will do that for us. I am wondering if you need to be assigned a maidservant to help you."

Her eyes opened wide. "A maidservant for me? I am the maidservant." She paused between stitches in the tunic before sewing again.

"You *were* the maidservant. Now you are a concubine."

"I know how to dress myself and care for my hair," Bilhah argued.

"I still know how to do those things. However, to improve Jacob's status and image, we accept help from others. We do our part. When we return with him to Canaan, he will be a prince or a king. We, his wives—"

Bilhah cleared her throat to speak, but I pushed on, not letting her speak. "And as a concubine, you must give up your pride and accept help from maidservants. I will assign Orna to be your maidservant."

"Orna is young."

"As you were when you came to be Rachel's maidservant," I reminded her. "You can train her."

"True. Orna will do. Thank you. When will you give her the assignment?" She tied a knot and cut the thread. "Reuben can wear this again." She shook it out before folding it.

"I suspect Simeon will fit into it better than Reuben. Both boys are growing so fast." I grinned, thinking about how fast my sons grew.

Bilhah tipped her head to the side. "Yes. This tunic will fit Simeon better than Reuben."

"I will assign Orna before our evening meal. All the maidservants are there in the kitchen then."

We went through my list of changes in her life. Bilhah accepted them with few complaints.

"I never learned to weave. Maybe later you can teach me. For now, it is not important. My healing will continue to keep me busy."

I cleared my throat. Only the most delicate subjects remained to be discussed. "You may know I claim Jacob's nights on those nights when Rachel suffers from her moon time."

"I will not conflict with you," Bilhah said, her ears becoming bright red. "My moon times have been the same as Rachel's for many years."

I nodded. "I suspected it might be that way for you. Thankfully, it is not for me. Otherwise, I would never have time with Jacob or have my children. It will be a problem for you, since she expects you to give her children."

"I hope she understands that and shares Jacob with me. If she does not, I will never give her children."

I nodded. "We will need to discuss this with her."

"And if she refuses to join us for the discussion?" Bilhah asked.

"We will find her wherever she goes to hide. This topic is much too important for you and her. I have heard of men slipping out after their wives are asleep to see their mistresses."

Bilhah cleared her throat and pulled at the neck of her dress.

"No. You are not a mistress. Your position is more formal than that. You are his official concubine, given to Jacob by his wife, Rachel. You have the right to be with Jacob at night."

Bilhah ducked her head. "She must allow him to spend time with me."

"I hope she remembers," I said. I had little hope of that. Rachel would not have thought that far.

When we settled everything else, I sent Bilhah to find Rachel.

"I know it is not something you want to do," I said, "but we need to talk with her. Will you invite her to come visit us?"

Bilhah rose from her seat and stretched. She would discover the joy of a child within her soon enough. "What shall I tell Rachel?"

"We have some things we need to discuss. Life in our home has changed for the women," I said, shifting my weight in my seat. "She needs to join in this discussion."

Bilhah nodded and moved toward the door, her head down and shoulders rounded.

"And remember, you are no longer a maidservant. Rachel changed that when she gave you to Jacob," I called after her.

She lifted her head and straightened her back. "Yes. Rachel changed my life. I should thank her."

I chuckled at this thought. Rachel would not expect gratitude. Or perhaps she would.

After a time, Bilhah returned to the sitting area, giggling.

I raised my eyebrows in question. When she did not speak, I asked, "Why the giggles?"

Between giggles, Bilhah enlightened me. "Rachel did not want to come because you called her. She is Jacob's first wife by choice."

I started to protest, but Bilhah raised a hand to stop me.

"I reminded her that choice does not have a say in this. Her eyes widened, and her face became red. I told her the purpose of our chat, and she became quiet."

Her giggles continued. "Then, I thanked her for giving me to her beloved husband. My life is better already now that I am Jacob's concubine. I have a larger chamber, fewer menial duties, and more rights, especially with Jacob."

She bent over with laughter. "Rachel had no retort, nothing to say, except that she will join us presently. She did not expect me to change so much."

I giggled with her, then sipped water to stop the hiccups the giggling caused. We settled into our chairs to mend again. It would not be kind of us for Rachel to come in and hear us laughing.

Rachel took her time, as I knew she would. She did not care that my sons would be ready for an afternoon snack soon and interrupt us. I had already warned Amina to take them outside after their snacks. I would see them later.

Rachel entered the sitting area as if this were her choice, looking around and acting surprised to find Bilhah and me waiting. I glanced at Bilhah, warning her not to giggle.

Rachel sat straight in the chair, refusing to relax. She set her feet to leap up. I leaned back in my chair and set my mending aside. Bilhah set hers in the basket, then sat back. She did not appear as comfortable as I had hoped. But she was new to this.

"You asked me to visit with you?" Rachel said.

I inclined my head. Two could play this game. "Yes. Now that Bilhah is Jacob's concubine and installed in her new chamber, we have discussed her changed role in our house. I will give Orna to her as her maidservant."

"Her maidservant?" Rachel cried. "She is *my* maidservant."

"You gave her to Jacob as his concubine. She may still be your maidservant, but she will no longer serve you as she has until now. Since Nita has served you while Bilhah was gone, she will continue to tend to your daily needs. Orna will help Bilhah. When we return to Canaan, we must show them how mighty Jacob has become. A maidservant for Bilhah will add to that."

Bilhah sat still. Her thumbs turned around each other, her only sign of discomfort.

Rachel leaned back in her chair. "That makes sense. But that is no reason to call me for a meeting. What is it you need me for?"

I inhaled. "You gave Bilhah to Jacob. As his concubine, she has a right to equal time with our husband at night."

"No, not equal!" Rachel cried, leaning forward.

I lifted my eyebrows.

"Bilhah is but a concubine, not a wife."

"And even the wife is not allowed fair time with her husband," I said.

Rachel colored. "He wanted me." She closed her eyes and lowered her head.

"And you want Bilhah to give you children. She must have time with our husband for his seed to settle in her womb. You must allow him time at night with her."

"She can take your time while I suffer my monthly moon time."

"No, Rachel, I cannot," Bilhah said. "We suffer from our moon time at the same time. You would not know, but we do."

Rachel chewed on her lip. "Yes. That will not help you give me children. I will take the first two weeks after my moon time. He can go to Bilhah for a few days in the week after that. He can go to Leah's bed in the week of our moon time, although I do not understand why." She shuddered. "Jacob loves me. He will be with me more than with either of you."

Bilhah ducked her head. "Then I may take Jacob to my bed for the rest of the week?"

"No!" Rachel cried. "He spent the last three days with you."

"Should we not allow Jacob to choose when to spend time with us?" I asked.

Rachel grunted. "He would spend all his nights with me, then."

Bilhah straightened in her seat. "Unless you remember how much you desire children to come through me and send him to my bed."

Rachel turned toward Bilhah, her face bright red. *Guilt, embarrassment, or anger?*

"I will remember. You will conceive a child for me."

"I will if you allow me time with Jacob," Bilhah said.

Yes, Bilhah. You will do well as Jacob's concubine. You are learning. But you learned earlier. You know how to handle Rachel as none of the rest of us do.

"Remember your responsibility," Rachel said, rising. "You will give me a child."

"If Jehovah is willing," Bilhah whispered.

Rachel stared at her maidservant, now her husband's concubine. "Yes, if Jehovah is willing," she said and swept from the area.

After Rachel's steps faded, I stared at Bilhah and sighed. "That went well."

Bilhah turned back to me. "As well as expected with Rachel. As long as she remembers she caused this change in our lives and allows me time with Jacob."

"We will not allow her to forget," I said. Bilhah would require my support in the coming months and years.

New Babes

Less than three months after the babe settled into my womb, Rachel intercepted me on the way to the garden to weed. "You carry another child. I see it in your glow."

I cringed, hoping it would be longer before she noticed. I straightened my back. "I cannot stop Jacob's seed from creating a child that settles in my womb. Nor is there anything I can do to encourage his seed to settle in yours. I pray every night that Jehovah will open your womb."

Rachel's face burned a dark red. I prepared to evade her kicking foot. Instead, she took a deep breath and blew it out. "You pray for me? You want me to have a child?"

Hurt filled me. *How could she believe I would not?* "You think I do not? I love you as I always have. I always desire the best for you. Besides, Reuben and Simeon need a brother, as will this little one."

Rachel closed her eyes, fighting back tears that trickled down her face. I touched her shoulder, and she fell into my arms. "I am sorry to be so jealous of you. My time will come."

"Jehovah will send you a child," I whispered.

She bit her cheek and closed her eyes. I touched her shoulder, and my sister fell into my arms. "I repent of my jealousy toward you and your sons every night. You have loved me since my birth. My time will come. Jehovah will open my womb and give me sons. May this child be another son for Jacob." Her tears fell onto my dress.

I patted her back and stepped away. "Your son will come when Jehovah wills it. Thank you for your goodwill."

Within two weeks, Bilhah did not come for the morning meal. Rachel asked Orna where her mistress was.

"Too sick to leave her sleeping pallet," Orna responded, oblivious to the joy and pain it brought Rachel, and poured hot water into a cup then dropped something in to make a tea.

Is that mint? Is she with child?

"What did you add to her tea?" I asked.

"Bilhah recommended mint. She says it helps sick stomachs."

I was right.

I nodded. "Mint always helps me. I keep mint in my pocket in the early days when I carry a child." I pulled a mint leaf from my pocket and popped it into my mouth.

Rachel gasped. "She is ... Bilhah is with child?"

I smiled. "She must be. Ask Jacob. He always knows before I do."

Rachel rubbed her eyes. Her anger must have given her a headache. What would Bilhah recommend?

Bilhah suffered from sickness for three months. After the first few days, however, she did not allow her child to slow her down. She continued as a healer and completed her chores in the house.

Her self-assurance increased each day. She sat in the sitting area with the rest of the family, joining in the discussions. Rachel tried to push her away once, but both Jacob and I reminded her that Bilhah had become part of the family when she became Jacob's concubine.

I spent time with Bilhah, helping her understand her new status, until she no longer deferred to Rachel's every demand. I smiled as she refused to give in to her former mistress.

Rachel spent more time in the weaving chamber, weaving blankets and fabric for clothing and wrappers for Bilhah's child. I spent time in the weaving chamber with my sister, weaving fabric for clothing and wrappers for my new baby.

Bilhah and I shared our experiences with our coming babies. She had participated in my birthing process as the healer, but had never experienced it for herself. Now was her time to enjoy the process.

Only two weeks after I discerned movement within me, Bilhah cried out. "What is that? I feel something."

"A little tickle of movement?" I asked.

Her jaw dropped as she touched her stomach over her unborn child and nodded. Wonder filled her face.

"Your little one is big enough now you can feel him moving."

Rachel leaned close. "May I?"

At Bilhah's nod, she set her hand on Bilhah's stomach.

"There," Bilhah cried. "Do you feel that?"

After a brief time, Rachel removed her hand, shaking her head. "I feel nothing."

"The babe is still tiny," I said. "Bilhah is only now sensing his movement. Give him time to grow. Then you can feel him move."

Bilhah and I giggled together like young girls, rather than mature women carrying babies. Rachel tried to stay with us. She wanted to share the experience, but how could she? She had not yet had a child move within her womb. Until she did, she could only listen.

At last, she leapt from her chair. "Oh, you two," she cried, and strode from the sitting area and out the door. I saw her stomping across the meadow toward the stream that bordered our land.

"It is hard for her," Bilhah said.

"I would not like to be the wife who is loved, but who has borne no children." I cradled my little one within me and looked across to watch Reuben and Simeon bend their brown heads, one dark, the other light, together to stack blocks. "I would like to have Jacob's love. Since Rachel has that, I will enjoy his children."

Bilhah nodded. "Someday Jehovah will open her womb, and she too will have children. We must trust Him."

Months later, the cramping and pain of childbirth overwhelmed me as it had twice before. When they crowded close together, I allowed Zilpah to find Bilhah to help me once again. I had wondered how she could help me, since her body had distended with her child, but she had assured me of her continued ability to do what must be done.

After Zilpah left, I focused on the pain and the movement of my child towards his birth. Bilhah hurried in, asking why I had not called for her sooner. I could only breathe through the cramping pain.

Later, Jacob's footsteps pounded up the stairs, heralding his coming. He soon held my hand, encouraging me.

As Jacob sat beside me after the birth, he kissed me. "You are an amazing woman. Three sons in four years. What will you call this son?"

I inhaled. Would he understand? "This time my husband will be joined with me in love because I have borne him three sons. His name is Levi."

His head jerked back. "I have always loved you, Leah."

"You love Rachel."

"I do, and I have loved her since I met her." Jacob closed his eyes briefly, then opened them once more. "But I love you as well. You are the mother of my sons."

"But you do not love me as a wife."

"I love you, Leah. You are a blessing to me." His face twisted, struggling to assure me of his love.

"Yes, you love me as the mother of your sons. I am not the woman you would choose as a wife." My hand moved to the scars on my face. "I am ugly. I wish I were not."

"You are not ugly!" His forcefulness surprised me. "You are a beautiful woman. I no longer see the scars. I see a beautiful woman who I am grateful has accepted me as her husband and the father of her children."

"But do you love me?"

His tender kiss showed me his love. Yes. He loved me. But he would always love Rachel more.

For several days after the birth, Jacob stayed with me and Levi, helping to care for our little son. When I joined the family once more in the evening, he left me for Bilhah. Her child would come soon, and he wanted to be a part of his delivery.

One night, near her time, Bilhah could not find a comfortable place to sit, twitching, and adjusting her seat. She would move her hand to her stomach, massage it, and pause. Her little one would come soon.

But Rachel and Jacob did not notice. Bilhah hid it well from them. I saw it, for I watched for the signs.

Rachel begged Jacob to spend the night with her. Reluctantly, he agreed. I wanted to say something, but Bilhah caught my eye and shook her head.

"Let them have this night," she murmured.

I knew Jacob would be unhappy with Rachel when I heard him leave the house. I watched him stride toward the animal paddocks. He should be with Bilhah, but it was not my place to tell him.

Zilpah did not come in to help me dress. I did not expect her. She would help Bilhah. For many weeks, Bilhah had trained her in how to help deliver a child. She had helped me during Levi's birth. I prayed for Jehovah's blessings on Bilhah and her babe.

I sat with Levi, patting his back after he ate, when the cry of another newborn echoed down the hall. Rachel had her child. I continued to care for my babe as I heard Rachel's cry. She needed time with Bilhah and her baby. She had claimed the child as hers.

When I heard Jacob's pounding footsteps fly past my chamber, I knew someone had finally sent for him. *Poor Jacob. He will not be happy to have missed the birth.* I shook my head. *Rachel would hear of his displeasure, though the rest of the household will not.*

I took Levi in his basket to Amina. "Will you care for Levi while I go meet Bilhah's babe?"

As Amina set Levi's basket near the other boys in their chamber, Reuben glanced up from his blocks. "Did Auntie Bilhah have her baby?"

"She did, and I am going to congratulate her."

"When can we meet the baby?" he asked.

"Later. He is your little brother, but he needs us to stay calm until he grows a little bigger. Remember how you took your noise and ran outside when Simeon was tiny? Both Levi and Bilhah's baby need that now."

Reuben nodded and returned to his blocks. I walked across the hall to meet Bilhah's babe.

"May I see the new baby?" I asked.

Jacob stood rocking and singing to the child. At Bilhah's nod, he set the babe into my arms.

"A boy?" I asked.

Bilhah's smile warmed the room. "Yes."

"He is beautiful." I kissed his little cheek, inhaling the fragrance only a newborn has. Levi had lost his already, and I missed it.

I snuggled him close and sang him a little song. "Mama Leah loves you, little boy. What is your name?" I glanced at Bilhah.

Jacob answered. "Dan. Rachel named him Dan."

I glanced at Rachel, who sat near Bilhah, with raised eyebrows.

"Jehovah has judged me," she said with a sigh. She must have repeated this more than once. "Still, He heard my plea and gave me a son through Bilhah."

I nodded and turned my gaze back to Dan. "He is a blessing to our family. Grow big, Dan. Levi needs a friend to play with."

Bilhah turned her radiant smile toward me. "I like it when you call yourself Mama Leah. It honors me." She turned to Rachel. "Will you honor me and allow our son to call you Mother Rachel?"

I glanced up in time to see tears filling Rachel's eyes. I had misjudged her. She was not as hard as I had expected.

"I would be honored. Blessed little Dan has three mothers. You," she nodded to Bilhah, "Leah, and me."

I bounced my head as I bounced Dan. "I like that. My sons will call you Mother Rachel, and you, Bilhah," I nodded toward her, "are Mother Bilhah. Expect the boys to use those names soon."

It would be no problem for them with Bilhah, but Rachel may be a challenge. She had rarely shown affection to them.

Miracle

Levi and Dan grew almost as twins. They often slept in the same basket while we worked during the day or sat as a family in the evenings. Reuben and Simeon played with blocks, building tall towers for their father to admire.

Simeon readily called the other two women his mother, but Reuben withheld his choice to call Rachel mother.

Then one evening, Simeon crawled onto Rachel's lap and gave her a sloppy kiss. "Love you, Mama Rachel," he said.

Her arms enfolded my little son. "Love you too, Simeon."

He grinned and slid off her lap.

After that, Reuben called her Mother Rachel. She glowed when my sons did. I did not understand how it would relieve some of her pain, or I would have called on my sons to do it sooner. It took Bilhah's love for me to see.

The four boys filled the house with noise and laughter. After a time, Rachel learned to laugh with them.

How would she accept the news that I carried another child? She had not exclaimed with joy when she learned of my others. I cringed at the thought of her stomping feet and jealous cries.

However, she did not. She did not weep, nor kick her stool, nor retire to her chamber. Instead, she gulped away her pain and continued to join us in our daily tasks.

"How are you doing this?" I asked one afternoon when we worked alone together in the weaving chamber.

"Doing what?" Rachel asked.

"You are not angry that I carry another child. How are you calm?"

Rachel's gentle smile warmed me. "My time will come. Jehovah has promised."

I hugged her. I did not know how she knew. Nor did I expect her to remain calm.

Our relationship returned to what it was before Jacob came to Harran for the next few years. I loved having a sister again.

Like his brothers, Levi grew rapidly. He loved his brothers, and they loved him. Reuben wanted to carry him around. I allowed him to do that upstairs or when we visited in the sitting area. Simeon wanted to carry his brother as well, but I did not allow him as often as I allowed Reuben. At almost two, Simeon was not as big nor as strong as three-year-old Reuben.

Even Reuben struggled to lift his baby brother after a few months. Instead, the two boys would lie on the floor beside Levi and encourage him to turn over, then lift onto his hands and knees, rocking with him until he moved forward. The boys' enthusiastic cheering echoed through the house. When Bilhah and Dan joined them, they encouraged little Dan as well, loving and encouraging him.

I loved it. I loved that my sons loved me.

Levi walked early, like his brothers. He toddled with unsteady steps about the house whenever I set him down. One morning, I helped Zilpah prepare the evening meal. Amina gathered our clothing, preparing to wash it later that day, leaving my sons in the kitchen with us.

Neither Bilhah, Dan, nor Rachel had come to the kitchen for a morning meal yet. *Is Bilhah sick with another child? She and Dan are normally here by now.*

"Stay with Levi, Reuben," I said. "Do not allow him to get close to the fire."

"The fire is hot," Reuben said.

"Yes. Do not let Levi get burned."

Reuben nodded, his eyes big at the thought.

I turned to mix the stew, cutting the vegetables to add when the mutton had browned.

"No, Levi!" Reuben shouted.

I turned as my littlest son toppled next to the fire, his hand falling into the hot coals. His scream of pain agonized me.

"Levi!" I shouted, dropping my knife. In no time, I dragged him from the coals.

Levi's cries of pain echoed through the house. While I swept him into my arms to comfort him, Zilpah filled a small bowl with cool water.

"Put his hand in this," she said, setting the bowl on the table.

I sat next to the table and set his hand in the bowl of water.

"Can you get Bilhah?" I asked Zilpah. "She will know what to do."

Zilpah nodded and raced from the kitchen. She ran up the stairs while I held Levi's little hand in the cool water. His screams became sobs.

The water warmed from the heat in his hand, and I dumped the water into the dishwater, then poured more cool water into the bowl. Levi howled. I patted his back.

"Mama is sorry you fell into that fire," I crooned. "This cool water will help it stop hurting."

Where is Bilhah? She knows what to do. Oh, Jehovah, bless my little son. Do not allow his hand to scar.

Reuben and Simeon stood beside me, crying with Levi.

"I told him to stay away," Reuben cried. "Oh, Levi. Do not hurt. Why did you run over there?"

"Levi hurt," Simeon cried.

Finally, two sets of feet pounded down the stairs.

I crooned to my baby, "Mother Bilhah will be here soon. She will know how to help you." I then touched Reuben's back. "It is not your fault. You did all you could to stop your brother. Mother Bilhah will help Levi."

Bilhah rushed into the kitchen. "Where is he?"

"Here."

"Oh, good. You have his hand in cold water," Bilhah said, slowing her steps.

"Zilpah had the sense to give me cold water for his hand," I said. "Will his hand heal?"

Bilhah took Levi's hand in hers, in the bowl under the water. She uncurled his hand so she could look at his palm. She inhaled a sharp breath.

"What?" I asked.

Bilhah shook her head. "He hurt his little hand."

"He fell into the coals."

"I can tell." She bit her lip.

His scream softened to a wail.

"Mother Bilhah will help you stop hurting," Reuben said. "She knows how to mend our hurts."

"Keep his hand in the cool water," Bilhah said. "I need to get some aloe." She stepped out the back door, returning soon with a thick leaf oozing with sap.

"This will help you heal, Levi," she said. She lifted his hand out of the water. His screech increased. "This will help stop the pain. It will not hurt," she soothed.

With gentle care, she dabbed his hand dry, then dripped the oozing sap from the leaf onto his injured palm. Levi's little palm shone bright red. I wanted to cry with him.

"I should have watched you more carefully," I said, tears filling my voice.

"I should have seen him," Zahira said, fighting back tears. "It is my duty to help care for your sons. I did not."

"No," Amina said, entering the kitchen. "I should have kept the children with me. It is my duty to care for your children."

"Babies move fast," Bilhah said.

"You had other duties today, Amina." I glanced back at her and tried to smile. "Reuben did his best to keep him safe," I said as Reuben's cries increased. "It is not your fault. Levi is fast."

"I tried to stop him," Reuben cried.

"I know. You did your best. Mother Bilhah will help him stop hurting. Listen. He is not crying as hard."

Levi burped and stopped crying, although little whimpers escaped now and then.

"The aloe helps cool the pain," Bilhah said. "He should feel better soon."

I stared at the ugly burn in my baby's palm. "Will it leave a scar?"

"Perhaps a little one," Bilhah said. "But I will do all I can to prevent it."

While she dripped more aloe over his hand, Rachel brought Dan in.

"Will Levi have a scar?" Rachel asked after gasping at the ugly red burn.

"I hope not," Bilhah answered. "Zilpah remembered to give Leah a bowl of cold water to cool it. I dripped aloe onto it."

She dribbled more of the aloe onto Levi's palm. "He will need a honey mixture applied soon. I do not want his hand to scar closed."

I fought down my gasp. *My son cannot have that disability because I did not care for him properly. Jehovah bless him.*

"Lebi," Dan whined.

Rachel set him to stand on the chair beside his brother.

"Lebi hurt?" Dan asked.

Levi lifted his tear-stained face. "Dan."

Dan hugged my little son, then took his uninjured hand while Bilhah smoothed in another salve, then she wrapped a loose bandage around his damaged hand, ensuring it would stay open.

"I would not normally bandage these, but Levi is a baby. I do not want him to eat the aloe."

"Will it make him sick if he eats it?" Fear gurgled in my stomach.

"No. But it does not taste good."

I sighed. "Then he will not eat it."

"I will examine his hand again soon," Bilhah said, bending to kiss Dan and then Levi on the cheek. "I will not allow him to have a scarred and damaged hand."

I pinched the bridge of my nose and closed my eyes. *If only someone had cared enough about me and my scars.* I sucked in a cleansing breath. *But 'if* only's*' and 'maybes' cannot change the past.* I ran my fingertips across the now-faded scars on my face. "Please help him. I do not want him damaged like me."

"He will not be damaged, and you are not damaged. You are a beautiful woman," Bilhah said.

"Jehovah will not allow Levi's hand to scar," Rachel said, running her fingers through Dan's hair.

"What will Jacob say?" I asked, dropping my head to my chest. "I allowed my son to fall into the fire."

Bilhah examined Levi's hand many times that day. After first gently washing it with cold water, she would alternate between soothing aloe sap and honey mixed with healing plants. Each time, she wrapped the hand in a soft bandage, making sure it would not pull together.

Levi whimpered as Bilhah worked on his hand. Dan sat with him, consoling his brother, and then played with the blocks beside him. Levi soon joined him, stacking blocks with his other hand.

The honey soothed him in a way the aloe had not and helped it heal. Later, when she applied the aloe, we had to catch Levi. He ran with his brothers into the sitting area with a block clutched in his bandaged hand.

"This is looking better already," Bilhah said. "But he will need to have the bandage and salve changed frequently. I do not want his hand to scar closed."

I bit my lip. "Do you need me to do it?" I asked. "I can if you give me some of your honey mixture. I can cut an aloe leaf."

"Tomorrow," she said, wrapping Levi's hand. "I want to ensure no sickness infects his hand. We do not want that."

I shook my head. "No! We do not want any sickness in his hand. How can I know if that happens?"

She ran her hand up his wrist and up his arm. "If red streaks up his arm like this, get me fast! He will need extra help."

I ran my fingers up his arm as Bilhah had. "Redness up his arm?"

"Yes. Those streaks show an infecting sickness. No, do not let them go higher than here." She pointed to the little bend marks on his wrist. "That infection can race toward his heart fast in a child."

I sucked in a breath and held it, not wanting to exclaim and frighten Levi and the other boys. I silently let it out. "I did not know."

"It happens, so watch him." Bilhah finished wrapping the bandage around Levi's little hand before settling into a seat to mend and watch our sons play together.

Near evening, as the maids set plates on the table for the evening meal, we stood watching Bilhah re-bandage little Levi's hand. Dan sat beside him, as he had all day, holding his brother's hand.

The fiery red blister filling his hand brought tears to my eyes. I wiped them away as Jacob returned from herding Father's flocks. He stood next to Rachel and stared at the blister in our son's hand.

He slipped into the chair beside me, nodding at Bilhah.

"What happened to Levi?" he asked as he pulled Levi onto his lap.

I chewed on my lip, fighting back my tears. "He stumbled into the fire this morning. His hand landed in the hot coals."

Jacob gasped. "The hot coals? Were you not watching him?"

His words, though soft, stung.

"I tried to stop him," Reuben cried. Fresh tears slid across his face.

"Reuben did his best to keep Levi safe," I said. I wrapped an arm around my oldest son. "It is not your fault, Reuben. Levi is fast. You tried."

"I tried," Reuben echoed.

"Of course, we watched him, but I worked with Zilpah to prepare this meal. Reuben was watching him as well, and chased him when Levi toddled toward the fire. I grabbed him out of the fire as fast as I could."

"Yes, babies are fast. You tried, Reuben," Jacob said. "Will he lose the use of his hand?"

I held my breath, waiting for Bilhah's response.

"It is early," she said, picking up the bandaging material. "It will not scar if I can stop it. I will do everything I know to do to prevent the scarring."

She wrapped Levi's hand once more, ensuring it lay open so it would not curl with the scar. "There you go, Levi. You are a strong boy."

"Lebi better?" Dan asked.

"Not yet," his mother answered. "But he will heal."

"If Jehovah is willing," Jacob said.

The meal was ready. I helped our sons clamber into their chairs, then I helped set food on the table. I found my place next to Reuben and Simeon, and waited for Jacob to pray over the food. Before he did, he set his huge hands on Levi's little head and prayed for his healing.

"Will Jehovah honor your prayer?" I asked after the prayer, my eyes moist with unshed tears.

He nodded. "As you trust and honor Him, Jehovah will bless our child." He handed Levi to me. Levi slurped in a sad breath, then giggled at Dan.

"Shall we bless this food now?" Jacob said.

Bless Levi's hand *and bless us to continue as a happy family.*

Levi woke screaming with pain after his nap, and again that night. Bilhah rushed in ahead of me to care for him.

Over the next two days, his pain reduced, and Levi's hand healed — faster than even Bilhah expected. Each time she put aloe or honey on his hand, it looked better.

"I do not understand," she said one evening, more than two weeks later, as we gathered for dinner. "I am grateful, but Levi's hand should not be healed as much as it is. Burns as bad as his take much longer to heal."

"It is nearly healed?" Jacob asked.

She nodded.

"It has only been two weeks since he Injured it, but he plays as though nothing happened," I said.

Jacob took Levi's little hand in his huge paw, turning it over. He traced the lines of the scar, closed it and opened it several times. "The scar does not affect his use of his hand," he murmured. "Jehovah has blessed us. He healed Levi's hand."

Bilhah could not hide her gasp.

"Little children heal faster than older people," she said. "Mama told me that, and I helped other children before coming to live with you. But, I never saw a child with a burn as bad as Levi's heal as well or so fast."

"Because of Jacob's blessing that first night," I said. "He promised Levi that his hand would heal fast without damaging scarring if we would trust Jehovah." I looked around the table. "I trusted Jehovah. Did you?"

Zilpah nodded in agreement. Bilhah bit the inside of her lip. Rachel closed her eyes as if in prayer. Reuben's head bounced up and down. Simeon gazed at everyone in wonder. Dan grinned beside Levi. Jacob watched the others as I did.

"Jehovah loves his little children," Jacob said. "He has healed our little boy. Let us give Him thanks."

We knelt next to our chairs and raised our hands in prayer as Jacob spoke the words of gratitude for us.

Four Sons

Bilhah carried another child, as I had suspected. She suffered less with this child than with Dan. Her care of Levi's hand brought us closer than we were before.

One day while Reuben was still not quite five, I took Reuben, Simeon, and Levi into the sitting area to read books. I picked a book from the shelf — a favorite of my boys— and read it to them. My sons needed to learn to read.

Reuben and Simeon sat on either side of me, leaning across my lap to look at the words of the book, while Levi sat on my lap.

"Please, Mother," Reuben begged. "I want to read. Teach me?"

I gazed at him. "I suppose you are old enough to learn." He was, but I wanted him thirsty to learn.

I read the book through, pointing at each word.

"Let me read it now," Reuben teased as I finished.

"Oh?" I asked. "Can you read this?"

He took the book onto his lap and ran his fingers over the words.

"Start here," I said, touching the beginning word.

With confidence, Reuben read the first few words, then twisted his face as he tried to determine the next word. Then he read it on his own.

"Good," I murmured.

Reuben read the story, with a little help, to his brothers and me. We clapped for him at the end of the story.

"I did not know you were learning as I read," I said as he finished. "You read very well, even on unfamiliar words."

Reuben grinned.

"I can read the story, too," Simeon said. "Let me read."

I lifted my eyebrows. "Can you?"

"Yes," he said and pulled the book to his lap.

I moved Levi to sit beside Reuben so I could see the words on the page.

"Simeon cannot read," Reuben said, his voice scornful. "He is still a baby."

"You wanted a chance to read. I let you. Now it is time for Simeon to try."

Reuben hooted. "He is a baby."

"Give him a turn."

Simeon ran his fingers across the words, telling a story similar to the one Reuben had read to him.

Reuben jeered. "You do not know how to read, Simeon. You do not read the words. You are making them up."

"That is how you learned," I said. "You do well, Simeon, for a child of almost three. You got some words right."

Reuben snorted.

I pointed to a letter on the page and helped Simeon recognize it.

"I heard stories from my mother of Eve teaching her little ones to read like this," I said to Zilpah, who dusted the tables. "Her grandmother saw a copy of her life story."

"I heard those same stories. I would like to read the little stories she wrote for those children to read, if I cannot read Eve's book," she said.

I nodded. "Those books would be helpful, and we would learn much about her life from them." I sighed. "Too bad they are lost."

Levi wiggled after a short time. That he sat so long to hear one brother read and the other brother try to read some on his own surprised me. I set him on the floor and shooed Reuben and Simeon away to play with the blocks stored in a nearby basket.

I leaned back in my seat, resting my tired back. "I should teach the boys more."

I thought about how to teach the boys throughout the rest of the day. By the next morning, I had a way of helping them.

After checking the sky to ensure the day would be clear and beautiful, I asked Zilpah to bring two flat pans outside, where I would meet her. Amina and I took the boys out to dig in soft sand.

Zilpah found us there. She grinned. "Perfect way to teach them without using the vellum. Obtaining that can be difficult."

"And expensive," I agreed. "My mother did this to teach me and Rachel our numbers and letters. No waste of vellum."

She set the pans on the ground, and the boys filled them with sand.

"Tell Auntie Zilpah thank you," I said.

"Thank you, Auntie Zilpah," Reuben said. Simeon repeated the words.

Zilpah stood and watched us for a time, while I directed Reuben to find a stick to write with. Simeon dug in the sand, pushing more into his pan. Levi ran his fingers through the sand, as a little boy would.

"Have fun with the sand," Zilpah said, giving us a little wave before she returned to her duties elsewhere.

I gave her a little wave. Amina sat on the sand beside us, trying to ensure Levi ate none of it.

I taught Reuben numbers and letters. Simeon watched and tried to imitate his brother. However, his hands were not big enough yet to do it well. He tired early and joined Levi. Reuben drew neat letters and numbers across the top, then wrote something beneath.

"What did you write?" I asked.

He shook his body importantly, then read, "Mother is the best. I want to herd sheep with Father."

"Nice," I said. "You did well. You will soon be old enough to go with your father."

In the next days while I waited for my next child to come, I sat in the sunshine with Reuben, teaching him to write and read. Simeon came often to join us and learned some basics. Reuben would need to read and write when his father called on him to work with the animals.

One evening, shortly after I began teaching Reuben to read and write, Levi climbed into Jacob's lap and set his hands on either side of his father's face. "See tower?"

"You built a tall tower," Jacob said.

"Simeon knocked it," Levi whined.

"I saw him bump into it. It looked like an accident to me." Jacob moved Levi to sit on one leg. "Tall towers fall easily."

He signaled to Simeon, who ran to him.

"Did you ask Levi's forgiveness for knocking his tall tower over?"

Simeon sucked in a breath and chewed on his lower lip. "No, Father, I did not. I bumped into it as I walked past it."

"I saw," Jacob said. "But Levi worked hard to build that tower. You should apologize to him and ask his forgiveness."

Simeon turned to his brother. "I am sorry I bumped into your tower. Will you forgive me?"

Levi grinned his baby grin. "Yes."

"I will help you build it again, if you would like," Simeon said.

Levi jumped off Jacob's knee, and the boys returned to building. Dan and Simeon helped Levi build another tall tower.

As I watched the boys play together, I suffered some early squeezing pains warning of my next child's impending birth that evening. I tried to massage the spasms without bringing them to the attention of the others. No one said anything then, but Bilhah frowned at me more than once. I shook my head slightly, not wanting the others to be aware of my discomfort. I expected her to come examine me that night.

After Bilhah's examination, I curled into my sleeping pallet, knowing my child would come soon. As I drifted toward sleep, a door softly bumped closed. Jacob passed my window, glowing in the moonlight. He slipped onto the pallet on my other side.

"May I sleep with you?"

"You are always welcome," I murmured.

His cool hand touched the bulk of warm stomach. I flinched. Before he moved it away, I caught it in mine. "Your hand is icy."

"I will move it."

"No, it is nice," I mumbled.

Before the moon dropped behind the mountain, I jerked awake with hard spasms, warning of the coming of my child. I bit back my moan and pressed on the babe. He had stopped kicking the night before, another signal of his coming.

I tried to sleep again, but another spasm rippled across my stomach. I yelped and smashed a hand over my face, trying to stay silent.

Jacob put his arm across me. "Did I hear you cry out?" he mumbled.

"It is nothing," I said. "Only a spasm."

"A birthing spasm?" Sleep no longer slurred his speech.

I breathed through my mouth. "Yes."

"Should you not call for Bilhah to come help?"

"I should. But she needs her rest."

He snorted. "You need Bilhah's help. It is good she is so close."

He struggled up and pulled his tunic over his head. "I will return."

Another spasm rippled across my stomach. I hoped Bilhah would come soon.

After that, I focused on breathing as the spasms came in waves across my stomach. Bilhah came to help me, but I remember nothing except the clenching pain until she said, "You have another boy."

Four sons! Jehovah blessed me with an abundance of sons. This one was healthy too, if his bawling gave us any hope of that.

Jacob knelt beside me after they helped me back to the pallet I did not remember leaving. "Four sons," he said, his eyes shining with tears. "You did so well today."

I nodded.

Bilhah placed the child next to me, and with some help, he suckled.

"What will you name our son?" Jacob asked.

I glanced at Bilhah and the maid, who were bustling around the chamber, cleaning the mess. "Later," I whispered.

"You are a beautiful woman, Leah," Jacob murmured. "I love you."

"You love that I give you sons."

"Yes, but I love your gentleness. I love the way you care for everyone else here. I love that you are the mother of my sons. But, I love you for you."

I smiled. "I have waited long to hear those words."

Jacob grimaced. "I know. It took much too long to know."

He sat staring at our son while Bilhah finished her cleaning.

"I will leave you to rest," she said.

"Send the other boys in when they wake," I murmured.

She nodded. "It will not be long. I will tell Amina."

She bundled up the dirty cloths and left my chamber.

"Now, my dear Leah," Jacob said. "What name will you give our son?"

I summoned strength I did not feel, for it took all my strength to give birth to this child, and whispered, "I praise Jehovah. His name is Judah."

"Judah?" Jacob repeated. "That is a good name. May he always praise our God, Jehovah."

I nodded.

"Now rest. You need to regain your strength."

"Who will care for Judah while I sleep?" My words sounded distant.

He bent over and kissed me. "You know I will watch over our son while you sleep."

"And who will watch over the flocks?" I mumbled.

His voice came as if from far away. "The hired men."

The thought filled me as I slept. I had given Jacob four sons.

Soft rustling woke me. I opened my eyes to see my three older sons peeking over the edge of the basket where little Judah lay.

"He is so tiny," Levi whispered.

"He is bigger than you or Simeon were," Reuben replied in a knowing voice. "Is he not, Father?"

"He is a big boy," Jacob whispered. "Do not wake your mother. She worked hard to bring him into the world."

They all nodded, staring at their brother. Jacob had not noticed I was awake yet.

"What do we call him?" Simeon asked.

"Judah," Jacob answered. "We praise Jehovah."

"We always praise Jehovah," Reuben said. He shifted his feet and dragged his hands through his hair.

"Yes, Reuben," I said. "We always praise Jehovah. I praise Him for each of you, my sons."

My sons and husband turned toward me.

"You are awake," the boys cried.

"We tried to be quiet for you," Simeon said.

"And you did well. Do you like your new brother?"

The boys nodded their heads.

"When he big to play?" Levi asked.

"Not for a while," Jacob said. "He needs to grow before he can play games with you."

"But you can talk to him and play quiet games with him now," Reuben said, straightening his back. He had waited for each of the other two to grow big enough to play with.

Amina slipped into the room. "You boys need to eat," she whispered. "You can come visit your mother and brother again later, after they have rested."

Each son kissed my cheek before allowing Amina to shoo them from the room.

Little Judah squeaked, then whimpered.

"He is hungry," Jacob said, lifting him from the basket. "And wet."

I reached for my child, but Jacob lifted a clean wrapper from the pile and changed Jacob's bottom before lifting him into my arms. "I am an expert at this."

"With four others, you should be," I said with a grin. "And soon you will have a sixth child."

"A sixth son," Jacob said.

"You always know," I murmured.

Judah's whimpering became a lusty bawl.

"And now, with these sons, I can renew my practice." His smile lit his face. He bent to kiss me. "I love you."

"I thought that was a dream," I said as I guided the babe to my breast.

Jacob brushed the hair back from my face. "No, Leah. It was no dream."

I remembered that day many times over the years. He did not often speak of his love for me, but he did that day. Those words helped me survive many difficult days.

Plans

Within three months, Bilhah delivered another son in the middle of the day. I sat with my sons in the sitting area feeding Judah. Dan played with Levi and the other boys while Amina washed the clothing that day.

Rachel swept into the area. "Would you like my help?"

Exhaustion filled me. Judah had not slept well the night before, cutting his first tooth, and I spent much of the night rocking and soothing him. I glanced up with sleepy eyes. "Please. I struggle to stay awake."

"Do you need to rest in your chamber?"

"No, I will lie here on the floor. If you are here, I can nap for a bit." I grabbed a blanket and pillow off a seat and lay on the floor.

"I will stay with the boys," she murmured. "You rest."

I mumbled my thanks and soon drifted into sleep with Judah sleeping beside me in his basket.

Zilpah woke me with the news of another son for Bilhah. Rachel took Dan up to meet his brother while I changed Judah. After I fed Judah, Amina came in to take my sons outside for a walk, allowing me to climb the stairs to meet the new baby alone.

I pushed Bilhah's chamber door open and saw Rachel and Jacob standing near Bilhah, gazing at the baby who lay in Jacob's arms.

They turned to me, and Jacob set the little boy in my arms.

After rocking and cooing at the baby's beauty, I asked, "What is your name, little one?"

"Naphtali," Bilhah said.

"Such a big name for a tiny boy," I said, lifting my eyebrows at Rachel. I knew she had claimed the right to name this child.

"With great wrestling, I have wrestled with my sister, and I have prevailed. His name is Naphtali."

Wrestled with me? In what way? I thought she had given away her jealousy.

Rather than saying anything, I nodded and repeated. "Big name for a tiny baby boy."

I loved watching Levi and Dan play together, and Judah and Naphtali were becoming fast friends, even as babies.

After dinner one evening, we sat together as a family. The older boys sat on the floor building towers. Judah sat on a blanket near us.

Judah sat near Rachel. She made a silly face at him.

He smiled.

She made another silly face, thinking no one saw her.

Judah smiled again, then giggled.

His giggle warmed me. I reached for him as Rachel picked him up. She lifted her eyebrows at me, and I sat back.

She hugged him close, then her face twisted. "He is wet."

I reached for him, but she shook her head and pulled a clean wrapper from the basket. I watched while she took her time changing him.

I waited for Judah to spray her, but she kept the wrapper over him. She must have watched me closer than I thought.

When she finished, she lifted Judah into her arms and grinned.

"Is that your first time?" Jacob asked.

"It is," she said. "But I did it."

I grinned along with her. "You did well." I hugged Rachel and Judah close until Judah squalled.

Rachel patted his back until he squirmed to get down to play with Naphtali.

Jacob offered his thirteenth sacrifice, thanking Jehovah for these last two newest sons. Father walked through the crowd, crowing about his daughters and their children, claiming Dan and Naphtali as Rachel's. Bilhah sat on the side, clenching her jaws.

"Do not allow my father to cause you distress. Your sons know who their mother is. It matters not what others say or do."

"It is frustrating. Laban knows the truth, yet he continues to say my sons are Rachel's. She claims them. She gave me to Jacob so I could give her children. But Dan and Naphtali are my sons. They do not belong to Rachel."

I slipped an arm around her. "We know. Your sons know. Ignore my father."

"I try, Leah, but his bragging hurts."

I hugged her.

We had one more year until Jacob would break free from Father's clutches. He would then have completed, as promised, the many years of servitude Father had forced on him.

I expected Father to discover another ploy to keep Jacob working for him. His wealth had multiplied many times in the years since Jacob had come to Harran. Father could not allow that wealth to diminish.

At home, we discussed the problem, although Jacob did not believe Father could cause him more problems.

"We need to consider preparations for our return to Canaan," Jacob said.

"Canaan?" I asked.

"You know I need to return to my home. Our life here has always focused on preparing us to return home."

"Your home," Rachel said.

"Yes," Jacob squeezed her hand. "You knew from the beginning of my plans to return home."

"And what will you do if Father uncovers our plans to leave?" Rachel asked. "You know he will not want you to go. You have increased his wealth."

"He should expect it. I have never hidden my plans to return home." Jacob nodded. "He will try to keep me here, although I have not heard from my mother yet. She said she would let me know when it was safe to return home. I may need to stay here for another year or two. I do not have enough animals. I must have enough to return as a prince, not a beggar."

"Father would have you continue in his service as a beggar," I said.

"I understand," Jacob said, brushing his fingers through his beard, "but Jehovah will not allow him to keep me here. He will provide."

We listed everything we would need to travel from Harran to Canaan. "We will need to plan and prepare food for travel for at least two or three months. I do not know how long it will take us to travel that distance with animals and children."

"How much time will we have to prepare?" Bilhah asked. "Such a journey will take time to prepare."

"We will have this last year, perhaps more," Jacob said. "I do not have enough animals to leave yet, and Jehovah has not yet commanded it. We will want to have our preparations completed before the day arrives."

I nodded and glanced at Rachel and Bilhah. *I am ready to leave tomorrow. I am ready to leave both Father and Mother. They have treated both Rachel and me with harsh greed.*

"We will weave material for tents if your men will bring us the wool and hair they find in the bushes," I said.

"And we can grow more vegetables," Rachel added. "We will need much more food. Will we have enough animals and herders?"

Jacob chewed on his beard, then gazed at me. "Reuben is young." He took a breath. "Not yet eight. I would wait for him, but I need to teach him how to care for animals before we leave. I will require his help."

"Already?" I said, gasping. "Reuben is barely six."

Jacob inhaled a deep breath. "I would allow him to continue his childhood another two years, but we cannot. I will soon enlarge my flocks and need his help. I will hire herders soon, but like your father when I first came to Harran, I need someone from our family to work with them to protect our interests. The animals must learn to love and follow our sons."

I swallowed the lump in my throat as Reuben left his brothers and stood next to his father's knee.

"Do you mean it? You will take me with you to tend the flocks?" he asked.

Jacob glanced at me. "Your mother must allow it. You are not yet the age of a man."

Reuben moved to stand in front of me. "Will you allow it, Mother? I have learned to read, write, and do my sums. Can I go with Father?"

"You are young. Too young to spend all day among the animals."

"Would you allow him to go if I promised to bring him home by midday for a time until he is strong enough to stay all day?" Jacob asked.

"I could stay all day," Reuben whined.

"Reuben," Jacob said with a growl. "We must convince your mother. It does not help when you whine and beg to go before she is ready."

Reuben turned to me. "I can come home at midday if you wish. Please allow me to go with Father."

I huffed out a breath. "You will grow tired of waking early and working hard. Once you begin, you cannot stop. Are you certain you are prepared for that?"

"Yes, Mother. Please allow me to go."

"Until midday only, until I know you can handle longer days. Do you accept that?"

Reuben nodded. "Yes, Mother. You will allow me to go with Father?"

I shook my head. "I prefer you stay home and enjoy your childhood another year." I held up my hands to stop his argument. "However, your father is correct. He will need you among his herders. The animals need to learn to love you, as you must learn to love them."

"Then I may go?" Reuben asked.

I wanted to shake my head and cry that he was only a boy, not ready to become a man. But if we were to leave Harran, Jacob would need a son working with him.

"Yes, Reuben. You may go. You will want to go to sleep soon. Your father leaves early in the morning."

Reuben whooped and kissed my cheek. "Goodnight, Mother. I go to my sleeping pallet now."

I grinned and glanced out the window. The moon hung low in the sky. "Goodnight, Reuben. Sleep well."

It broke my heart to lose my little boy already.

Difficult Command

Within three months, Jacob used the first tent material Rachel and I wove to make a large weaving tent for us and made four new big looms so we could weave tent materials for our travel to Canaan. We set the tent behind the house, so it would not be apparent to others that we planned to leave.

Jacob hired men to help as his flock increased. He also hired more women to help in the house. At the end of the week, his men brought us bags of wool and hair, gathered from fences and bushes, to spin and weave. When they sheared the animals, they brought us bags of wool and hair, which kept us busy spinning and weaving through the year. Some we kept for our needs. The rest we sold to help our family.

Along with the new herders, Jacob hired two more girls to help in the house, Pili and Yedida, whom we called Dida. They freed us to spend more time weaving and spinning.

In our preparations to leave Harran, my stomach did not grow with another child. Jehovah promised Jacob a large family. I had given him four sons. Bilhah had given him two more. But I did not believe I had done enough.

I prayed to Jehovah about the problem, but no child settled in my womb. Instead, a whisper entered my soul. 'Give Zilpah to Jacob as a concubine. She needs a man to care for her and protect her. She will give him the sons you cannot. You will give him children again, but for now, give Zilpah to Jacob.'

No! It will give him one more woman to come between Rachel and me. How can I?

'It is my will.'

The whispering left me. I knew Jehovah's will, but I fought to obey.

How can I do this? Rachel struggles with two others in Jacob's life. How will she handle another?

Jehovah commanded this. Why *should I complain? But Jehovah does not have to live with Rachel.*

What will Zilpah do? She asked for a man of her own years ago. When Rachel asked Bilhah to become Jacob's concubine, I promised her I would never ask this of her. Will she understand?

Finally, after a week of arguing, Jacob came to my chamber. He noticed my tear-stained face.

"Why the tears? Has someone hurt you?"

I shook my head. "No. I have left off giving you children —"

"You have given me four healthy sons," Jacob said, embracing me.

"I know, and I am grateful for them. I have received a message from Jehovah. I have fought it for a week."

"You must obey if it comes from Jehovah. What message did you receive?" He kissed my brow and moved to kiss my lips.

"I am to give Zilpah to you as your concubine. She will give you more children."

Jacob's face pulled back from mine. "You are to do what?"

"I am to —"

"I heard. But why? I have three women already and six healthy sons. Why would Jehovah demand I take another?"

"I was told Zilpah needs a man to protect and care for her. She will give you sons I cannot. I will give you more sons later, but now, I am to give Zilpah to you."

Jacob's shaggy head shook back and forth. "Why? Why would Jehovah demand this of me? I accepted you, for your father insisted. You have become a woman I love. I took Bilhah because Rachel demanded it. I care for her. How can I take another concubine? Rachel will ..." He buried his head in his hands.

"I know. I have argued for a week against this. It is hard enough for me as the first wife when Rachel is so jealous. Rachel has learned to control her jealousy most of the time. But ..." I lifted my hands and sighed.

Jacob encircled me with his arms. His strength warmed and comforted me. "I know. Sometimes, the commands of Jehovah are confusing. Why would He expect me to add another woman to our family?"

I stuttered something. He kissed away my words. "We do not know what Jehovah knows. He understands what will come to us and what is best for us now. He does not always expect us to understand. He expects us to obey."

Jacob's kisses reminded me of his love for me. This remarkable man could love another woman. "Then we will do it?"

He set his forehead against mine. "Yes, we will do it. The Sabbath is six days from now. I recommend you talk with Zilpah and prepare her before then."

I nodded. *Will she understand? Will she see this comes from a command from Jehovah?*

Jacob kissed me again. We would enjoy this last week before he took another woman.

The next morning, after I watched Jacob and Reuben stride toward the paddocks, Zilpah entered my room.

"Did you have a happy night with Jacob?" she asked. "You have been extra tearful this week. Did he help you resolve your problem?"

I looked into her beautiful dark eyes. She had been with me since my tenth birthday, supporting me, helping me through all the challenges of life. Although I am a tall woman, I stretch to look into her eyes.

"He did. I have left off having children. My womb is empty," I said as I sat on my stool, waiting while she brought a cloth filled with cool, herb-filled water that soothed my eyes.

Surprise filled her eyes, as I expected. Greater surprise would fill them after I shared with her the resolution.

"Are not four sons enough for a woman?"

My gaze dropped to my hands, pleating my nightdress. "I miss having a babe in my arms." I pulled the nightdress off.

"Judah is still a babe, barely weaned." She lifted a dress from the hooks that held my dresses. "Will this dress do?"

I nodded, not looking at her choice. She always chose beautiful dresses for me to wear. "I have received a message from Jehovah. One Jacob has agreed that we must obey."

I lifted my head in time to see her eyes widen. "Oh, what message is that? Of course, you do not have to tell me. It is none of my concern."

"But it is," I said, standing to allow her to drop the dress over my head.

I waited as she pulled it down and tied the bows at my waist. "Jehovah has commanded me to give you to Jacob as his second concubine. You need a man to protect and care for you." I gazed into her face.

Zilpah fought to control the emotions raging within her and showing on her face. "You were commanded?"

I nodded.

"To give me to Jacob?"

I nodded again.

"And he has agreed."

"He questioned my message, but yes. He agreed."

Zilpah bit her lip and inhaled. "Sit. I will prepare your hair for the day. Shall I braid it or leave some hanging down your back? When?"

I stared into the polished brass mirror. "Do we have cleaning to do today?"

Zilpah shrugged. "We are to clean the sitting room today, and the men delivered more wool this morning to spin." She held her face still, anticipating my answer to her question of when.

"Then braid it and pin it up, out of the way of the spindle." I settled onto my stool. "I know I promised I would never do this, but Jehovah has commanded. I will announce my giving you to Jacob on the Sabbath. That will give you time to adjust to the idea and prepare. I had hoped you would have received the same message."

Zilpah frowned. "The thought crossed my mind. I dismissed it. Why would you cause more trouble with Rachel? And why would you bring another woman into the family when you have so little time with Jacob already?"

I sighed. "I would not. As you said, I have four beautiful, healthy sons. Jacob continues to come to my chamber. More children will come to me as Jehovah wills. But only the three of us will know this came from Jehovah. Everyone else will hear I feared I would have no more children and gave you to Jacob. I will say your children are mine, but we will both know they are yours, given to you from Jehovah."

"I dreamed of a man who loves me for myself," Zilpah said as she twisted my braid around my head and pushed pins in to hold it there. "There was a man ... I thought perhaps Yitzchak would want me. But he died before he could ask Jacob for me. I want a husband. I want to be his only wife."

"I understand," I whispered. "I had the same hopes and dreams. I wanted a husband who loved me more than any other woman. My father changed that for me when he insisted I take Rachel's place." Tears slipped down my cheeks. "I apologize for the loss of our dreams. Jehovah knows what is best for both of us. I believe now He arranged for me to marry Jacob first. He is giving you a kind and gentle man who will love you."

As she pushed the last pin into my hair, tears traced the lines of Zilpah's face on either side. "I wanted a man to love me. I did not want your husband. I see how difficult it is for you, for Bilhah, and for Rachel. I hoped a man would talk to Jacob and ask for me."

"Jehovah knows our needs. He will bless you."

"Even though Jacob has three other women?"

"Even though he has three other women to love." I knew Jacob would love Zilpah. "Wear your best dress. You choose, but you will want to look beautiful for Jacob."

Zilpah murmured something as she left my chamber. I knew her confusion but knew Jacob would care for her.

Another Concubine

Jacob and I loved each other more ardently and deeper that week, knowing the changes that would come to us on the Sabbath. Neither of us desired this, but we accepted Jehovah's will.

I wondered which dress Zilpah would choose to wear, but waited to learn. On the Sabbath morning, Jacob kissed me. "I will return to you when I can. I honor you for your obedience."

He dressed carefully. I did not ask, but knew he had prepared a place to spend the next days with Zilpah. I slipped a dress over my head, and he tied it at my waist. "With four children, you are still slim and beautiful."

My hand touched my face. "With these scars?"

"What scars? Those faded long ago." He moved my hands and ran a finger along my face. Then he kissed each cheek, and then my lips. "I will return to you. We will have more sons when Jehovah wills it."

I smiled a crooked smile. "We must trust Jehovah."

Zilpah did not come in to help me that morning. I hoped someone helped her dress and prepare. The day would be memorable for her.

She wore the blue dress I had given her for the last sacrifice. She had not worn it since. Her eyes and hair shone. Jacob would love her.

I fidgeted during the service, thinking through the words I would use. I glanced at Zilpah, whose hands sat still in her lap, hiding her anxiety. She deserved a man like Jacob. She deserved Jacob.

At last, Daniy completed his sermon. As always, he asked if anyone had needs or announcements. Before anyone else could rise, I strode to the front of the congregation.

"I find I have stopped bearing children. Jehovah promised Jacob many children." I waved to Zilpah to come stand beside me. "Zilpah has been my friend and maidservant for many years." I nodded to Jacob to come stand on my other side.

I waited until he moved to the front. "Now, she is to become Jacob's concubine, joining Bilhah." I looked into her eyes. "I give you to Jacob as his concubine and my sister-wife, to give Jacob the children I cannot." I set her sweaty hand into Jacob's cool hand and stepped back.

Jacob looked into Zilpah's eyes. "Will you have me?"

Her eyes glistened with unshed tears of joy. Warmth filled me as she whispered, "Yes."

"Then I take you as my wife and concubine, to be mine forever."

He led Zilpah through the congregation and out the door. Whispers from the crowd followed them.

As I returned to my seat, Rachel's stare bore into me. She would not understand. I had to trust Jehovah.

However, as I dropped into my seat next to my sons and Reuben gripped my hand, Rachel leaned toward me. "I know your pain."

I could not lift my head and acknowledge it. She did not know. I clenched and unclenched my hands. Even as Jehovah commanded this, it hurt.

During the three days while Jacob and Zilpah were becoming a couple, I called on Pili to serve me as a maidservant. On the morning Zilpah and Jacob were to return, three mornings later, I warned her I would call her to a meeting with my sister-wives.

I assigned Zilpah to a chamber near Bilhah's, since the two women were close friends, and invited her, Bilhah, and Rachel to meet with me in the sitting area after she had settled her possessions into her new chamber.

I sent Simeon, Levi, and Judah with Amina to walk outside. I suspect Bilhah sent her sons with Orna. Then I went to the sitting area and worked on my mending. I could depend on mending to keep me busy if I did not have spinning.

This time, when we met to make new assignments, Rachel joined us. After the other three women settled around me, I sent for Pili and Dida. They waited nearby, knowing I would call them.

"Pili," I said. "I assign you as my maidservant. You have served me well in the last three days." I turned to Dida. "You will now serve as Zilpah's maidservant. Your other assignments will change. We will discuss them later."

"Maidservant? For me?" Zilpah asked, setting her hand on her chest.

I grinned at her. "As I explained to Rachel when she gave Bilhah to Jacob, we must all have maidservants when we return to Canaan. They must see Jacob's wealth. Our maidservants add to his status."

I sent Dida and Pili off to their chores, promising them I would ask Jacob to hire more maids.

We discussed different household responsibilities for Zilpah as I had with Bilhah. Among her duties, Zipah took over responsibility for the bees Bilhah had enticed to make a home in our garden. We would need the honey on our journey.

We became four women loved by Jacob.

Zilpah conceived in her first days of being with Jacob, as Bilhah and I had done. She delivered a son before the fourteenth sacrifice. I helped Bilhah with her delivery and experienced childbirth from the other side. I learned to love Zilpah and her child in a way I never expected.

Jacob, as he had done with me, sat beside her, urging her on, and carried her back to her sleeping pallet.

As she fed her son his first meal, Zilpah gazed at me. "What will you name our son?"

Surprise filled me, for I did not expect her to ask.

"This child is yours as he is mine," she said. "As my mistress, it is your right to name him."

Zilpah and Jacob waited for my answer.

I had considered a name and searched through the records for the perfect name, wondering if she would give me the opportunity to name her child. "A troop comes. His name is Gad."

She bent her head to return her gaze to her son. "Gad. A good, simple name for a son. He shall lead a troop of men who follow Jehovah."

Jacob now had seven sons. Would he fill my womb again with more children?

We gathered at Father's home soon after for the annual sacrifice offering gratitude to Jehovah for safety and remembering the years since Jacob began working for Father. Jacob also gave thanks for Gad. This was his fourteenth sacrifice. He had paid his debt to Father for both me and Rachel.

We expressed our joy in songs, smiles, and laughter throughout the day. We hoped Father would free Jacob from his service so we could travel back to Canaan and meet Isaac, Jacob's father, and Rebekah, his mother. I wanted to meet Esau as well, for Jacob had shared many stories of their adventures together while they were young boys.

What would our lives be like today if Esau had come with Jacob? Would he have seen an acceptable wife in me and married me? I will never know. I will not wonder about it again. Jacob has given me four sons and another through Zilpah. I am grateful.

As we celebrated, we could not avoid Father's frown.

"He will miss Jacob," Zilpah said. "He has increased the size of his flocks many times over each year."

"And he will want Jacob to continue increasing his wealth. Father has never considered him to be the husband of his beloved daughters." I said, cocking my head to the side. "Jacob deserves to increase his own wealth now, not continue to serve as a hired man for our father."

"What will your father do?"

I pursed my lips. "I do not know. But Jacob will not allow Father to use him as he has for the past years. He will find a way to make our lives better."

Near the end of the celebration, while we and our believing friends packed up to take our tired children home, Jacob sat with Father in deep discussion. I wanted to wander by, to hear what passed between them, but dared not. I helped clear away the last of the food while Father's men servants took down the tables.

Soon they had everything put away except the table where Jacob sat with Father. We four women, our sons, and Mother stood a distance from them in a tight, silent, little knot, watching and waiting.

My sons had played hard and were ready to sleep. They sat at my feet, drooping in exhaustion while I rocked little Judah.

At last, the men pushed their chairs back and stood. Father extended his hand, and Jacob took it. They had reached an agreement. Mother strode across the field to join Father.

I wanted to hear about their agreement, but the boys were tired. Jacob took Dan from Zilpah's arms and put an arm around Rachel. "The boys are tired. We will discuss this after the children are asleep."

After tucking our sons into sleeping pallets or baby baskets, we gathered in the sitting area. The four of us women found seats and waited for Jacob to speak.

He sucked in a deep breath and allowed the air to escape before he spoke.

"You know my plan to return to Canaan and my family there. I have a responsibility to return and care for my mother."

We all nodded. We had discussed this often in the past year.

"Will we leave soon?" Rachel asked.

"We cannot leave yet. Laban agreed to accept that a portion of the sheep should be mine. Although I have increased his flocks many times in the past fourteen years, he only allowed to have given me the oldest ewes to keep us fed and cared for. He has carefully refused to provide enough to add to my wealth, keeping me dependent on him." Jacob snorted. "Laban would have no wealth now if I had not come to Harran."

"What will you do?" I asked, leaning forward.

The others leaned closer as well.

"I reminded Laban of my assistance in increasing his flocks in the years since I took the responsibility for his flocks. I then asked him when I could provide for my growing household."

Rachel glanced at my stomach, searching for a suggestion that I once more carried a child. I did not. Then she glanced at Bilhah and Zilpah, searching for symptoms of another child.

She sighed. "What will he give us?"

Jacob leaned back in his seat. "I did not *ask* Laban to give us anything. I negotiated with him for a part of his flocks, the ones whose wool is less acceptable to sell. The animals that seem to be less valuable. I suggested he allow me to take the speckled cows, the brown goats, and the spotted sheep as payment for my continued care of his flocks."

"But few animals have those colors, and they will not bring you the wealth we need to leave," I cried, then covered my mouth with my hand.

"Not normally," Jacob agreed. "But there are more of those colors within his flocks than Laban suspects. Jehovah will bless me with more animals as I continue to bless and help Laban. And the colored wool is in greater demand recently."

"Father will claim all your flocks if you keep them together," Rachel said, pulling on her ear.

"I told Laban I would move my animals away from his. If he finds any not speckled, spotted, or brown, he could consider them stolen."

We women gasped.

"He will search your flocks for sheep?" Zilpah asked.

"Unless they are newborn animals, he will find none that are not mine. I will go out tonight with my man, Demas, and separate the animals before Laban changes his mind."

"Will you take Reuben?" I asked.

Jacob shook his head. "No. Let him sleep. Morning will come early for him."

Rachel leaned back and sighed. "Be careful. Father will change the terms."

"As if he has not done so before?" Jacob said with a growl. "I will work longer hours, tending to my flocks and Laban's. I cannot mix them. But I have trained his herders well and have hired a man to help with mine." He sighed. "I will work longer hours for a time, and when the young come, it will keep me among the animals much longer. Be prepared."

"And Reuben? Will he be given greater responsibility among the flocks?" I asked. "Will you include him more?"

"Reuben loves our animals. He will do well to keep them safe with our herders." He stared ahead, seeing nothing. "He is young, but has learned well. Perhaps Simeon is old enough now to help."

"At six?" Rachel asked.

"Yes, I will include him in the learning soon."

"Our sons must learn their father's business," I murmured.

Jacob looked toward me. "I will not take Simeon every day. He is still a little boy. But he will need to join me when he can. When we are more settled with Laban, I will take him more often."

"When will you take my sons with you?" Bilhah asked.

Jacob turned toward her. "When they are old enough to help without endangering themselves and me."

Rachel's eyes lost focus. *What is she thinking?*

Her eyes focused once more on me. "Your sons will help us."

Jacob leaned forward and took my hand in his right hand, Rachel's in his left hand. "Thank you for understanding. Our wealth will increase now that Laban has agreed to allow me flocks. We will soon be ready to go home."

"One more thing," Jacob said, leaning forward. "We need to increase our plans for our departure from Harran."

"What more will we need?" I asked.

"Tents for each family and our servants," Jacob said, touching a finger to enumerate. "Bedding, travel tables, cushions, and animals to carry them."

"We have some of that prepared," Bilhah said.

"We will need dried food. And servants to help with the trek, men to herd the animals and women to assist you, my wives, and our children."

"Do we not have enough servants?" Rachel asked.

Jacob shook his head. "Not yet. And I need larger numbers of animals. Perhaps they will be ready in a few years. It will take a few more years for my flock to grow big enough to take back to my father."

"What more can we do to prepare now?" Zilpah asked.

"We need more tents," he said.

"We have woven fabric for tents," Rachel said. "And we can weave more."

Jacob unfolded his long legs and stood from his seat. "But I must leave now."

"We will miss you at dinner," I said.

"I will return for dinner, but I may leave again, as I must now, to ensure our flocks are bedded and safe."

"Do we have paddocks for animals?" Bilhah asked.

"We have some, but they are old and need work to keep our animals safe." He pulled us to our feet, hugging each of us, beginning with Zilpah. "I am grateful my women understand. I appreciate your efforts to get along. It makes my life easier when I have to deal with Laban."

I glanced at Rachel. She grimaced. We would continue to strive to love each other.

Simeon's Request

One afternoon soon after the sacrifice, I sat in the sitting area, spinning as I often did.

"Mother?"

I looked up to see Simeon standing by my knee. "Yes, Simeon?"

"Can I go with Reuben in the morning? He said I would be a help."

I peered at my second son, examining him. *How did he grow so* big *so fast? I had agreed to allow Jacob to take him. Was it time?*

"You are not eight, not yet a man." I said, measuring his height against my remembered vision of Reuben at that age. As tall, maybe taller. "What does your father say? Are you old enough to help with his flocks?" I leaned forward to brush a lock of hair off his forehead.

He shook his head, causing the lock to fall back over his eye. "Reuben was six when he started helping Father."

"Have you asked your father?"

He sucked in a deep breath and nodded. "He says I can go with Reuben if you agree." Longing filled his gaze. "Father says mothers are careful with their sons."

I chuckled. "He would know. His mother took extra care to watch over him."

"Can I go, mother? Please?"

Jacob had warned me this would happen soon. Too soon for me, but Amina would have an easier time with only Levi and Judah. Especially as Dan, Naphtali, and Gad often joined my boys. We needed another nurse to care for all these children.

Simeon liked to run and play. Would he settle enough to care for the flocks? Some animals were *much bigger than* he was. I shuddered. *What will I do if a big animal runs over him?*

"I will listen to Father and the herders," Simeon said, as if hearing my thoughts. "I will watch for the animals. They will not trample me."

"They trampled a herder last month," I said with a shiver. "He is still recovering. How will you avoid a big animal if he could not?"

Simeon gazed into my eyes. "Father will give me a father's blessing as he gave Reuben. Jehovah will protect me. I am among Abraham's posterity."

I opened my eyes wider. "I did not know your father gave your brother a blessing."

He nodded his head solemnly, as one much older would. "He did it the first day in the meadow. Reuben tells me of times when the animals have come close, but none have hurt him."

I knuckled my eyes. "They came that close to him?"

"But none touched him. Jehovah blesses him." My little boy sounded like his father.

Levi came to stand next to his brother, his eyes wide.

"Would you be willing to start by helping Reuben only in the morning? Amina and I need you to help us with little Judah."

He folded his arms across his chest and let a sigh escape. "If I must, but not for many more weeks. Reuben needs me to learn to herd the animals so I can help him."

I set Judah on my lap and put my hand on Simeon's shoulder. "Then you can go help Reuben when your father decides it is time."

"Yippee!" Simeon shouted.

Levi tugged on my skirt. "I want to go too. May I help Father with the herds?"

I smiled at my young son, not yet five. "You may go with Reuben when you are as big as Simeon."

"I am big enough. May I go tomorrow?" He pled.

"Not tomorrow, son. I need you to help me and Amina with Judah. He will need a big brother to teach him. He will need you to help him learn how to be a kind brother like you. Can you do that for me?"

His lower lip quivered.

"And when you are bigger, you can join Reuben and Simeon with your father, helping herd the flocks."

"I am bigger now. Can I go?" Levi asked.

"Not today or tomorrow. Not next week. But you can go when you are bigger. I am certain Dan will want to go with you when you go, and Dan needs to grow some more as well."

Levi twisted his mouth around, thinking about my words. "I will stay and help Judah. He will need me to teach him to read and write. We can make tall towers."

"He will," I said, smiling at my little son. "Why not make a tall tower with Judah now?"

He plopped at my feet, called Judah, and pulled the blocks to him and started building.

After dinner that evening, we moved as a family to the sitting room while the maidservants cleaned the kitchen. The older boys sat on the floor building towers.

Simeon left his brothers and came to stand near us and touched Jacob's knee. "Father?"

"Yes, son?" Jacob said.

"Mother says I can go with Reuben to learn how to care for the flocks in the mornings. Can I go tomorrow?"

Jacob's eyes found mine.

I nodded. "He is young. Are you certain he will be safe?"

"I will watch over him," Reuben said from where he was building a tower on the floor with his brothers.

"If Reuben will help teach you," Jacob nodded to Reuben, "then you may go with us tomorrow. We rise early, though. Can you do that?"

Simeon's head bounced with excitement. "Yes. I can rise early."

"You will want to go to sleep early, then," I said as Amina came into the room.

Simeon ran to Amina. "Can we go to our sleeping pallets now? Father says I may go with Reuben to care for the flocks tomorrow."

Amina's eyebrows lifted, and she turned to me. "Is that right?"

"It is. Not all day, but he can go in the morning." I turned to Jacob. "I suggest you bring him home early. He has not learned to work yet."

"I planned to bring him home for the midday meal."

"I can stay all day," Simeon cried.

"Reuben only stayed part of the day for the first days," Jacob said.

"It is hard work," Reuben agreed. "You will be ready to come home for your midday meal."

"I will not." Simeon folded his arms and stomped a foot.

"Simeon," I warned. I did not want my children to become unruly, as my sister had. Our mother had thought her little tantrums were funny when she was little. We no longer thought them funny.

"Yes, Mother." Simeon huffed out a breath. "It will not tire me."

"We will see," Jacob said. "For tomorrow, at least, I will bring you home at midday."

"Yes, Father." Simeon did not look happy.

"Cheer up," Reuben said. "You can go with me tomorrow."

"I can." He turned to Amina again. "Can we go to our sleeping pallets now?"

"After prayers," Jacob said.

We prayed together, then Simeon turned to Amina once more. "Now?"

Amina shook her head and laughed a short laugh. "Yes, Simeon. We can go now. Come, Reuben and Levi. It is time." She bent to scoop Judah into her arms.

"Not tired," Judah cried.

"Maybe Amina will tell you a story if you go without crying," I said.

"Will you, 'Mina'?" Judah asked.

"If you get in your pallet fast," she said.

The boys hurried out of the sitting room ahead of her.

"You will care for him?" I asked when the boys were gone from the room.

"I will," Jacob said.

"And will you give him a father's blessing as you gave to Reuben?"

Jacob sucked in a breath. "I did not know you knew about that."

"Simeon told me. That blessing helped me agree. Simeon is so young."

"I will bring the boys to your room in the morning before we leave and give him a blessing then. Will that settle your concerns?"

"I would like that."

Rachel cleared her throat.

"This is for the boy and his mother," Jacob said before she could say anything. "I will come to you early, Leah."

I smiled. I would have private time with my sons and husband.

I heard Reuben and Simeon bouncing down the steps, Reuben shushing Simeon. "You do not want to wake Mother," he whispered.

A grin filled my face, both for my considerate older son and my eager younger son. They would return after eating.

Judah, at two, had weaned and moved into the boys' room months earlier. I continued to wake early as I had when he needed feeding.

I sat beside the window and watched the sun rise before Jacob opened the door and herded my two older sons in with a reminder to stay quiet.

"We are here so Father can give me a blessing," Simeon announced in a whisper.

"I wondered if he would remember," I said, glancing up at Jacob.

"I remembered. I rose late this morning." He yawned.

"Long night?" I asked.

He nodded. "Rachel."

"Say no more," I said with a hand-muffled laugh.

Jacob shrugged. "We should do this. The men are waiting." He moved the stool from in front of my dressing table to in front of me, then waved for Simeon to sit.

Jacob set his hands on our son's head and called on Jehovah to bless and protect Simeon as he worked with the animals and throughout his life. He promised him blessings of safety, family, and joy if he remembered to obey the commandments of Jehovah, his father, and the others who would teach him.

I swallowed my emotions, recognizing Simeon's manly desire for me to hide them. When his father removed his hands from his head, Simeon fell into his father's arms and thanked him. Then he hugged me.

"We must go," Jacob said. "The herders wait for us."

My men left, and I sat alone, watching Simeon bounce beside his father. *Bless my Simeon, please, Jehovah. Keep him safe and bring him back to me.*

By midday, I sat at the table with Simeon's favorite bread and meat waiting. Before I could worry, Jacob entered with Simeon.

"How did you do?" I asked. "Did you learn anything?"

"Sheep can be stubborn," Simeon said.

I cleared my throat and glanced at Jacob. "Oh?"

"They would not follow me as they do Reuben."

"Oh." I looked at Jacob over Simeon's head.

He grinned. "Our sheep follow the one they love. For now, they love Reuben. It will not take them long to learn to love Simeon."

"Will they tomorrow?" Simeon asked.

"Not tomorrow," I said. "I need you to help me with Judah while Amina helps wash our clothing."

Simeon's lower lip slipped out.

"Simeon," Jacob said. "You agreed."

"Yes, Father. I am happy to help Mother tomorrow." He turned to me. "But can I go with Father and Reuben the next day?"

"We will see if you are helpful tomorrow," I said.

"I will help you lots."

Jacob grinned at me and grabbed bread and meat from the table. "I must return to the flock." He looked at Simeon. "Eat and rest. We will discuss when you will go with me again tonight."

"Yes, Father," Simeon said, climbing onto his chair and eating.

Jacob left and I sat with Simeon. Before finishing his bread and meat, his head bobbed against his chest.

"Watch Judah for me, Amina, will you?" I asked.

She nodded, and I lifted Simeon into my arms.

"My little man is worn out."

"Not," Simeon said.

I carried him to his room and laid him in his pallet beside a sleeping Levi.

I was right to allow him to stay only *for the morning.*

Each time Simeon went with his brother and father after that, he stayed a little longer until a few months later, he stayed all day. By then, I had adjusted to losing my little boy to the flocks, but I continued to miss him.

In the following months, as Simeon grew, he worked with his brother and father caring for the flocks. He sometimes came home with bruises on his arms, shoulders, and back. I called Bilhah to help.

She would bring her healing ointments to help ease the pain and color of the bruises.

One day, after observing Bilhah heal many of these bruises, I asked, "Simeon, what are you doing to be bruised like this?"

He looked up at me from watching Bilhah. "The big bulls like to bump into me when we feed them. They must not see me." He shrugged. "I am growing. Soon they will know I am there and stop bumping into me."

"Can you not see them coming and stay out of their way?" Bilhah asked.

"I do," he replied. "But they crowd in on me. They are funny. I will try harder to avoid them."

I tousled his hair. "I would be happier if you would avoid these big bulls and the bruises they leave."

Simeon ducked his head. "Yes, Mother. But they are nice guys."

"Nice?" I cried.

"How can you call them nice when they bump into you?" Bilhah asked.

"They rub against me, looking for hugs and love," the little boy said. "They like it when I rub their noses and backs. How can you not love big animals who want loving?"

Bilhah shook her head and looked at me over Simeon's head.

"What are we to do with you, Simeon?" I asked.

"Love me like I love the big bulls," he said.

How could I not love this courageous, loving son of mine?

Children

Although Rachel fought her jealousy, our love grew strong while we waited for Jehovah to call us to move to Canaan. She became grim when Zilpah conceived another child. Zilpah bloomed with her second child. Rachel faded, even as she worked to maintain her cheer. I found myself concerned about her health.

Not many months after Simeon joined his brother and father herding the animals, Zilpah gave birth to a second son I named Asher. It was not much more than a year after giving birth to Gad. When asked why, I told others, "Happy am I, for the daughters will call me blessed."

However, another child did not fill my womb, and Rachel continued to pray to Jehovah to bless her with her first child. We found compassion and our lost companionship in our shared childlessness.

Some days, Rachel's patience thinned, and she struggled with everyone having children except her. On those days, she stayed in the indoor weaving chamber, away from me and the others.

One day, I entered the weaving chamber to keep her company. She moved, facing away from me.

"I cannot listen to you speak of your sons today," she said, tears filling her voice. "Please let me work alone."

I touched her back and left, going instead to the weaving tent with Zilpah and Bilhah.

We continued our preparations for the day when Jehovah would tell Jacob to go home. We all spent much of our free time spinning or weaving.

As we shared a meal after Jacob's fifteenth annual sacrifice, Mother suggested we use mandrakes to cure our infertility. Mandrakes are difficult to handle, causing the skin to burn and itch where touched by the plant. But some thought a tea made from the root, or carving the root to look like a child and putting the carving under a sleeping pallet, would relieve childlessness.

I shuddered at the thought. I prayed Jehovah would send me another child without such dreadful endeavors.

During the harvest, Reuben heard his grandmother's suggestion and spoke to me about it. I warned him about the potency of mandrakes. "I would prefer not to resort to their use," I told him.

One afternoon, he brought me an armful of them from the fields. I shuddered, but noticed he had wrapped a rag around them to protect himself.

"Give me some of your mandrakes," Rachel asked.

Her demand filled me with anger. "You have taken my husband every night. And now you will take my son's mandrakes?" I set my fists on my hips and glared at her.

Her voice sweetened. "If you give me some mandrakes, I will send Jacob to you tonight. I do not need all your mandrakes, just a few."

"You will sell our husband for a few mandrakes?" My frown deepened.

"Tonight and tomorrow?" she suggested.

"Mother?" Reuben asked, drawing his eyebrows close together. "Do you want me to give them to her?"

I glanced at Reuben, then returned my gaze to Rachel. "Give her three. If that is not enough for her, it is not Jehovah's will to give her a child."

Reuben separated three mandrakes from the bundle within the rag and handed them to her. "I hope this is worth the pain you give my mother," he muttered.

"Rueben!" I cried.

"But Mother."

Rachel grabbed her mandrakes in her apron to protect her hands and arms from a burn that would cause fierce itching.

"This is between Rachel and me, Reuben. We will resolve this, as we have since long before your birth." I stared at my son until he ducked his head, then turned to Rachel. "Two nights for me. You will not complain."

She bit her lip and swallowed. "I will not complain."

After she left, I told Reuben to take the mandrakes away. I did not need them. Jehovah would bless me with another child in His own time.

He grinned. "But you will have two nights with Father. I succeeded."

"Reuben!" I laughed.

He grinned and took the mandrakes away.

When Jacob returned from the fields that evening, I took him to my chamber as I had in the early years of our marriage. We enjoyed our two nights together. Jacob remembered his love for me and promised to share his time with all his women better.

During those nights, I conceived another son, Issachar, "Because Jehovah compensated me for giving my maidservant to my husband," born in the ninth year of our marriage.

In the next years, I gave Jacob another son, Zebulon, "For Jehovah has given me payment. Now will my husband dwell with me," who was born before Jacob's eighteenth sacrifice, almost eleven years after we wed.

Of course, Jacob continued to love Rachel and spent more nights in her chamber than with any of the rest of us. On one of the few nights he spent with me, I conceived one last time.

One morning during the months I carried Dinah while Gad leaned against his mother, asking when he could join his older brothers, Rachel came to eat the morning meal with us. Her face lost its color when Nita brought food to her. She jumped from her seat and rushed out the kitchen door. Bilhah followed her outside.

Zilpah and I exchanged a questioning glance.

When Bilhah and Rachel returned, Rachel pushed a mint leaf into her mouth. Understanding dawned. Jehovah had finally opened her womb.

We cheered for her and encouraged her in her sickness, in the few times she had the strength to leave her chamber. Her age did not help her overcome her struggle with nausea.

I visited Rachel in her chamber each day, where we would spin fibers into threads and yarn and discuss our coming children. Some days, when I entered her chamber, Rachel sat with a small table across her lap, covered in parchment, ink, and a pen.

"What are you doing?" I asked.

"Writing the story of my life," she responded. "Eve, Sarah, and many others wrote their stories before the end of their lives. Grandmother spoke of seeing Eve's. Perhaps my children will read my story and appreciate my struggles."

"This is not the end of your life!" I cried.

She lifted a shoulder in a slight shrug. "Who knows? Besides, it gives me something to think about beyond the sickness of my stomach."

"Your children will love reading your story," I said, praying she would live long past the birth of this child.

Perhaps someday, *before the end of my life, I will write my story.*

I gave birth to Dinah a little more than a month before Jacob's nineteenth sacrifice in Harran. Rachel missed the sacrifice, too sick to leave her sleeping pallet.

Two days after the sacrifice, Rachel struggled to descend the stairs to join us in the sitting area. Dan and Naphtali hurried up the stairs to balance her.

She had spent six months in her sleeping pallet while her child grew within her. Her muscles had grown weak and had not adjusted to the weight of the baby within her.

We welcomed her back into the family with joy. She even asked to hold Dinah. Eleven children were noisier now. Jacob insisted Rachel would give him an eleventh son.

The noise dwindled to silence when Jacob asked, "Are we ready to move to Canaan soon?"

Everyone focused on Jacob and the discussion.

Rachel answered first. "Zilpah and the others tell me we have woven enough cloth for tents and more to trade. We have almost everything we need to travel."

Jacob nodded. "Excellent. I will send the last of the tent fabric to the tentmaker." He turned to Zilpah. "Do we have enough honey?"

Zilpah sat taller. "We have many extra pots of honey. We will have enough for healing and eating. We should have some to trade if needed. I can prepare the bees to move with us."

"Fine," Jacob said, leaning forward. "And food? Will we have enough, Leah?"

I shifted in my seat. "We have many dried fruits, vegetables, and meats packed into baskets, ready to load onto camels when you decide it is time to leave."

"Remarkable. We will want to have enough food for everyone." Jacob turned toward Bilhah. "How are your healing supplies? Will you have enough?"

She nodded. "I will, as long as no one falls into the fire before we leave." She glanced at Levi, who shuddered. "Some accidents use more supplies than others. If we travel without accident or battle, we will have plenty."

"Will Jehovah call on us to leave soon?" Rachel asked, massaging her swollen stomach. "I hope to give birth before we leave."

"Jehovah has not called us to leave yet," Jacob gazed at each of us in the family circle. "But the time will soon come. Be prepared to leave with little notice."

We would not leave soon enough, but I agreed. Rachel needed to give birth and regain her strength before traveling to Canaan.

Joseph

In those years, all our older sons, from Simeon to Judah and Naphtali, who were then in their eighth year, joined Reuben and Jacob herding the animals. The boys enjoyed the time in the hills with the animals. Our herds grew, even as Father changed his agreement each year, striving to increase his flocks and decrease Jacob's.

One evening after Dinah's birth, I asked the boys which animal they preferred to work with. They spoke all at once.

"Naphtali," I said. "Tell me which animal you love."

"Father only allows me and Judah to herd the sheep and goats," Naphtali said. "I love the sheep. They are gentle. Father says they represent Jehovah. I love them more for that."

"Sheep are loving," Reuben said. "I still love them."

"Which animal is your favorite now, Reuben?" Zilpah asked.

"The camels. I spend most of my time with them now." He pulled on his ear. "They are awkward when they rise from the ground, but they walk with such grace and can carry heavy packs for long distances. We need our camels."

"I like camels," Issachar said. "They are gigantic."

"They are too big for me!" Judah said. "I prefer the goats. They eat everything. My problem is keeping them away from things they should not eat. They are smart and strong, and they love me, and I love them."

The boys all murmured their appreciation of the goats.

"I want to herd the goats," Asher said, running to stand in front of Jacob. "Can I go help Judah with the goats, Father?"

Jacob set a huge hand on Asher's little shoulder. "When you are bigger. Your mother would not approve of my sending you out to herd goats yet. Grow another year. Then you can."

"Which animal do you prefer to work with, Levi?" Bilhah asked, drawing attention from Asher's frown to Levi.

Levi glowed as he looked at Bilhah. "You know I love the horses. They know I love them, and even the wildest stallion comes to me when I call. He noses my palm for the carrots I keep in my pocket."

The pocket he carelessly slung across his shoulder was always dirty inside. He never had a clean cloth when he needed to wipe his face or nose clean.

"I love to feel the wind blowing in my hair as we fly across the plain. They are amazing animals."

I was not the only one to envy him, for murmurs of encouragement filled the sitting area.

"And you, Simeon?" Zilpah asked. "Which is your favored animal?"

"I still love the kine and bulls," he answered. "Those big bulls still come to me so I can pet their noses. They love me, and I love them. They can pull wagons that the horses would not."

Someone had to love the bulls.

"I love those big bulls," Gad whispered.

"When you are big enough, you can help Simeon," Jacob said.

"Will we have wagons when we leave?" Bilhah asked.

"A few," Jacob answered. "We have some things that will ride better in a wagon. And the bulls will travel better if they are busy pulling a wagon."

"And you, Dan?" Rachel asked.

"Mother Leah, I have found my place with the donkeys," Dan said. "Donkeys may not be as big or as beautiful as horses. They cannot carry all that the camels carry, but they are strong and capable. I can carry messages to Father on the back of my donkey without a saddle. He is much more comfortable than Levi's horse."

Levi raised an eyebrow. "Horses are majestic. Donkeys are unimpressive."

Dan lifted his chin. "I like donkeys. Someone must."

Zebulon tugged on my skirt. "Mother?"

"Yes, Zebulon. Which animal do you like best?" I asked.

"I like the lambs and kids. They play with me when Father takes me to see the animals."

We all grinned.

"That is why all my sons begin with the sheep," Jacob said. "Sheep are gentle and loving. I can trust my little boys with them."

"Can I go help you now?" Gad asked.

"Not until your mother agrees. She has to be ready to let you leave her."

"I am big. Can I go?" Gad stared into Zilpah's eyes.

She shook her head. "Not yet. Soon, but not yet."

Jacob would need Gad soon. He had taken all our sons to work with the animals and in the fields earlier than most men in Harran. He needed his sons.

Three weeks later, I woke up early to Jacob banging on Bilhah's chamber door. "We need you. Rachel's child is coming."

Dinah opened her brown eyes and fussed.

I lifted her from her basket. "You are wet, dear daughter. I will change you, then we need to see that your brothers get off to work with the animals."

I spoke to her, explaining what I did as I had with her brothers. She watched me with a serious expression. Certain she understood my words, I continued as I changed her wet clothing. "Mother

Rachel is finally giving birth. She will give you another brother to love. One you can grow up with."

I pulled off her nightdress and removed her bottom wrapper. "You will have eleven brothers. Your brothers will love and protect you. You are a blessed little girl." I tied her wrapper on.

"We will need to see to your brothers. All your other mothers are busy with Mother Rachel. She waited many years to give you this brother." I pulled her dress down over her head. "I wonder what she will name her son."

I wrapped a blanket around her and lifted her into my arms. "We need to go see that your brothers are ready to go help with the animals."

I carried Dinah down the hall to the chamber where all the boys slept. Our older sons had dressed and were sliding their feet into sandals.

"We are almost ready to leave," Reuben said.

"We heard Father call to Mother," Dan added. "We will go help the herders without him today."

The younger boys still slept, as they always had.

"I will prepare your morning meal," I said, leading them down the stairs.

When we entered the kitchen, Amina had their morning meal on the table and a lunch for each of them wrapped in a cloth.

"Thank you, Amina," I said, sinking into a chair to feed Dinah.

She turned with her eyebrows raised. "I do this every morning. Are the other boys still sleeping?"

"They sleep on," I said.

I joined the boys at the table eating a bowl of grains as they ate their food, grabbed their lunches, and rushed out the door with a hurried kiss on my cheek as they waved goodbye to Amina.

"Enjoy your day," Amina said.

I finished my grains and stood with Dinah. "We will be in the sitting area. You can bring the other boys there after they eat, if you like. Then you can have some time alone."

"I will do that."

I took Dinah to the sitting area and laid her on a blanket on the floor to kick and play. I pulled out my spinning and worked while I watched her.

Amina brought in the boys. Gad lay beside Dinah and talked to her. The other boys pulled out the blocks and built towers. We had a pleasant time together. Then I heard the cry of a newborn babe.

"You have a new brother," I told them.

"Mother Rachel's baby came?" Asher asked, looking up from his tower.

"When can we see the baby?" Issachar asked.

"When they come get us," I said. "Mother Rachel will need to rest awhile before she is ready for visitors."

The boys nodded and returned to their blocks.

Later, Amina returned. "Nita said Rachel would like you to meet her son, Leah."

"You will watch the children?" I asked.

She sat beside the boys. "Yes. Nita will let me know when Rachel is ready for these boys to meet her son."

I took Dinah up the stairs and down the hall, tapped on Rachel's chamber door, and entered. I swallowed an unexpected lump. Jacob sat near Rachel on her pallet, rocking the tiny child.

"You finally did it," I said.

Rachel glanced away from Jacob and her baby. "At last. Jehovah has finally given me a son."

"What did you name him?"

"Joseph. Jehovah has taken away my reproach." Her tired smile warmed the room. "And He shall give me another son."

Another son only? You deserve at least one more. You waited a long time.

"Excellent," I said. "You deserve another son, and many daughters. Joseph is a mighty name. He will grow to add to our family."

Jacob's eyes lost focus as he spoke. "He will be one who fulfills the promised covenant."

Joseph will fulfill the covenant? What of Reuben and my other sons?

"All my sons will have a share in the covenant," Jacob added, as if he heard my inner complaints, "as long as they remember to obey Jehovah's commandments."

May all my sons obey.

We Prepare to Leave

Rachel never regained her full health. We eased the burden of household chores, allowing her to return to helping, but never asking as much of her. I wanted us to enjoy a long life together.

At last, when Gad reached six, Jacob took him with his brothers to help with the animals. He loved the sheep and spent his time with them.

One Sabbath, not long after we celebrated Jacob's twentieth sacrifice and thank offerings to Jehovah, Rachel waited near the back of the sanctuary with Joseph while Jacob spoke with Daniy about his sermon. Joseph walked around the seats, chattering to her while they waited.

Our brother, Chayim, spoke with his friend near her. Her frown deepened as she listened. I wondered what she had heard.

We returned home soon after. While the children played, Rachel shared what she had heard with Jacob.

He called his four women and seven older sons together. "We must prepare. Laban's sons plan an attack on me. Jehovah will not allow it, but He may soon decide it is the time for us to leave Harran."

We all gasped.

"Our brothers would not hurt their sisters and sons," I cried.

"I heard them speak," Rachel insisted. "Their anger and greed have grown beyond caring for us."

"What do they have to be angry about?" Simeon asked.

Rachel spoke again before Jacob could. "They think your father has taken the animals that should belong to them. They believe all the animals are Father's, and he should give them all to our lazy brothers."

I lifted my eyebrows. "That bad?" I asked, remembering her frown.

Rachel nodded.

I struggled to believe, but knowing my brothers, I knew she spoke the truth.

"I am wealthy," Jacob said, "but Laban has changed, considering me his servant, not the beloved husband of his daughters."

He never has.

"Father speaks ill of you when we go to his home," I said. "Yesterday, when I visited Mother, he stormed into the house, complaining that yet again you had taken what was not yours."

Jacob shook his head. "Prepare yourselves. The day will come soon for us to leave."

"Have you heard from Jehovah?" ten-year-old Levi asked.

Jacob glanced up at the boy. "I have not, but the spirit warns me. It warned me years ago that your mothers should weave tent material."

"I remember watching Mother weave with Issachar lying in a basket beside her," Judah said.

"And Mother," Dan said. "She came into her chamber proud of having learned to weave."

I grinned. "Your mother and Mother Zilpah learned to weave with few problems."

"Are the tents prepared?" Bilhah asked.

"All is ready. They wait on the other side of the field. The day will soon come for us to leave Harran. I suggest you begin packing now," he said.

"Can we get more baskets and trunks from Mother?" Rachel asked.

"No!" Jacob jerked backward. "Do not tell anyone outside of this house. Talk with the maidservants. They may have more baskets. When I hired them, I warned them we would leave sometime. They all agreed to go with us. But do not tell your father or mother. Your father's willingness to support me has changed. He is no longer happy to have me tend his animals. He is not to know until after we are gone."

I would not share with them. I have waited thirteen years for this. Even before Father insisted I marry Jacob in Rachel's place, he had not treated me as one with any sense. I knew then how angry Rachel would be. Anger would have filled me in her place. But Father insisted we do it his way. I am ready to leave him far behind. I hope Canaan is far enough away.

Rachel frowned. "Mother should know."

"No," Jacob said softly, although heat filled his voice. "Avagail loves Laban, and she is afraid of him. If she knows, she will be obliged to share it with him. It is better she does not know."

I knew then I would have to watch Rachel. She would want to go visit Mother and tell her goodbye. She would cause Jacob problems.

In the next five days, I had to stop Rachel four times as she walked out the door to go visit Mother. "You cannot go. Remember?" I reminded her. "Jacob does not want Mother to lie to Father, and she will tell him of our leaving."

"I want to speak to her one last time," Rachel cried when I stopped her for the fifth time, little Joseph in her arms. "We may never see her again. Do you not desire to say goodbye?"

"Yes," I said with a nod as I stood in front of the kitchen door, preventing her leaving. "But I listen to our husband, and he said we should not share with anyone outside our home. It is not safe."

"Not safe?" Rachel whined. "Not safe to speak a last word with our mother? If it were Dinah, your heart would break."

Dinah, little Dinah. Jehovah had blessed me with a girl to love at last.

"Yes, I would cry many tears of grief if she had to leave without telling me. I hope her father treats her husband better than our father has treated ours. He is a brute willing to do anything to get his own way."

"I will not miss Father," she said. "I will never forgive his treatment of me when I should have married Jacob." She tried to dodge past me to open the door.

I moved, keeping her in front of me. "And Mother will tell him we are leaving if you go see her. Father will be angry with us and with Jacob."

"I will not tell her we are going." Rachel stood panting. "She misses Joseph."

"Mother will know something is wrong, and you will tell her. She always knows." I leaned against the door. "You know you cannot go. Are all your baskets and trunks ready?"

We had dragged and cleaned baskets and trunks from storage for our possessions. We had more than I expected. Packing them had kept Rachel busy the first three days. Still, she had tried to elude me each day.

"They are full and ready. When will we leave?"

"When Jacob decides it is safe. Trust him."

Rachel sighed and turned to drag herself up the stairs once more. I would not miss the stairs.

Men had taken all the baskets and trunks except our bare essential needs, moving them to the barns near the far field. We knew we would leave soon. We had watched each day since the Sabbath for Jacob's messenger, who would give us the word it was time to leave.

Early on the sixth morning, a messenger from Jacob arrived, telling us he needed to speak to us at the far fields with all our children. Father seldom came to those fields, making it safe for us to leave from there.

The time had come for us to go.

Most of our sons had gone to the fields to work with the animals with Jacob that morning. Issachar and Zebulon, three and two, trotted along beside me and Bilhah, while I carried Dinah and Rachel carried Joseph. Asher trotted beside Zilpah as the four of us women followed the messenger across the track and through the fields, staying away from other homes.

When we arrived in the far field, the older boys had helped Jacob bring all the herds together, ready to follow them down the trail. Men had loaded camels and donkeys with the tents and our packed baskets and trunks. The last of our baggage had come in a small wagon, pulled by the big bulls, and men worked to load much of it onto the animals.

"Your father's love for me is gone," Jacob said as we came to stand with him. "He no longer considers me a son, the husband of his beloved daughters. Instead, he thinks of me as a servant who built his flocks, making him wealthy, but not one to consider."

His hands clenched and unclenched. "Jehovah, the God of my father, has been with me. I have served your father with all my power, helping him for the last twenty years. In that time, he has changed my wages ten times, but Jehovah did not allow him to hurt me."

I nodded. "We know. We agree." Father had not been a faithful master.

Jacob swept his hands out, recounting his grievances against Father. My head bobbed along with Jacob's words. I had watched Father change Jacob's wages each year, promising him a color he thought would be rare, and cursing Jacob and threatening him with Harran's city guard for theft.

Rachel moved close and tucked her hand in the crook of Jacob's elbow. "Father is covetous. We understand."

"An angel came to me," Jacob continued after running his hand over his eyes. "He told me Jehovah has seen how Laban treats me. He reminded me of my anointing before I came to Harran and the vow

I made at Bethel. He commanded me to leave this land and return to the land of my father."

Jacob gazed at Rachel, then at me. "What will you do? Will you go with me or stay with your father?"

"Father took everything of ours away. He forced me to marry you when you expected to marry Rachel. Neither you nor I desired the marriage, though now I am grateful," I said with intensity. "There is no inheritance here for us."

"None," Rachel agreed. "We are considered strangers to him rather than his daughters. He sold us and used all the dowry that honor demanded he give to us for himself. It should have been ours. Do as Jehovah has commanded."

Jacob turned to Bilhah and Zilpah, who stood beside Rachel and me. "What will you do? Will you go with me?"

"Laban sold us to you as maidservants and slaves to his daughters," Bilhah said.

"There is nothing to keep us here," Zilpah added. "We have not seen our families for many years. They no longer count us as daughters and sisters."

"We will go with you, our husband and father of our sons," Bilhah said with a firm nod.

Jacob brushed his hands together, then called to his men to bring the camels. He helped me up into the padded saddle sitting in front of the hump, then handed Dinah up to me.

"Wanna ride my own," Zebulon cried when he saw Issachar mount a tall camel.

"You are too young to ride alone," I crooned as Jacob lifted him onto the camel with me. "We will have a wonderful time together on my camel. I suspect there are treats for us to eat in this bag."

When I showed him the bag behind us, he stopped complaining. The camel rose in its jerky pace to its feet.

Rachel sat on her camel while Jacob handed Joseph to her.

Soon, we were all mounted. Jacob sat on his camel and raised his hand, the signal for us to move out.

I glanced around for my sons, expecting them to lead smaller herds of sheep and lambs, followed by the herders and their dogs. Instead, they too sat on camels as beloved sons of the master. Herders followed the animals with their dogs, following behind us on our camels.

I settled in for a long ride.

Confrontation

I sensed Jacob's desire to ride as far from Harran as possible that first day. However, he halted our ride to rest and eat at midday. He stopped before the sun set, allowing his servants to set up our tents before dark.

As he often did, Jacob went to Rachel's tent that night, and each of the next five nights. I expected nothing different. He had spent the last nights of our life in Harran with me, since Rachel suffered from her womanly curse.

We reached the Euphrates River on the second day. I feared it would be too deep for the animals, but its flow had reduced, rising only past the camel's feet.

Our sons dismounted and led herds of animals across the river behind their father. Jacob set Gad in front of our baggage on a tall camel. He complained at first, insisting he was big enough to take his sheep across the wide river, but when he saw the difficulty the littlest lambs and calves had in the water, he settled back against the baggage and stopped arguing.

After crossing the river, Jacob led us down the trail a short distance where we dismounted to rest while our older sons returned to the river and helped lead the animals safely across.

It took the rest of the day for all the animals to cross the river. Although some young animals fought the currents that swept them down the river a short distance, we lost no animals in the crossing.

After resting the animals and people that night, we continued our journey toward Mount Gilead. The rocking camels should have put us to sleep, but as we traveled, we peered behind us many times, expecting to find Father and our brothers following us. In the seven days it took to travel from Harran to Mount Gilead, we expected him to race into our camp and attempt to drag us home at any moment. Only our little ones slept on the swaying camels.

When we arrived at Mount Gilead, Jacob stopped our caravan. He wanted us to rest, and he needed to offer a sacrifice of gratitude to Jehovah. I hoped Father had given up on us. I feared we were not far enough away from him to be safe.

He had no love for us. Why would he force us to return to him? Without Jacob, we would become an encumbrance on his wealth. He did not care about Rachel or me. Our children were only a symbol to the people of Harran of his immense wealth. We daughters were no longer his beloved daughters.

I put Dinah down for a nap in my tent when a cry rose from the guards. Dust rose in a vast cloud behind us.

Someone followed us.

I stood with the other women, our youngest sons gathered in a knot around us, while our men surrounded us, watching as riders emerged at the base of the dust cloud.

Father.

And my brothers.

Racing ahead of their men toward our camp.

Jacob joined us, wrapping an arm around Rachel who leaned against him. "All will be well," he said. "We have nothing to fear. Jehovah is with us." He turned to the four of us women. "Take your young children and wait in your tents. All is well."

I turned toward my tent, knowing Dinah slept there, but stopped, searching among the milling boys for Zebulon and Issachar. Bilhah and Zilpah took their young sons from the group and shooed them to their tents as well. As always, Rachel stood on her tiptoes to kiss Jacob before carrying Joseph with her to her tent.

At last, my two younger sons joined me, grumbling that they wanted to stand with their brothers. Our older sons arranged themselves in a loose circle behind their father.

I sucked in a breath and prayed for their safety.

Each of us stood in our tent doorways, waiting and watching to see what Father would do. Issachar and Zebulon stood with me in the door of my tent, watching Father and his men pull their horses to a stop in front of Jacob.

Father's horse reared up, pawing at the air. Dust rose in a cloud around the horse's feet. He settled his horse before climbing off and standing in front of Jacob. He took a wide stance, as always, with my brothers and his other men ranging beside and behind him. This would not be pleasant.

"Why have you stolen away from my fields without telling me?" Father said in a roar from the excitement of the chase. "Did you also take my daughters away as captives with the sword?"

"Your daughters, my wives, came with me willingly. I left at Jehovah's command," Jacob replied in a low and even voice.

How could he express confidence in the face of Father's rage? I shook my head and listened.

"Why did you flee in secret with no warning? I would have held a feast and celebrated our time together with songs and laughter." Father inhaled.

He lies. He would not have celebrated us. If he had wanted, he could have celebrated with us many times in the past twenty years. He did not.

Jacob stared into his eyes and shifted his feet, preparing to respond.

"You did not allow me to kiss my grandchildren or my daughters goodbye." His false whine sickened me. "You did a foolish thing."

"It may appear foolish to you," Jacob said, at last inserting himself into the discussion. "I had reason to leave without sharing with you."

"You left when you knew I would be gone," Father shouted.

"Yes, for you would have prevented my leaving. You knew since my coming that I would return to my home. Every time I have suggested I would leave, you found a reason to keep me."

Father stamped his foot, much like Rachel did when she did not get her way. "Bah. I would have given a feast for you."

Jacob shook his head. "When did you care enough for my wives and me that you gave a feast in our honor?"

"Every year —"

"I offered sacrifice, and you allowed it. Your men set up the tables. My wives and the women who worshipped with us provided the other food. When did you kill and roast a sheep or a steer for us? I will tell you. Never." Jacob's voice, so often controlled and soft, became loud and strident.

Father stepped back, then stepped forward again. "When did you ask?"

"Why should the husband of a man's beloved daughters request a feast in their honor?"

Jacob and Father stood like wild camels in rut, about to attack each other.

Until Jacob huffed out a breath and dropped his voice. "The time has come for me to return home. I must visit my mother once more."

I want to meet Rebekah. Jacob told me so many lovely things about her.

"With all your family?" Father asked.

"I must return to take my place as a son of Isaac. I will not return to Harran. I must take my family with me." He turned and walked toward his sons, then returned to stand in front of Father. "We have overstayed our welcome. Your sons see me as unacceptable competition. They believe I have taken their inheritance. They planned to hurt me. I left before they could."

Father turned to stare at his sons. "Hurt you?"

They lifted their hands and shook their heads, trying to show their innocence.

"I will deal with you later," Father growled before turning back to Jacob.

"They told me you were stealing my animals." He gazed toward the brush paddocks holding our animals, his jaw set firm. "You have many more than I expected."

"They are mine. Each time you changed my pay, Jehovah blessed me. The ewes and other female animals gave birth to the ones you promised me, making them mine. If you honestly remember the covenants we made, you will see these are mine. I took none of your animals."

I glanced at the multiple herds of animals, none plain, as Father had insisted were his. They were all multi-colored, all as he had given to Jacob to decrease his wealth.

Father's clenched fists relaxed somewhat. "My sons think everything I have should be theirs, and none yours. I shudder to think what would happen to my daughters if I left them in their brothers' care."

"They are mine. I will care for them." Jacob's insistence sent warmth through my chest. "My wives and my children. I will protect them from any who would hurt them."

Father nodded his agreement. "I agreed to give you my daughters, but I did not agree to give you all my wealth."

"All your wealth?" Jacob ran his hands through his beard. "Have you looked at your flocks lately?"

Father waved a hand toward our paddocks again. "I see all you have claimed for yourself. Shelomiy says —"

"Shelomiy says many things. Few are accurate. I have many because you agreed I could have them." Jacob threw his hands in the air. "When you return, go look at your own herds. You have many more than I do. We had to build new paddocks to hold all your animals."

Father's bushy eyebrows rose. "More paddocks?"

"How else would I protect them all? Your wealth in animals continues to be greater than mine. When did you last inspect your animals?" Jacob set his hands on his hips, ducked his head, and shook it.

"Shelomiy —"

"Do not always accept the word of a son who would cause your daughters and grandsons to become beggars. You have lost none of your wealth by sharing some with me and your daughters."

Father swallowed the words he had planned to speak. He nodded toward the tents we, his daughters, stood in front of, then turned back to Jacob. "I know you have longed to be home with your father for many years. But why would you steal my god images?"

Images

God images? What god images? Mother said they kept the images of the local gods to hide their belief in Jehovah. Others from Harran who came to visit would not know of their true beliefs. Did they believe in Jehovah or the *gods of Harran?*

Mother loved the images she kept in her chamber, claiming they helped her conceive each of her children. Had she given those images to Rachel?

I tried to remember the last time I had seen them there. It had been years. I had thought she had found the error in her beliefs and put them away.

Jacob leaned back, opening a space between himself and Father. "I did not take your images. Why would I? I believe only in Jehovah. They are not here. Search my camp among our goods. If you find them, whoever has them will die."

I sucked in a harsh breath. *Would he kill Rachel if he found Mother's images among her goods?*

Father, Jacob, and Father's men entered Zilpah's tent. It took some time for them to search her baggage, but when they left her tent, from Father's grim look I knew they had not found his images.

They then entered Bilhah's tent. Once more, they found no images among her baggage. Father's frown deepened.

Next, Jacob, Father, and his men came to my tent. *Father would not believe Rachel would have his images.*

I held onto Zebulon and Issachar. "Dinah sleeps. Please do not wake her," I whispered.

Father nodded and held a finger to his lips as he turned toward his men. Still, they searched through all my possessions, lifting my sleeping daughter to search beneath her. They found no images among my possessions.

Finally, they entered Rachel's tent. I stood still, praying to Jehovah to protect my sister if she were guilty. Why would she have those?

As Jacob stepped out of Rachel's tent, stormy frustration filled his face. "What have I done? What is my tresspass? What is my sin that you have pursued so hotly after me?" he stormed at Father.

Issachar tugged on my skirt. "Mother? Why is Father so angry?"

I turned from the tent opening. "Your grandfather blames him, saying one of us took his images."

"Like the one Mother Rachel kept in her chamber?"

The innocence of children always surprised me.

"Yes, dear." I bent to touch his lips. "But Grandpapa does not need to know you saw it there. Say nothing about it."

With big, round eyes, he nodded. "Is it so terrible?"

"Yes, son. Very terrible. After Grandpapa is gone, I will explain it to you."

His nod was somber. "Yes, Mother."

"Why not go with Zebulon and practice your reading?" I said. "He would love to hear a story."

My little son turned and walked across the tent and plopped beside his younger brother and read a book to him.

I sighed and turned back to my husband and father's argument.

"You know I found nothing," Father said, clearing his throat.

"For the twenty years I have lived with you, your ewes and she-goats have not cast their young away, and the rams of your flock I did not eat," Jacob said, his frustration tightening his jaw and voice. "I brought the animals torn by beasts to you. I took the loss because you required the losses from me, whether the animals were stolen by day or by night."

We had often heard this complaint when a beast had entered the fold at night during the time the flocks were in the care of the herders, tearing at the sheep and goats. Father never accepted responsibility for the loss, never accepted the loss because his herders ran rather than protecting his animals. Every time Father expected Jacob to absorb the loss, taking the meat from the injured animals for himself, even when his daughters suffered from a lack of food.

"I suffered during the day in the heat of the drought, and in the frost at night. I did not sleep when waiting for the ewes and the she-goats to bring forth their young. For what? To hear you complain when a ewe or she-goat did not survive."

Jacob walked away from Father, then turned. "I have served you for twenty years. Fourteen of those were for your two daughters, when I contracted only for seven years to earn Rachel. But I accepted Leah and learned to love her, and worked another seven years. And in the last six years while I worked with your cattle, you changed my wages ten times!"

Father cleared his throat and stepped back, preparing to speak, but Jacob continued. "If you had not feared the God of my father, the God of Abraham and Isaac, my father, you would have sent me away before now with nothing. I would have no sheep, no goats, nor any other animals. Worse, you would have kept my wives and children, sending me away with empty hands. You would have taken them from me now if Jehovah, the God of my father, had not warned you against it. Jehovah has seen my afflictions and the labor of my hands and rebuked you last night."

Father stepped forward, lifting a hand to set it on Jacob's shoulder, but he flinched away.

"These are my daughters, and the children are my children," Father said. "These cattle are my cattle. All you see is mine. But you can take them. What can I do today to these my daughters or unto their children? I can do nothing to hurt you, for indeed, the God of your father spoke to me last night. He warned me to take heed of the words I speak to you, whether good or bad." He shrugged and lifted his hands, as if asking permission. " Come. Let us make a covenant, you and I. Let it be a witness between you and me."

Jacob paced away, returned to stand in front of Father, then paced away once more.

Zebulon came close to me and held my hand.

Jacob bent to pick up a stone, which he brought to Father. "This will be a pillar as a witness of that covenant."

Father called on my brothers and his men to gather more stones, while Jacob asked his servants to do the same. Although my brothers grumbled, they helped make a heap of stones.

As they worked, I slipped out of my tent and found our maidservants. "Prepare a meal for my father and his men."

The maidservants stirred up the fire and set to work preparing a meal. When the men completed the heap, the servants brought the food to the men, who ate it, using the heap as a table.

"This heap is a witness between you and me today," Father said. "We shall call it Galeed and Mizpah, a lookout point. Jehovah watch between you and me when we are away from each other. If you afflict my daughters or take other wives besides those you now have, our covenant will end."

With two wives and two wife-concubines, why would he desire another wife? *We had no concerns that he would break* his *covenant with Father. He had not wanted to marry me, and argued against Bilhah and Zilpah. I had no fear of Father's wrath.*

Father continued. "This heap and this pillar we have set between us is a witness. I will not pass beyond it to harm you, nor will you pass it to harm me."

"It shall be done," Jacob said. "I will offer a sacrifice to seal the covenant."

While we women and our children ate, Jacob went among the flocks to choose a ram to sacrifice. We watched from the base of the mount as Jacob sacrificed it, then fed Father and all the men with him.

That night, Jacob came to my sleeping pallet.

"I do not complain, but why are you here rather than with Rachel?"

"She suffers from the custom of women."

Grateful for the darkness in my tent, I lifted my eyes in surprise. She had suffered that a week earlier. It proved to me she used it as an excuse to avoid Father finding his images in her baggage.

I did not complain and enjoyed Jacob's attention.

Early the next morning, as Father prepared to leave, he took Rachel and me in his arms and kissed us, blessing us and all our children. He ignored both Zilpah and Bilhah. They scowled after him as he mounted his horse and waved to his men and rode away.

"Do not concern yourselves with him," I said. "Father is a horrible, selfish man. You do not deserve his disdain, nor should you care about it."

I did not deserve it either. As I returned to my tent, I breathed a sigh of relief. I no longer needed to fear the man.

I do not know what Jacob said to Rachel about the images. When we left Mount Gilead to travel onward toward Canaan and Mamre, two images stood next to the pile of stones.

We stayed there at the foot of Mount Gilead two more days, giving Jacob time to offer another sacrifice to Jehovah. Early on the third morning, we rode once more on the trail to Canaan.

Esau Comes

Jacob needed to meet with his twin brother, Esau, and receive his forgiveness.

In the twenty years he spent in Harran, Jacob had not heard from his family. He still feared Esau had not forgiven him. He expressed his fears as the family prayed together, fervently begging Jehovah to soften his brother's heart. Still, his hands quivered when he thought of Esau.

After we passed through the River Jordan, nearing the land of his father, he sent messengers out in search of Esau. They returned days later, racing on lather-covered camels.

Jacob stopped his camel in anticipation of the message. I went with the other women and our sons who pushed our camels forward to better hear the report.

Jacob handed the leader of the messengers a flask of water, allowing him to take a long drink before asking him questions.

The messenger wiped the splashes of water from his beard and handed the flask to the next man before speaking. "We met Esau, your brother, and shared your message with him. He sent us ahead with his message."

Jacob inhaled. "And what message did he send?"

"Esau comes to meet you with four hundred men."

Jacob's face lost its color beneath his tan. "Does he come to destroy me?" he whispered. "Does he still hate me after all these years?" He ducked his head in silent prayer.

Jehovah, soften Esau's heart. Bless him and Jacob, *that he may find forgiveness.*

Jacob lifted his head. "Demas? Where is Demas?"

Demas had worked beside him almost since he had arrived in Harran. Now, as his oldest and wisest servant, he walked among the flocks as he always did.

"He is with the flocks," Reuben reminded Jacob.

"I need him," Jacob said. "Send for him."

Reuben waved to a small boy on a donkey. "Go get Demas."

The boy rode away.

The short, squat man with a tangled beard and windblown hair ran behind the messenger sooner than I expected. Concern filled his dark eyes. "You require my presence?" he asked, breathing hard from his run.

Jacob handed him his water flask before speaking. When Demas handed it back, Jacob said, "Yes, Demas. Esau comes. I will not have him attack and destroy all my family and flocks. Divide the flocks into two parts. I will send Leah and Zilpah and their children with you and one flock to the west. I will take Rachel and Bilhah to the east with me. If Esau destroys one camp, the other will escape."

Demas bowed. "It will be as you command."

Jacob sent my sons, Reuben and Simeon, who had more practice, to help divide the flocks. When they returned, Jacob directed Zilpah and me to take our children and our possessions to the west, separating us from the others.

Zilpah shuddered, and tears trickled across her face as she waved goodbye to Bilhah.

I nudged my camel closer to Zilpah's and set my hand on her arm. "Still your fears. Jehovah commanded Jacob to come here. He would not send us into the wilderness for Esau to attack and kill us."

"But Jacob fears him." She wiped at the tears on her face.

"With reason." My camel swayed away, taking my hand from her arm. I guided my camel around a boulder in our path. "Esau threatened to kill Jacob before his parents sent him to Harran. They sent him there as much to protect him from his brother as to find a wife."

I smiled, thinking how Jacob had found two wives and two concubines.

"A brother would kill his twin?" Zilpah asked, shuddering.

"He may threaten it, even consider it. He may even follow through. Jacob left to ensure Esau could not. We do not know if Esau continues to carry his grudge against Jacob. All I know is Jacob has done what he believes to be right. We can only hope that Esau no longer hates his brother."

My six sons joined the guard that night, and I pulled Dinah onto my pallet. Although I spent most of my nights without Jacob, an icy shiver of loneliness crept up my back after Zilpah and I prayed for protection and softening of Esau's heart.

Early the next morning, however, Jacob sent his men to gather our group back together with his. He had spent the night communing with Jehovah.

Rather than divide his family again, he sent gifts to his brother of goats, sheep, milk camels, cattle, and donkeys, sending each group in separate, small herds. He hoped the gifts would win his brother's forgiveness.

He gave each set of herders the same instructions. "When Esau asks whose animals these are, reply saying they belong to your servant, Jacob. They are a gift for my lord Esau. Jacob comes behind us."

The goats and their herders left. After a short time, Jacob sent the sheep, and later, each of the other herds of animals. It would take time for Esau to meet and accept all the herds. We camped there and waited through the night.

How would Esau accept the flocks? I prayed he would accept them with the same love Jacob sent them.

As we got up early the next morning, dust rose along the trail in front of us.

Esau and his men.

Jacob dressed with care, wearing a light blue tunic and a deep blue robe over it, both falling to his knees and covering his muscular shoulders and arms. His hair, now a medium brown, hung in long curls down his neck and around his ears. His matching beard now held streaks of gray and flowed to his chest. Intelligent, azure eyes peered out from his sun and wind-tanned face. New lines around them hinted at his stress. He wore hastily dusted sandals and kept his shepherd's crook nearby.

The rest of Jacob's family wore deep blue, showing they were part of his family. The boys wore deep-blue robes, the same color as their father. His women and Dinah wore deep blue dresses. I wound my braid on my head and covered it and my face with a sheer blue tichel. I did not like the taste of sand.

Rachel allowed her hair to fall across her shoulders, but she also wore a deep blue tichel to protect her mouth and hair. Both Zilpah and Bilhah had braided their hair to keep it out of the way. However, they also wore blue tichels to keep the sand out of their mouths.

Jacob gathered his family near and shared his plans. "I am sending each of you ahead to greet Esau. I hope this will help gain his forgiveness."

We nodded, hoping Jehovah had given him the best way to assuage Esau's hurt.

"Zilpah, you and your sons will go first to meet my brother." When she nodded, he turned toward Bilhah. "Bilhah, you and your sons will follow Zilpah."

She bowed her head in agreement.

He turned to me next. "Leah, you and your sons and Dinah will go next —"

"I can do that," I murmured.

"— and Rachel," he turned to her as if I had said nothing, "you will go last with Joseph. I want each of you to leave a space between you and the family group ahead of you. I will come last to greet my brother. I hope his heart is softened by your beauty, and he will welcome me home."

Zilpah gulped.

Last concubine first, beloved wife last. Jacob would keep Rachel and Joseph until *the end. I pray nothing happens to any of us.*

Zilpah held her sons' hands. Gad and Asher straightened their backs and marched forward as if to their death. Perhaps they were. I saw Gad's fist clench. He could do little against four hundred men.

Bilhah followed with Dan and Naphtali. Her sons were older than Zilpah's, and stood taller, walked with greater strength. They stayed close to their mother to protect her.

I followed next, leaving enough space between us so the dust Bilhah and her sons kicked up would not cover my dress. I wanted Esau to see me as Jacob's wife, not as a dusty traveler.

I held Dinah in my arms, planning to set her on her feet when we neared Jacob's twin. My sons walked with me in a shielding circle. They murmured to each other to stay strong and fear nothing. Jehovah was with us. My heart throbbed with joy for my sons.

I heard Rachel following behind us, with only one set of footsteps. She too carried her little son, Joseph.

We had not walked far, Zilpah had neared Esau. He had dismounted from his camel, when racing footsteps overtook Rachel. I glanced back to see Jacob bowing near the earth. He ran and stopped to bow again between Rachel and me, then bowed once more when he came in line with us. He raced toward his brother, stopping four more times to bow low.

Jacob stopped and knelt one last time after passing Zilpah. Esau ran from his camel to meet Jacob and lifted him from his knees. He threw his arms around his brother, embracing him as the long-lost brother he was.

My sons and I stopped walking when we reached Zilpah, Bilhah, and their sons. Rachel soon joined us, watching and waiting.

"Jacob, my brother," Esau wept. "I have missed you."

"And I missed you," Jacob sobbed. Tears from both men mingled in their beards.

At last, they broke their embrace. Esau turned toward us and swept his hand in our direction. "Who are these?"

Jacob cleared his throat. "These are the children whom Jehovah graciously gave me, your servant."

He then beckoned us to come forward. We stepped forward in the order we had walked. Jacob introduced each woman and her children to his twin brother. Esau lifted us from our bow, kissed our cheeks, and spoke kind words to our sons. He kissed Dinah on the forehead and teased her until she smiled. After kissing Rachel on each cheek, then tickled Joseph until he giggled.

As we women and our children stepped back, Esau turned to Jacob."What do you mean by sending all those gifts of animals?"

"To find grace with you, my lord," Jacob replied, dipping his head.

Esau's curly red hair shook with his head. "For me? I am your brother, your twin brother, not your lord. I have enough and more for myself without your gifts. Keep your animals for yourself."

Jacob's brown curls shook. "No. If I have found grace in your sight, receive my gifts. I have seen your face as if I had seen the face of Jehovah. Better yet, you are happy to see me. I beg you, take the gifts I sent to you. Jehovah has blessed me with abundance. I have enough."

"No," Esau said. "I have enough. Jehovah has blessed me."

"And he has blessed me. You are the lord of Canaan. Please accept my gift."

The brothers turned and walked away from us, arguing about the gifts. When they returned, Esau had agreed to keep the flocks sent to him by Jacob.

"I will lead the way home. We will soon be with our father. Joy will fill his face to see you once more."

Jacob's face turned grave. "And our mother? What of her?" He reached for Esau's hand.

"Mother watched for your return all these years, yearning to see your face." Grief filled Esau's face. His smile drooped. "We lost her only last month. Her last words were of you."

The joy on Jacob's face crumpled. Sudden tears streamed across his face. "Last month? I missed her?"

Esau's muscular arms encircled his brother once more, his tears mingling with Jacob's. "She sent messages to Harran, but no messengers returned with word of you. She prayed you still lived, but her illness overtook her. Her joy at your return would have revived her."

I would have loved to have left earlier — *last month, last year. But Father would not give us permission. Jacob asked, he begged, but Father refused. This is also on Father's head.*

Sobs shook Jacob's shoulders. "I should have left Harran sooner."

"You could not have known about Mother's illness. It happened suddenly. You had no way of knowing." Love filled Esau's words.

But they did not comfort Jacob. "The spirit warned me to leave earlier," he wept. "I chose not to have a confrontation with Laban. I could have left earlier, but my children were too young to travel far and fast, especially if Laban chased after us. I waited for them to grow. I waited for a day when Laban would not be near us to notice our going. If I had been willing to enter a conflict, we would have arrived home in time to kiss her cheeks and introduce my family to her."

Esau continued to pat Jacob's back, repeating the words, "You could not know."

"I did not listen. And because I was unwilling to confront Laban, I lost the opportunity to kiss my sweet mother's face one last time."

"Jehovah has given you abundant blessings. Trust Him. Mother trusted Him to protect you while you were gone from us. Look!" Esau swept his hands out to the multitude of flocks grazing on the grass near us. "You are blessed with flocks." He turned his gaze toward our knot of wives and children. "And look at your family. Eleven sons follow you as you serve Jehovah. You are blessed."

Jacob wiped away his tears and smiled warily. "I am extra blessed to have found you here, willing to welcome me home."

"Come," Esau urged. "I will ride ahead with my men. Ride home behind us. We will protect you."

Jacob kicked a stone near his foot. "No, I cannot. My children are young." He waved at Dinah and Joseph. "They have never traveled so far, and could not travel as fast as you and your men. They would not arrive healthy. And I have many young among my flocks. These would not survive your fast pace."

Esau cleared his throat and kicked a stone toward the one Jacob kicked. But Jacob spoke before he could. "No. Go on ahead. Tell Father I come. I will follow at a safer pace for my children and animals."

Once again, a gentle argument between the brothers ensued. Esau tried to convince Jacob to accept some of his men as guards, but Jacob claimed we had enough guards. We would travel at a safer pace.

At last, Esau agreed and leapt onto his camel, which rose from its waiting place. He signaled to his men and rode away with shouts of joy.

I hoped to meet Jacob's father, Isaac, soon.

A Bear

We followed Esau at a slower pace. Our animals had too many young to race across the countryside at Esau's pace. Our little children could not race ahead.

We stopped in the land of Succoth, a distance from Esau's lands. We had too many animals to share the land Esau claimed. Jacob purchased land, and he and his men built us a home and barns, sheds, and stables for our many animals. Jacob told us we would stay there until our sons became men.

After he had us settled into a house and the animals into barns, he announced to the family his plans to visit his father, finally.

"Why did you wait so long?" Bilhah asked when he announced his journey.

"I needed you in a safe place before I left you behind," he said. "Father loves Esau more than he loves me. Mother stood between Father and me, preventing arguments and helping me succeed. She loved me as Father loves Esau."

Our sons murmured soft comments to each other.

"We would have been safe in our tents," Reuben said.

"The men of Succoth needed to know me and know I would protect my family and take vengeance on any who might consider harming them. They know that now."

I would not want to have those men attack us.

"When Father promised Esau his blessing for a bowl of venison stew, Mother helped me deceive him," Jacob continued. "Then, when Esau learned he had lost the birthright he had sold to me for a bowl of stew, his first thought was to take my life. Mother heard of it and warned me I should leave. She cried to Father and convinced him to send me to Harran to find Laban and perhaps a daughter to marry."

"He had two daughters," Judah murmured.

"Yes, he did," Jacob said, turning to him. "And I am grateful for both of them."

"He should have sent Esau to Harran," Zilpah said.

"He should have sent us years earlier. Mother encouraged him to send us for several years, but there was always something else to prevent it. When Esau married a Canaanite woman, Mother feared I would also find a Canaanite woman if she did not send me away." He swallowed. "It did not help that Esau threatened to kill me."

"How would it have changed all our lives if Esau had come with you?" Rachel murmured.

She thinks she would have had Jacob to herself, as if Esau would have had me. Jehovah knows our needs. We both needed Jacob.

"We can never know," Jacob said. He took a deep breath. "I am the second son, not loved in the same way as Esau, the first child. Yet Father blessed me with amazing blessings before I left home, confirming the blessings Mother and I had gained for me using guile. Then, I thought he might love me."

Dan glanced at Naphtali and whispered, "We will never receive those blessings."

"You will receive blessings from Jehovah as you obey Him," Jacob said, gazing at Bilhah's sons. "I did everything to gain his love. I obeyed him. I obeyed Jehovah. I do not know if Father loves me yet." He shuddered. "I do know I love you and will bless you with all Jehovah allows as you obey Him."

Gad nodded and took Asher's hand. "We will obey."

"I expect that from my sons," Jacob said with a firm nod. "I will leave for Mamre in the morning. Demas is responsible for the animals. Each of you boys who have herds to care for, take your instructions from him. I am leaving men to protect my herds and family. Stay safe."

Reuben and the older boys crowded around their father, asking him questions, before he sent them to their chambers to sleep. After a few more instructions to his women, we, too, found our chambers. As usual, Jacob went with Rachel.

We watched Jacob and his small band of men ride away the next morning before returning to our chores.

Our sons rose early each morning to tend to their animals. We missed Jacob, but continued to care for our home and animals.

Jacob's return was joyous. We had missed him.

I doubt I had ever seen Jacob so happy in all the years since his coming to Harran. "Father welcomed me with open arms, showering me with his love," he exclaimed. "He missed me almost as much as he misses Mother." He sighed. "He loves me. But Father agrees. Our sons need to be stronger before we return to live near him."

"We are strong," Reuben cried.

"And grown," Simeon agreed.

"You are growing and strong, but you need to grow bigger and stronger to join the men who protect your mothers and sister. As you work in the fields, tend to the animals, and fight off wild beasts, you will grow stronger. And we must allow your younger brothers to become strong as well. When we move to your grandfather's land, we will need to prove our strength to the Canaanites."

My older sons grumbled, but they returned to their responsibilities in the fields and with the animals.

One afternoon in the third year we lived there, Simeon, Judah, and Gad came into the house carrying Naphtali between them on a robe, calling for Bilhah.

I rushed to the entrance of our home to see why they had shouted.

"We need Bilhah fast," Judah cried. "Naphtali is hurt."

Bilhah ran in with her basket full of healing supplies. "What happened?"

I lifted the bloody edge of his robe and gasped. Blood covered his back. I stared up at Simeon.

"A bear." Simeon said.

Bilhah gulped and fought back her tears. Her youngest son fought for his life. She directed them to take him into the kitchen and set him on the table where she could minister to him.

Her gasp filled the room when she peeled back the ragged robe. "How did this happen?"

"A sow bear scratched him," Judah said.

She filled a bowl with warm water and dropped herbs into it. With a clean cloth, she swished the herbs through the water, then started cleaning dirt from the wounds.

"You know how Naphtali loved his sheep. He hunted a ewe that had slipped away to give birth. He found her with her newborn twin lambs in a thicket." Simeon shuddered. "He lifted a lamb and stepped from the thicket to take it to Reuben. He did not see the bear cubs following their mother along the path."

My heart hurt. *What happened?* "Bear cubs? That is not safe."

"No," Simeon said. "He stumbled over a cub. It squalled, and the sow turned to chase Naphtali."

Bilhah sucked in a breath, but kept cleaning the gouges on her son's back.

"He tossed the lamb to Reuben as the sow caught up to him, raking his back with her claws."

"I did not believe she would let go of him," Judah said, gulping a big breath.

"She finally left Naphtali, bleeding into the dirt," Simeon said. "I took my robe off, and we rolled him onto it and raced home with him. We knew he needed Bilhah's help."

Bilhah pressed against a deep scratch, working to slow the bleeding. "And the lamb and its mother? Did they live?"

"While we got Naphtali onto my robe, Reuben retrieved the second lamb and called to the ewe. He took them to the paddock." Simeon shuddered. "Gad watched for that sow bear. We feared she would come back to get us."

I shuddered.

Bilhah filled a needle and handed me another. "I will need your help to stop this bleeding."

I clenched my jaw and pressed the needle through Naphtali's skin on either side of the scratch and started sewing. I soon could poke the needle through his skin without cringing.

Although he had passed out from the pain of the injury and Bilhah's herbs, Naphtali moaned.

"This is your robe, Simeon?" I asked.

"I had nothing else. I had to get him here fast."

"Both robes will need to be replaced," I said.

"He needed our help," Simeon protested.

"I know. I will make new robes for you both."

"I will replace Naphtali's robe," Bilhah said between clenched teeth.

I nodded. "Yes. He is your son. You should do that."

I returned to stitching the deep, long scratch. The sow's claws had left so many scratches.

We finished stitching the scratches, and I leaned backward, stretching my back. How did Bilhah do this for so long? This time she did it for her son.

"Will Naphtali live?" Judah asked.

I turned my gaze to Bilhah, seeking her answer.

Bilhah lifted an eyelid. "Yes." Bilhah slowly bobbed her head. A small sob escaped. "Most of the scratches have stopped bleeding." She pressed her cloth against a scratch. When she lifted a corner, the scratch continued to bleed.

"Press here," she said. "I need to clean this again, or he will get sick."

I pressed on Naphtali's injury while Bilhah refilled her bowl with more warm water and herbs. As before, she swished the herbs around with her cloth, and prepared to clean Naphtali's back.

She dripped the herb-infused water onto the scratches and dabbed at them, working to clean the last of the dirt from them. Then she smoothed honey into the scratches.

Issachar came into the kitchen. "Will Naphtali live?"

Bilhah stepped away from the table and rubbed her back. "He will live. It will take time for him to heal. We need someone to move him off the table."

Issachar helped Simeon and Judah lift his brother off the table and carried him to lie on a pallet Zilpah and Rachel had prepared in the living area.

Naphtali spent many days there in the middle of the living area, tossing and turning from the pain. Bilhah sat next to him, massaging honey into his wounds as often as necessary.

Bilhah watched for streaks of red. They appeared.

In our rush to stop the bleeding, we had not washed away all the filth from the bear's claws, nor did we remove all the bits of dirt and fabric from Naphtali's shredded robe.

Bilhah and I took turns washing his scratches and smoothing more honey into the worst of his wounds. After many days, the streaks disappeared.

Jacob and Reuben helped Naphtali mount the stairs to his pallet, where he spent more days healing. After a week, he came down the stairs to sit with us, reading stories to Dinah and Joseph, and helped Zebulon write. I sewed Simeon a new robe and Bilhah made Naphtali a new robe in the time it took for him to heal.

While Naphtali healed, Esau raced through our gates with two hundred men.

"I came to see my brother and his women," he called.

Jacob stepped into the setting sun to welcome his brother.

He sent a servant to slaughter a steer to cook to feed his brother and his men. I set the women servants to preparing more food.

Naphtali welcomed his uncle. When Esau wrapped his arms around him for a hug, Naphtali flinched.

"Naphtali is recovering from a bear attack," Jacob said.

"I did not know," Esau said, frowning. "Did I hurt you?"

"Not much," Naphtali said.

He enjoyed sitting with his uncle and retelling the story of his bear encounter and basking in his uncle's presence and love.

"The women will love your scars. You can tell them an excellent story," Esau said, then leapt on his horse. "Stay strong."

By the time Naphtali had healed enough to return to the animals, Issachar had passed his sixth birthday. I stood beside Bilhah with tears of joy sliding down our cheeks as we watched our sons stride toward the paddocks.

Two years later, Naphtali presented Bilhah with the bear's fur. "I waited until her cubs had left her and lived on their own before I killed her. This fur is for you. You kept me alive."

Joseph Works

Esau returned to visit almost every year after that, leaving his sons at home, responsible for their mothers and animals. Reuben teased him about bringing a son next time, but he never did.

Rachel did not allow Joseph to join his brothers in the sheep paddocks when he reached six years. She protected him until his complaints grew too strong.

"I am Jacob's son," he argued. "All my brothers left their mothers at six. I am now seven. I must take my place with them and learn to care for the animals."

"We will ensure no accident befalls him," Reuben said.

"How can you do that when Naphtali carries the scars of the bear?" Rachel cried. "You could not keep that sow from clawing Naphtali's back."

"That happened far from the paddock, where Naphtali went on his own. When we saw he was gone, we went to find him. We will stay with Joseph and keep him safe."

Joseph dropped to his knees. "Reuben and the others will help me. Father will give me a blessing as he gave the others. Jehovah will protect me. Please allow me to go. I look like a baby to my brothers."

Rachel glanced at me. "How did you allow Reuben to leave you so early?"

"I could not fight Jacob. He needed my son to help, as he now requires your son's assistance."

"Then I should allow him to go?" Her face twisted, begging me to tell her no.

"I know you want to keep your son close, but you must let him grow. He needs to learn to work hard."

"He can learn that —"

"No, Rachel," Jacob said. "Joseph cannot become a man with his mother holding him back. You must allow him to join his brothers. I will give him a blessing. Jehovah will keep him safe."

Rachel scowled, but she gave in.

"I can go tomorrow?" Joseph cried.

"Yes. For the morning, as your brothers did." Rachel sighed.

"I am older than they were," Joseph complained.

"And you will obey your mother. You can go in the mornings only for a few days," Jacob said. "You will be happy to rest in the afternoon."

Rachel wept the next morning, pacing from the window to the door, never able to settle enough to spin or weave. She would sit and pick up her spindle, then leap up and stare out the window. At last, Jacob and Joseph walked through the door.

"The sheep loved me, Mother. None of them pushed me over," Joseph said, excitement spreading from him through the room. "I am not tired. Let me return this afternoon. Please, Mother?"

"Joseph," Jacob murmured. "We talked about this."

Joseph gazed up. "Yes, Father."

"I am happy you are home," Dinah chirped. "We can practice our writing and numbers."

Joseph smiled. "We can do that. As long as Mother does not send me to my room to sleep."

"No," Rachel said. "You have not required an afternoon sleep for more than a year. Writing and working with numbers is an excellent way to spend your time."

Jacob returned to his work, and the children sat at the table to eat. When they finished, they bounced off to read together.

Not long after that, all our sons worked with Jacob in the fields and with the animals. Joseph joined them every day. Rachel continued to do all she could to keep him close to her and away from danger.

Jacob and the other boys stayed with Joseph, protecting him when he went out. But Rachel did her best to keep him from doing anything dangerous.

When Joseph was ten, Issachar grumbled to me about Rachel. "She treats him like a baby. Why will she not allow him to be the man he can become?"

"Joseph is her only child," I reminded him. "She waited many years for him. She fears she will lose him."

"Jehovah will watch over him as He cares for Zebulon, me, and the others."

"I pray Jehovah continues to protect all of you."

"He should do what he can without Mother Rachel's permission."

"Would you do that?" I asked, staring into his blue eyes.

"No. I do not need to do that. You trust me. Mother Rachel does not trust Joseph to stay safe. She will cause someone to be injured."

"Give him time and space. He will learn. He must live with his mother."

"It is time for her to let go," Issachar said with a growl.

I hoped Joseph would stay safe.

"Does he do well?" I asked.

"All the animals love him. He is gentle and they sense his love. Even the camels come to Joseph's call." Issachar shook his head. "They do not come to me."

"Watch Joseph. Rachel will let him go sometime."

In the next months, each of my sons came to me by themselves, complaining that Rachel did not allow Joseph to do everything they did. They fought for their brother, then they wondered if he could do the harder work.

I tried to temper their unhappiness, for Rachel's health had never recovered from Joseph's birth. She clung to him as she clung to life.

Lion

Our sons grew, becoming powerful men. My oldest four enjoyed hunting in the desert. They brought us wild meat to add to our diet. One day when Judah was eighteen, they returned with the pelt of a lion Judah had killed.

Judah boasted of killing his first lion alone.

"You did not kill him alone," Reuben teased. "We were with you."

"You threw no javelins nor shot any arrows at this lion," Judah said, grinning wide. "Look at this skin. Only one place where my javelin pierced his skin."

"We chased him toward you," Levi said, laughing with his brothers.

Judah leaned back, his smile wavering. "Chased him toward me? You left me alone! But my aim was straight. I killed him."

"What would we have done if you had missed?" Simeon said, shaking his head. "Father would never forgive us if we had allowed that lion to injure or kill you. I was ready to kill him for you."

Judah's grin returned. "You did not need to. I hit him in the heart."

Jacob strode to the kill and stood beside Judah. "You did this?" He pointed at the lion's skin.

Somehow, Judah grinned wider. "He came roaring at me. I waited until he was close enough so one javelin would be enough. It hit him in the heart. He fell at my feet."

Jacob hugged him. "Good for you, son. But do not hunt lions alone."

The brothers cried out together, "He did not!"

"We were prepared to kill it before the lion got close," Reuben said. "I had my arrow ready."

Jacob turned to Reuben. "Why did you allow him to stand in front of a lion? You are the oldest. You should know better."

Reuben stared at his father. "Judah insisted he could kill it himself. He was never alone. We were all prepared to shoot our arrows if he missed."

Jacob frowned.

I wanted to touch Jacob. *Reuben needs your approval as you needed your father's approval.*

Rachel cried out and fell to the ground. Before I could get to her, Joseph stooped beside her.

They murmured together while Jacob sucked in a breath and, as if hearing my thoughts, slapped Reuben on the back. "You did well. Your brother has the skin of a lion, and everyone is safe."

Joseph's murmuring to Rachel lifted above the sound of the men. "Lions? You, Mother? I did not know."

Jacob rushed to her side. "Lion? You? When?"

She looked at him and shrugged. "Weeks before you came to Harran, a lion attacked when I went to the well. The sheep surrounded me while the herders chased him away with their crooks. I think one even shot an arrow at him."

I remember that day. She was frightened for a day, then excited by the experience.

All our sons surrounded Rachel as she told them her story.

"Now it frightens me," she finished. "I am a mother who fears for our sons."

My head bobbed with hers. I feared for our sons, but did not want to discourage them.

"We are safe," Judah said in a soothing voice. "I killed the lion."

Jacob glanced at him. "This time. Rachel is correct. Do not put yourself in danger without reason. We will need every one of you to help protect us soon enough."

Judah's joy slipped from him. "I thought you would be proud of me."

Jacob stood and took him by the arm. "I am, son. But I need you to protect our family. The time will come when I will need your strength. Do not put yourself in danger for no other purpose than to prove yourself."

Judah bit his lip. "I wanted a lion skin to warm me in the winter."

Before I could say anything, Rachel stood and walked to where the lion skin lay in the sand. "Your lion skin will make a warm blanket." She ran her fingers through the fur. "It is soft."

I swallowed. I had waited to step forward to congratulate my son.

"I am surprised by its softness," Simeon said. "This will keep you warm. Perhaps you can find a woman with this."

Judah ducked his head. "Not yet. I have to wait for you and Reuben to marry first."

All the young men guffawed as Reuben colored. "There is a young woman ..."

I hope my sons find respectable *women — who worship Jehovah.*

Soon after, Esau rode into our compound again with his men. Judah showed him his lion skin and shared the story.

"You killed this lion?" Esau asked.

Judah puffed out his chest. "With the throw of one javelin."

"He was an enormous lion," Esau said in his confident voice. "You had wonderful aim. Few men can hit a lion running toward them. Congratulations, young man."

Judah threw out his chest and swaggered off to brag to his brothers.

"He is an excellent young man," Esau said.

"Yes," Jacob said. He watched Judah make his way across the compound. "He is. But he is often proud."

"Nothing wrong with a little pride," Esau said, lifting his eyebrows.

"A little is fine. Too much ..."

I hoped Judah would control his pride.

Attacks

Two years later, after almost ten years in Succoth, Jacob moved us once more to the small city of Shalem. Most of our sons had grown larger, almost able to stand with our men to protect us.

This time we lived in our tents. Jacob did not build us a permanent home. I suspected he planned to move onward before long. But he told us Jehovah had warned us to stay out of the city.

Instead, he purchased a plot of land from Hamor and settled us in our tents outside the city. We were happy to have the best of the city without having our children exposed to its wickedness and women.

Succoth had markets, but we lived far enough from the city that we did not go to its markets often. Outside Shalem, we lived close enough to enjoy access to the markets. Zilpah could find fresh food to serve our family, and Bilhah purchased scarce herbs and other healing plants. We continued to depend on our gardens, but some food was only available in the market.

Shortly after our first visit to the market in Shalem, Rachel struggled with severe nausea. She could not eat without being sick. Zilpah took broth to her, and she struggled to keep it down.

Bilhah took her mint leaves, helping to resolve her sickness, but she continued to suffer from weakness. Then, she admitted she carried a child. She had conceived before we left Succoth, and now, outside Shalem, her body rebelled.

"After all these years," I exclaimed when she told me. "Jehovah has blessed you with another child."

She grinned from her sleeping pallet, where Jacob insisted she spend most of her time. "Jacob tells me it is another son. Jehovah promised him many sons. I suspect he does not think eleven sons is many enough."

I laughed. "No. Twelve is a complete number. He must have twelve sons."

She giggled with me, then stopped, fighting to breathe. "I fear I am too old. I do not regain my health as I should." Her joy slipped from her face like rain. "Will I live to see this child? Will I live to see him grown and married?"

"He will be born," I said. "Of that I am certain. Jehovah would not give you a child after all these years and then take you from us. You will live to watch him grow."

"Jehovah willing," she said.

"I pray Jehovah is willing," I added.

The nausea left her, but she did not regain her strength. I worried about her. At first, we wove together when she could, planning for her child. But then her health got worse, and she stayed on her sleeping pallet. I visited often, hoping to encourage her to live.

Jacob brought her a writing table, parchment, pen, and ink when she requested them. She sat as long as she could each day, working once more to write her life story that she had started while carrying Joseph. As she weakened, Rachel said she needed to finish writing her story.

Dinah and I were happy to find the market. We went there often to look at pretty things for sale. She met other young women there, young women she could gossip with about girl things, young women with whom she could share the trials of being one of the youngest in a large family.

The young women in Shalem batted their eyes and giggled each time one of Dinah's brothers escorted us to the market. Soon they invited her to visit them in their homes.

At thirteen, Dinah bloomed. She laughed and shared little stories with me, reveling once more in having eleven handsome brothers. They loved and protected her. We found happiness for about four months.

Until one day she did not return.

Dinah left to visit her friends early one morning with a group of guards to protect her since all her brothers had gone with their father to help the camels give birth.

I stayed busy weaving throughout that day. Everyone needed new clothing. As the sun set over the western mountains, concern filled me. Dinah had not ducked into the weaving tent to tell me about her visit. At last, I threaded my shuttle into the warp threads of the loom so it would not become lost, and then left the small tent to search for her.

I found no sign of her return.

I went back outside, seeking her guard. Zamir dragged his feet as he walked toward me. "Mistress Leah, we cannot find her."

"Cannot find her? Find who?"

"Dinah. We returned to Shalem as she requested, to bring her home."

"Bring her home? Why did you not stay there with her as her father commands?"

"We tried, Mistress Leah, but Dinah was insistent that we leave her there. Her friends would keep her safe. We tried to stay, but she shouted at us."

"I will talk to her when she returns. Did you ask for her at her friend's home?"

"The man who opened the door told us she had left. We went to other homes she had visited before. None admitted to Dinah being there. We returned to tell you."

I wanted to hit him, tear out my hair, scream into the wilderness, race into Shalem and demand the family of her friend tell us where my daughter was. Instead, I stared at Zamir. "What will you do now?"

"We knew you would fear for her, as we do. We came here to see if she came home alone and to tell you of our plans. We searched the camp. She is not here. We will return to Shalem now to search more closely."

I nodded and watched him plod back to his horse. The guards stepped into their saddles and rode away. Only then did I allow myself to react. I stumbled to my tent and fell onto my sleeping pallet and wept.

Later, I could no longer endure suffering alone. *I need Jacob. He will know what to do. He can find our daughter. He will be with Rachel. He is always with her.*

I stumbled from my tent to hers and scratched on her tent door.

When she came to the door, I wailed, "Is Jacob here?"

"Not tonight. He is at the camel paddock. The camels are giving birth."

"Not tonight!" I cried. "I need him." I stood in the center of the living space of her tent. My hands fluttered in the air. I did not know where to put them.

"What happened?" Rachel asked. Concern filled her voice, but my fear overwhelmed me. "Who is hurt?"

A shudder shook me. "No one is hurt. None I know of. But Dinah did not come home." I sank to the floor in a heap and wrapped my arms around my knees. My hands covered my face and the tears I no longer wiped away.

Rachel sank to her knees next to me. "Dinah did not come home? Did she go to Shalem to visit her friends?" She rubbed my back.

I could only nod through my tears.

"Did she not take men with her to protect her?"

I struggled to speak, choking on my tears. "She sent them home this morning, telling them to return to escort her home before dusk. The men did not find her and returned without her. She was no longer at the home where they had left her. Oh, Dinah, where are you?" I lowered my head onto my knees and allowed the sobs to wrack me.

Rachel continued to rub my back. "Perhaps she went to another girl's home?"

I lifted my head. "They searched all the homes. They could not find her. Oh, Jehovah, keep my daughter safe." Once more, I dropped my head to my knees.

Rachel's hand soothed me, but I could no longer hold back my weeping. "I will send a messenger to Jacob," she said. "He will know what to do."

"Please send a messenger," I stammered through my tears. "What if someone kidnapped her? What if they killed her? Oh, Dinah!" Sorrow took over, and I wailed louder.

Rachel struggled to her feet and left, and I sat with tears pouring over my face, sobbing. "Where are you, Dinah? Why did you not come home?"

Fear swept through me, and I could not control my grief. I sat in the middle of Rachel's tent, weeping.

After a time, cool air blew across my face. Rachel had returned. However, she did not come alone. Zilpah and Bilhah dropped to the floor beside me and massaged my back, speaking soft words of comfort.

Rachel took her time joining us. Her child did not allow swift movement. Looking back, it surprises me she could help me at all. "Jacob will be here as soon as he is available. The messenger sped away as fast as his donkey could carry him."

My head bounced up and down, unable to control my sobs. The three of them patted my back and attempted to soothe me until there were no more tears.

Rachel handed me a warm, damp cloth and suggested I wash my face. The warm cloth felt good. We moved to cushions and sipped the herb tea she poured us.

She rang a soft, tinkling bell, calling for Orna. Her maidservant entered, and Rachel spoke soft words into her ear. Soon, Orna brought us tea and cakes. We ate the cakes and remembered my beautiful daughter. Some memories brought us to laughter. Others left me sitting in silence, thinking of her. After a time, we stopped speaking, drooping our chins against our chests and drowsing on our hands.

A noise outside startled me awake. The men were home. I rose and stepped out the door. The golden haze of dawn greeted me. I wanted to see Dinah as well.

Jacob slid off his horse and opened his arms. I rushed into them. My sobs returned as I shared my fears. Our sons stood in a semicircle around us. Their strength encouraged me. What would they do to bring their sister home?

"Let us go find her!" Simeon cried.

"We will tear every house apart if they do not give us back our sister," Levi shouted.

Dinah's other brothers joined them, filling in the circle, grumbling and threatening Shalem with battle.

Jacob raised his hands and called for his sons to settle down. "You cannot run into the city and attack. We do not know where Dinah is. Whoever has her may hurt her if we attack now."

"We will insist they return her," Simeon shouted.

"We must do something," Zebulon said.

My stomach cramped at the thought. *Will they deprive me of my sons as well as my daughter?*

Jacob turned to him. You eleven boys—"

Reuben and Simeon shouted at their father, saying almost together, "We are not boys. We are men."

"Look at your younger brothers. Would you take Joseph and Zebulon to attack a city with many more men than we can take to battle, even if we take all our men with us? Would you risk the lives of your younger brothers?"

Simeon's eyes sought Joseph, a large young man, but still a boy at thirteen years. He then found Zebulon, not quite two years older. He swallowed. "We will leave them behind. They can guard our mothers."

Even Reuben growled at that.

"We do not have enough men to consider overcoming all the men in Shalem," Jacob said, keeping his voice low and calm. "You would lose Dinah, all my sons, and their mothers. The men of Shalem would attack and destroy us all."

"Then what will you do?" Simeon demanded. His voice twisted with contempt. "Pray?"

"Yes. I will pray for Jehovah's help. He will help me know how to get your sister and my daughter back. Now, go to the fields and harvest the oats. Our animals will need food."

Grumbling, our sons found their tools and stomped off to the fields, even young Joseph.

I looked at Rachel and shrugged. I did not want her to lose her son to get my daughter back. I did not want to lose any of my children.

Vengeance

Jacob took me to my tent and sat with me while I lay in my sleeping pallet and sobbed myself to sleep.

He had to be as tired as I was. He had not slept during the night any more than I had. Perhaps he would turn to Rachel and her sleeping pallet to rest. I shrugged as darkness surrounded me. Knowing Jacob, he would find a quiet place to pray.

He kissed my cheek. "We will get Dinah back. Trust Jehovah."

In my sleep, I prayed to Jehovah. I dreamed of Dinah injured in all the many ways it could happen. Mixed with dreams of Dinah's pain, I dreamed of Rachel losing her baby. I woke with my heart pounding and covered in sweat.

I rose and found the urn with cool water and poured myself a drink. As I drank, men's voices, urgent and demanding, caught my attention. I dragged my brush through my hair, washed my face, and changed my dress, then stepped to my tent door and opened it enough to hear the men's words.

"My son, Shechem, desires your maid as his wife."

I know that voice. But from where. I racked my brain as I listened.

"Dinah is a beautiful girl. Is she safe?" Jacob. I knew his voice.

"She is well," the unknown man said. "You are my friend. I would not lie to you."

"Hamor, you have been good to me," Jacob said.

Hamor! The one who sold us this land. He acted like an honorable man. But is his son?

"But I must have my daughter returned to me before I can consider giving her to your son."

"Shechem loves your daughter and does not want to give her up."

She is too young for this!

I stepped out of my tent and leaned against the tent pole. A sound caused me to look toward the fields. All our sons marched from the fields toward the men who sat beneath the terebinth tree in front of our tents. I edged forward, wanting to hear what our sons would say.

"Where is our sister?" Simeon demanded.

"She is safe with my son, Shechem," Hamor said.

"Safe?" Reuben asked. "Why would Dinah be with Shechem?"

Hamor sat taller, unwilling to allow my sons to intimidate him. "Shechem loves Dinah. He asked me to get your permission to marry her. He said she was wonderful last night."

Rachel, Bilhah, and Zilpah came to stand beside me. Our sons' grumbling echoed through the camp.

Jacob raised a hand, stilling their voices. "She was *wonderful* last night. Did he defile her?"

Our young men rumbled even louder. I heard their anger. Mine matched theirs. No man had a right to defile my daughter!

Jacob's voice lifted once more. "Did he?"

Hamor stammered an answer. "No, no. I do not believe he did."

"Did you or did you not?" Jacob's voice was dangerously calm. Shechem must be here with his father.

But Hamor spoke for his son. "He may have. He should not have. But he wants to redeem his mistake. He wants to marry your daughter."

Rachel caught my arm as I stepped forward. "Jacob will handle this," she whispered. "Stay here."

I struggled against her grasp, but she refused to let go until I stopped fighting. *Where did she get the strength? Why is she out of her sleeping pallet?*

"Jacob will resolve this with Jehovah's help," Zilpah whispered.

I listened to our sons complain, angry at their sister's defilement. I cheered for every argument.

Hamor lifted his voice above the sound of my sons. "My son longs for your daughter. I pray you give her to him as his wife. Make marriages with us, your sons to our daughters. Dwell with us in our land. Trade with us and become wealthy."

I lifted my eyebrows. "How much more wealth do we need?" I whispered.

A younger voice rose above the murmurs of my sons. Shechem? "Let me find grace with you, Jacob and Dinah's brothers. Whatever you ask, I will give. Ask as much as you desire for a dowry and gift. I will give it. But give me the damsel to be my wife."

I choked. "Now he asks, after he has defiled her."

Zilpah touched my arm. "Listen," she whispered.

Simeon spoke for his brothers. "We cannot do this, for it is a sin to give our sister to one who has not promised his life to Jehovah with circumcision."

A silence filled the camp, as though everyone held their breath.

Simeon continued. "We will consent to this *if* you will be like us. *If* every man in your city will be circumcised, we will give our sister to you, we will take your daughters as our wives, we will dwell with you and become one of your people."

A silent space ensued, as though son and father gaped at each other.

"But if you will not do as we demand, and be circumcised, we will take our sister and leave." Simeon's words echoed through our camp.

"Is there no other way?" Hamor asked.

"No!" Simeon and his brothers' voices echoed across our camp.

"We must speak with the other men of our city," Hamor said after gulping. "We cannot agree to this for them. Give us time to speak to them."

"Take your time. Three days," Simeon said with a drawl. "Will that be long enough?

I wondered why Jacob allowed his sons to take over. Perhaps he nodded in agreement?

"But our sister may not remain in your home." Simeon's voice hardened. "Send her to her friend Ismet's home, where she will be safe. Do not defile her again." He sounded angry and dangerous.

"She will go to Ismet's home," Hamor said, overriding Shechem's objections. "We will need the time to discuss this with the men of Shalem."

I stepped forward as our visitors and their men moved to their horses, watching them argue as they walked.

"Do not fear, Shechem," Hamor whispered. "The men of our city desire to increase their wealth as they trade with this man."

Three days later, Hamor returned, agreeing to all Simeon had demanded.

I breathed a sigh of relief. I would see my daughter again. I would help her heal from her defilement. They would have to return her so I could prepare her for her marriage.

They set a date for the circumcision rite, asking Jacob to assist, although they did not return Dinah. I spent the night in tears.

Three days after the circumcision, Simeon and Levi brought Dinah to me.

However, it was not a joyful reunion.

I led her to a stool where she sat, shivering. I thought perhaps she quaked with fear. Had Shechem hurt her? Blood had covered her brothers when they left her with me. Did it frighten her?

"Did Shechem not take you to the house of your friend, Ismet?" I asked in a low, calming tone.

"No," she growled. "Shechem used me again and again that night, laughing and boasting that my brothers and father had given me to him."

She sat on the stool, shuddering and unwilling for me to touch her, not to brush her hair, nor to wash her face, nor to help her change her clothing.

She stared at a spot on the floor in front of her. "Mother, it was horrible ... and wonderful. They slew Shechem and Hamor first, and took me away from that place." She glanced up at me, fierceness filling her eyes. "I followed them through the city. The screaming, the shouts, and the pain of the men, too sore from their circumcision to lift a hand to fight back as my brothers took their lives, enraptured me. Oh, they deserved it, but my brothers! How do they justify this to Jehovah?"

I smothered a shuddered gasp. *How could my sons be so* violent? *How is this, my beautiful young daughter, taking pleasure in their pain?*

I stretched my hand forward to brush the hair from her eyes, but she flinched away. "How could they do such a thing? They shouted about protecting your honor."

"My honor?" A bitter laugh passed her lips. "I lost my honor that first night when Shechem lured me to his home, giving me strengthened wine, so that I did not know what he planned. I was a maid, a virgin. I can never be a virgin again. I cannot find a man who will take me for myself. I will always be the defiled one, the harlot." Dinah stared at me. Anger filled her whole being. No tears filled her eyes, only hatred and pain. "I despise Shechem. He deserved to die."

"You do not think their circumcision was enough of a penalty?" I fought to stay calm for her, as my stomach churned.

Her eyes glittered. "They deserved that pain. At first, they moaned and groaned like little boys whose fingers were caught in a bear trap. But it lasted longer. They were still moaning on their sleeping pallets when Simeon and Levi barged in. They had no chance against the sharpness of their swords."

I swallowed past the lump in my throat. I did not expect her to find pleasure in their deaths. "But so many? They did not all deserve death."

Dinah turned her fierceness on me. "Do they not? Hamor convinced those men to accept circumcision, telling them that when my father and brothers came for the wedding feast, they would take their lives. They believed themselves stronger than us." She pounded her fist into her palm. "They expected to divide up all our possessions, our animals. They would all become wealthy from what we have."

She breathed in short, fast breaths, as if she had run a distance. I reached out to touch her face, but she pushed me away.

"They believed we had gold and jewels hidden in our tents. With that and our many animals, they would become wealthier than any had dreamed." She shoved a lock of hair off her face. "I told them we have no gold or jewels. They only laughed, telling me, of course I would say that. They planned to keep me, and take you, Mother Rachel, Mother Bilhah, and Mother Zilpah, along with all our maidservants as their slaves. I will not become a slave to any man."

I inhaled a sharp, deep breath and exhaled. "No. They were wicked men. But should not your brothers have left their vengeance to Jehovah?" I asked, sitting across from her on a cushion. "What happened with them?"

She took a deep breath to control her breathing. "Simeon and Levi came alone. After they rescued me and killed Shechem and his father, Hamor, they brought me out of the house to send me home." Dinah swallowed. "But the men at the gates of the city lay in their gore. I could not leave. Instead, I followed behind them, watching them destroy all the other men."

I chewed on my lip, wanting to cry out in horror, while needing to hear my daughter's story. "Blood and gore flowed through the streets. The stench became overwhelming. Women wept, begging Levi and Simeon to have grace on them, to forgive their men, and to allow their men to live. Levi growled at them. 'Did you have grace and care for my sister? You knew Shechem held her? Did you beg your men to free her?'"

The horror of my sons' acts gagged me. I struggled to settle my stomach. How could they have allowed their anger to lead them to such horrors? "Did the women answer?" I whispered.

Dinah snorted and shook her head. "No. They, like their men, wanted our animals. They wanted our women as slaves. They had no mercy for me. They begged me to speak to my brothers and stop their rampage. But why would I do that? They did not beg their men to protect me." She blew out a breath.

"Even their women?" I asked in a whisper.

"If Hamor's wife and daughters were an example of the others, they encouraged them in their plans to destroy us. Perhaps Ismet begged for my freedom, but after Shechem took me, all my supposed friends accused me of betraying their friendship to take their brothers. I was a harlot after all."

"No! Never. You were taken unwillingly." I stared at her face, seeking to find grief there. I saw only hard resentment.

"Reuben found me standing among the gore near the market. He ordered Simeon and Levi to bring me home. By then, the deed was done. There was no more vengeance to oversee. I allowed Simeon to pull me behind him on his horse. As Levi and Simeon brought me home, they promised each other to return and help gather the animals to add to our flocks."

Servants carried in buckets of hot water and poured them into the tub Amina dragged from the edge of the tent, filling it. When they had filled the tub, she and I encouraged Dinah to step into it and wash away the horrors of her time in Shalem.

Reluctantly, Dinah removed her filthy clothing and stepped into the tub.

I sat off to the side while Amina washed Dinah. Although my hands twitched, needing to move and disperse my agitation, I could not assist. I settled them in my lap and watched. I needed to be available for her when her hard shell shattered.

Amina helped Dinah wash the dirt from her body, then helped her wash her long, dark brown hair, which looked much like mine. As she rinsed away the soap, the bleating of sheep and goats echoed through our camp.

Dinah shot out of the bath, grabbing for a towel.

"Wait long enough for me to finish rinsing your hair," Amina growled.

Dinah's argument ended when she saw my frown. "Hurry then." She returned to the bath and impatiently allowed Amina to rinse the soap from her hair.

"It is clean," Amina said shortly afterward, patting Dinah's shoulder. "You may leave."

Once more, Dinah left the tub, grabbing her towel.

"Clothing?" I asked, lifting my eyebrows.

She dragged a dress over her body and shoved her slippers on her feet before rushing from our tent. I followed, amazed at her intense need to see the spoils from her enemy.

But there were more than animals. Babies squalled in their mothers' arms. Women stared ahead, saying nothing as they walked through the dust of our camp. Children whined, kicking the dirt away from their dragging feet. Girls of Dinah's age slunk with sullen resentment behind the others. Ismet glared at Dinah as she passed, then spat at her feet.

I thought those girls were her friends, but how could a friendship continue when Dinah's brothers destroyed their fathers, their village, their way of life?

"What will Father do about this?" Dinah asked. "Will he keep them?"

My stomach sank. Smoke rose from the direction of Shalem. Our sons had burned it in their anger. *How can we dress and feed this many more people? But if we do not, many will die. What will Jacob do?*

Decisions

As the sun fell toward the western mountains, Zilpah scratched on my tent door.

"I apologize, Leah, Dinah," she said. "But Jacob has returned from the fields. He wants a family meeting in Rachel's tent."

Her tent. Family meetings should be held in *my tent.* I glanced at Dinah. *Perhaps her tent is better. Rachel overexerted herself in my behalf last night and should not leave her sleeping pallet.*

"Dinah as well?" I asked.

"Yes. He specifically requested that Dinah come."

My stomach dropped. *What now? Would he support our daughter?*

Zilpah strode off to tell someone else to come to the family meeting. I turned to wake Dinah.

She shuddered, already awake. "Father wants me to be at the meeting?"

"He must want to know what happened to you," I said, brushing her hair off her face.

"If I must." She rose from the pallet and changed her clothing while I brushed and braided my hair again.

We trudged from our tent to Rachel's, entering after Judah and Reuben. We found seats on the pillows scattered around the sitting area of the tent. After sitting, she sniffed, then tears slipped across her cheeks. I reached for her hand. She let me hold it.

Only Dinah's soft sobs filled the space.

Jacob came into the tent and glanced around. He nodded to me, then opened his arms to Dinah. She rushed into his embrace, absorbing his words of comfort. He let her go, and she returned to her seat next to me. I took her hand and squeezed it as she calmed her tears.

My sons did not smile, nor did the other sons. Simeon and Levi sat near me, stiff on their cushions, looking uncomfortable.

They should be uncomfortable after what they did.

My other four sons, along with the other five from the other mothers, were no more comfortable than Simeon and Levi, though they had less to fear from their father.

Jacob took his seat next to Rachel and held her hand in his.

Not today. I have no time for jealousy today. His concern is for Rachel and her baby, and our daughter.

"What happened here today?" Jacob asked. "Why do we have women and children sitting around campfires?"

I kept my eyes on Jacob, not looking at any of my sons. I would not give him cause to disregard me for what my sons did.

"Reuben?" Jacob asked, as he often did, calling upon his oldest son first, as the one responsible for his brothers. "What is this about?"

Reuben shifted in his seat near me. "We brought the women and children of Shalem here to protect them. There are no men left there who can do that."

Jacob's thick brown eyebrows crunched together, becoming wiggling caterpillars. "No men in Shalem? What of Hamor? Where is Shechem? The men who sit at the gates? Where did they go?"

Reuben sat still, not responding.

"Reuben?" Jacob dropped his voice lower, sounding more dangerous.

Reuben lifted his head. "Dead. You must ask Simeon and Levi. Only they know what happened."

Jacob's gaze darted toward my second and third sons. "Simeon? Levi?" Question and concern filled his words. "What did you do?"

I refused to stare at my sons. They did not answer their father.

He growled their names once more.

I felt Simeon shrug. "Should we allow Shechem to treat our sister as a harlot?"

No! My daughter is no harlot. They had to do something.

"What did you do?" Jacob's growl made me wonder about their actions.

"You did nothing," Levi spat.

Levi must learn to have more respect for his father.

"You allowed them to keep Dinah," Levi continued. "You left her there with them, knowing they held her. Defiled her. Treated her as a harlot. We would not."

"You did not trust me to resolve this problem?" Jacob asked, speaking low. "Rescue my daughter?"

Levi and Simeon shifted on their pillows.

"What did you do for her?" Levi asked once more.

"Simeon?" Jacob asked, demanding an answer.

"You said nothing when we insisted they make covenants with Jehovah, including the circumcision," Simeon retorted.

"I had other plans, but had no time to share them with you. You marched in demanding their circumcisions. You were correct. She cannot marry an uncircumcised man, but you had no right to make the demand."

"Dinah is our sister!" Levi cried.

Jacob continued as though Levi had not interrupted him. "They would be sore today, three days after a circumcision. I intended to meet with them tomorrow when they could once again think of something besides their injured bodies."

"What plans?" Levi demanded, becoming louder.

"We will use quiet voices here," Jacob said. "We will not share our family problems with those who are camped outside."

Levi sat back, seething, but sitting still beside me.

"It no longer matters what my plans were. You took away my right of vengeance. What did you do?"

Simeon sat even straighter, boastful words poured from him. "We waited until today when the men of Shalem would have no ability to protect themselves. Then, we took vengeance on them. They planned to take more than our sister. They wanted our animals and our women. They planned to overcome us during the night and kill you and all your sons. They would take Mother, all your wives, and concubines, as servants or slaves. All our menservants and maidservants would become their slaves." He took a deep breath. "We could not allow that."

Dinah suggested a similar plan came from the men of Shalem. Did she hear it from Shechem and Hamor or from *Simeon and Levi?*

Jacob stared at Simeon as he recounted the potential crimes of the men of Shalem. "What makes you think this would happen?" His growl sent a shudder through me.

Simeon tossed his hair back. "I have a woman friend among their people, Nameem. She warned me of their plans."

"When?"

"After Shechem took Dinah."

"You knew where she was when Hamor came seeking her hand? And you did not tell me? Why?"

"I could not. You already sat with our enemy when I came to share the information with you." Although I could not see him, I sensed Simeon's earnestness.

"And your demand that they become like us?"

Simeon blew out his breath and sucked in another. "A ploy. I knew we could overwhelm them and take our vengeance on them as they recovered. They could not lift a sword to protect themselves."

Once more, Jacob's eyebrows beetled together. "It was not your right to take vengeance. It was mine. Why did you not share your knowledge with me after Hamor and Shechem left, before their circumcision? Why did you not allow me to choose our vengeance?"

"Would you have killed them all as we did?" Levi asked, his frustration apparent. "We two, Simeon and I, went into Shalem and killed every man. All are dead because we took upon ourselves the right of vengeance for our sister. Would you have gone with us? Would you have taken our brothers?"

A sharp gasp echoed through the tent.

Jacob leaned forward in his seat. "No. I am a man of Jehovah. I would not have murdered them." He sat back. "You have made me stink in this land and in all the lands around us. There are many men surrounding us. We are few compared to the hundreds of men in the other lands. Do you think we can stand against hundreds and live?"

Slave to Shalem or slave to those others? I would not be a slave. What have you done, my sons?

Simeon's chin hit his chest. "We did not consider the men of other lands. We expected they would understand."

Levi's anger had not yet cooled. "Would you have us allow Shechem and Hamor to treat our sister as a harlot?"

Jacob controlled his anger and hurt at his son's actions. It was too late. He turned to Dinah. "We will discuss this alone. You have much to tell me."

Dinah ducked her head. "Yes, Father."

"What shall we do now, Father?" Reuben asked. As Dinah's oldest brother and the oldest son, he supported his father in his actions. "We brought the women and children here for their protection. Neither they nor their animals would be safe from wild animals or men without men in their city."

Jacob set his head in his hands and sighed. "We shall discuss this with them, give them choices." His head turned on his neck, rocking back and forth. "You have made enemies of these women and children. They will always remember we took their husbands and fathers. They will not see it as a blessing that you brought them here. You brought them as plunder. You claimed them and their wealth. What more can they think?"

"Simeon and Levi brought their wealth here," Judah said.

"For their safety," Reuben added.

Jacob turned his way. "And did you push the women and children here? Or herd the animals to our paddocks?"

Judah bit his lip. "I helped with that."

"You are as guilty as Simeon and Levi," Jacob said, struggling to hide his frustration.

"We did not kill those men!" Naphtali cried.

"You willingly accepted the plunder."

"To protect them," Reuben repeated, leaning forward.

Every son stared at his father.

Jacob shook his head. "You have made me stink. I go to speak with Jehovah."

"But you have not eaten," Zilpah said.

"Nor will I until I receive an answer from Jehovah." He turned to his wives and concubines. "Are all the women and children cared for? Have they eaten? Did any receive any injuries?"

"I went among them searching for any injured," Bilhah said. "I cared for all I found."

"I fed them," Zilpah said. "We provided them with blankets and food."

"They are confused," Bilhah added. "I will do all I can for them."

He turned to Zilpah. "Find their leaders tomorrow." He glanced at me and shook his head. He turned to Rachel. "Take Rachel if she is able. Talk with them. Find out what they want us to do with them." Jacob stood. "We will leave this land. When I return, we will give them what they want if we can. Leave them here, take them with us, or take them to family in other lands. Find out tomorrow."

Zilpah nodded.

How can we do what they want? *What if they choose to stay here? Who will protect them? But how can we take them with us? They will hate us. How can we trust them? I am glad Jacob asked Rachel to talk with them.*

The next morning. Dinah joined me in the weaving tent. We would need more tents and blankets soon. Besides, Dinah needed to do something besides lie on her pallet, crying and feeling sorry for herself. I set her to work on a blanket, then prepared the warp to weave fabric for tents. If any of the women of Shalem stayed with us, they would need tents.

We worked together, saying little to each other, allowing the silence to heal our pains, until Joseph bent to enter. "Father is back. We meet at Mother's tent. He sent me to get you."

"Does he want me there?" Dinah asked.

"Why would he not?" Joseph asked. "You are part of the family."

A tear trickled down each of her cheeks. "After my defilement?"

"That was Shechem, not you," Joseph said. "You are part of the family. Come with me."

Joseph and Dinah had always been close. She needed his friendship and love now more than ever.

I followed the two young people across the short distance to Rachel's tent and entered behind them. As we had the day before, I found a place to sit on a comfortable cushion. Jacob sat near Rachel, who once more lay on her sleeping pallet. His head bounced off his chest.

"Is Father asleep?" Dinah asked in a whisper.

"No," Rachel whispered back. "Although he is exhausted."

"Did Jehovah hear him?" Dinah whispered.

"Hush," I muttered in her ear. "We are here to learn what Jehovah commanded us to do."

"Father," Joseph murmured from his place near Rachel. "Everyone has gathered. We are all here. We wait for you to share what you learned from Jehovah."

After a long pause, Jacob lifted his head. "Jehovah spoke to me."

I shivered as his gaze halted on Simeon and Levi.

"You have caused us many problems. Thank Jehovah, for he has a solution to these problems. You will pay a penalty for this."

Simeon and Levi cleared their throats. They had seated themselves near me once more. I hoped they would find courage in their souls.

But Jacob did not allow them to speak. "We have much to do." Turning to Rachel, he asked, "What do the women of Shalem desire us to do for or with them?"

"Zilpah and I spoke to many women until we were certain. Noora is their leader. She was Hamor's wife."

I glanced at Dinah, who frowned. *She cannot like* nor *respect Noora. Not after her time in the woman's home.*

"So she has training in leading cats?" Jacob asked.

"Cats?" Rachel asked.

"Unhappy women are like cats. You are never certain how they will act." Jacob did not smile at this.

I sniggered behind my hand. My sister and our maidservants, now Jacob's concubines, sometimes acted like cats. As did I, if I was honest with myself.

"The women look to her as their leader, as the men looked up to Hamor," Zilpah said.

Not a good thing to say now. Dinah grimaced.

Rachel glanced at Zilpah, who nodded. "Most of their women desire to stay with us. They will give themselves to us to be our servants, as we offer our protection, and if you will teach their young sons to be animal herders."

Most? Who does not want to stay? Are they lost to madness? How can they protect themselves against wild animals and men?

Jacob nodded his approval. "That is good. We will need their sons' help with so many more animals. And the women who do not desire to stay?" He gently tapped his fingers against his knee.

"Young women who believe they can survive in the burned city, among the lions, have asked to stay, but Noora begs us to deny their request," Rachel said.

"We cannot stop them. If they choose to leave us, we will help with the supplies."

"And weapons to protect themselves?" Issachar asked.

"Perhaps. However, I believe we need all the weapons we have. We are in danger." Jacob stared around the circle of expectant faces, stopping once more on Levi and Simeon. "We are to travel to Bethel. We can no longer stay here. Too many lands surrounding us are led by angry men. We are no longer safe."

Even I joined the others in glancing at Levi and Simeon, wondering what their punishment would be.

Jacob continued. "Put away all the strange gods from among you and become clean. Wash and dress in clean clothing. Do all you can to be clean, for we travel to Bethel tomorrow. I will make an altar and sacrifice to Jehovah once more. He who answered my cries on the day of my distress, and continues to bless me."

A murmur of appreciation filled the tent. We would continue our travels to Bethel, and on to Mamre. Perhaps we could settle there and not travel again. I prayed it would be so. I had no strange gods, but I had earrings I wore in Harran. Would that be enough for Jehovah?

"My words need to be shared with all within our camp. Reuben, call those within the camp together, especially the new women. They will have brought their gods with them." Jacob turned to Naphtali and Zebulon. "Go to the outer fields. Help the herders put the animals in paddocks for their safety and then bring them here as quickly as possible." He looked around at us all. "We leave for Bethel tomorrow. We can no longer stay here. The men from the surrounding lands will desire to take our lives. Simeon, Levi?"

The two young men lifted their heads and stared at their father.

"We will discuss this later, after we are on the trail."

We filed out the tent door behind Reuben. I stood close to Jacob and Rachel with Dinah by my side, watching the women and children of Shalem and our menservants and women servants gather. Their low rumble warned us of their concerns and interest in Jacob's plans. Most of our people knew Levi and Simeon had caused problems between us and our neighbors.

Zebulon and Naphtali returned with the herders sooner than I expected. These men joined the others at a respectful distance from Jacob. He stared around, and at a nod from Naphtali and Reuben that all had assembled, he stood on a table to be heard by everyone.

"We grieve with you for the loss of your men, your homes, and your previous lives. We would prefer your men had not lusted after our animals. However, we are no longer safe here, none of us." Jacob spread his hands out, encompassing the women of Shalem and all our servants. "Men from other lands will hear of your loss and come seeking a portion of your wealth, your children, your animals, and seek to take you into slavery."

He paused and gazed into their eyes as the women murmured.

"Rachel tells me you choose to stay with us. We welcome you, although we know you prefer not to have needed to accept our assistance."

The women murmured among themselves once more.

Jacob continued, "Our journey will not be easy. We do not know what the men of other lands will do. If you are to become part of our community, you will want responsibilities. We will soon give you assignments when we begin our travel."

That would be me. I will give them assignments. I will have to move among them to learn about *their abilities and interests. It will take some time to assign all these women. Can I? Can I set aside my anger and grief for Dinah to do this? How can I not? These women and their children deserve compassion and forgiveness.*

"You will become full members of our little community. Some of you have already stepped forward to help in our cooking tents. I commend you."

As he gazed into the faces of those women, their hard anger softened.

Lifting his eyes to our maidservants, menservants, and herders, he spoke again. "Welcome the new women and children as you interact with them. Their young sons will soon join you as they learn to care for the animals."

He lifted an arm and swept it south. "We serve Jehovah and obey his commandments. We leave here in the morning. Today we prepare. As you pack your possessions, go through them. Bring all your strange gods, your images of the gods you worshiped elsewhere. Anything that will cause Jehovah to withhold his protection must be removed and left here. We must become clean again. Wash yourselves and change your clothing. Prepare to come before the Lord our God, even Jehovah, who will save and protect us."

Once again, the crowd murmured among themselves.

"When do we receive our assignments?" Noora asked.

"Soon." Jacob turned and glanced at me. "Leah will make the assignments, probably along the trail, as we have much to do before then. We will protect you as you become one of us. Now, go. Bring your images to me."

The crowd scattered, some faster than others, but soon all had returned to their tents or campfires to prepare.

Jacob took Dinah's hand. "We need to talk."

She glanced at me, then followed him as he helped Rachel to her tent. I watched them until he led her away from the bustle of our camp.

I returned to my tent to pack and search out anything Jehovah would not approve as I waited for Dinah's return.

The sun had moved a span across the sky before Jacob brought Dinah back to me.

"You will heal of this," he said and kissed her cheek.

"Yes, Father." Dinah brushed tears from her face. "Thank you for understanding."

"I am your father. I must understand. I love you."

Jacob left to help prepare the camp for moving. I turned to help Dinah. I knew of no strange images she might have had, but insisted that I go through Dinah's possessions with her. She revealed three.

"I purchased them because I thought they were cute," she said.

Her words did not mislead me. "It matters not why you have them. They must go no farther with us."

"What do you have that will offend Jehovah?" she demanded.

"I will leave my earrings. I no longer need them. Do you have any others?"

She chewed on her lip, then bent to dig in a trunk once more, pulling out one more item. "I have this. Is it unacceptable?"

She held up a fat-bellied woman, a fertility goddess.

"Yes. That is one of the worst. Is that all?"

She lowered her eyes. "I have these," she reached into another bag. "Shechem gave them to me, promising he would marry me." She held ornate gold earrings. "Must I give them to Father as well?"

Yes! Yes! Yes! You must not keep anything from that experience!

I swallowed the pain the earrings brought to me, fighting back the shouts. I swallowed again and softened my voice. "What do you think Jehovah will want? Will he want you to have this to remind you of your defilement?"

She frowned, then rounded her shoulders back. "No. It is not something I desire to remember. They will go to Father, too."

I retrieved my earrings while she gathered up her images and earrings. Then we strode across the space between our tent and the oak tree on the edge of the camp where Jacob had dug a hole for them.

He kept his face emotionless as Dinah handed him her images.

"Is this everything?" he asked.

"Yes, everything," she said.

Jacob glanced up at me.

I nodded and smiled.

"Thank you for bringing them," he said with a nod and set our offerings in his hole.

Dinah and I returned to our tent and filled our baskets and trunks with all our possessions, preparing them to travel once more. She stopped to wipe away tears frequently.

I had hoped we would not be required to leave this place, that Jacob would build us a home and prepare paddocks and barns for the animals. However, it was not to be. Dinah had gone into the city. Shechem had defiled her. Simeon and Levi had taken it upon themselves to take vengeance on the men. We could no longer stay.

Dida helped us with our packing after she completed hers. It took us most of the night. When Jacob gave the signal to mount our camels, I wrapped a rope around me, holding me fast to the saddle. My camel would rock me to sleep as we traveled south once again toward Bethel and the land of Esau and Jacob.

I worried about Rachel. *How will she manage riding a camel? She has grown large with her child. Will she be safe?*

Assignments

We traveled toward Bethel, watching around us for attackers from other lands. Jacob assigned Simeon and Levi to ride with the guards at the back of our long line of people and animals, forced to eat our dust and watch for armies seeking to overwhelm us.

Among the many plundered animals our sons had driven in front of them to our camp were camels, which gave most of the women of Shalem camels to ride. To give rides to those without a camel, we moved some of our baggage onto donkeys.

After I was certain Dinah rode beside Zilpah and Bilhah, I fell back from my place behind Jacob to ride among the women and children of Shalem. I listened to each of them, hearing their history, learning their skills, their preferences for assignments.

Many times I swallowed bile that made its way into my throat when women complained about their losses. Yes, their lives had changed. They were alone. Women in their city had little to say about what their men did. I understood that. But these women had said little or nothing to their men about their excessive greed and the use of my daughter. How could they support men who defiled a young girl?

A few women offered me regrets for Shechem's actions. I accepted the regrets, but it hurt.

Those regretful comments helped me turn to the others and offer them greater kindness. I would not treat them as slaves. Some may need to serve us, but we would treat them all with compassion and kindness. I needed to subdue my anger for what happened to Dinah and soothe their anger. Perhaps that is why Jacob gave me the assignment.

I pushed away my pain. My responsibility was to help them integrate into our community and to give them assignments.

Knowing their men had wanted me and our women to become their slaves, and suspecting many of the women agreed, made it difficult at first. But the women cried about their wicked husbands. They spoke of learning about Jehovah. Their softened hearts shone through the dust the camels and donkeys kicked up.

Noora had convinced the young women to stay with us, though they said they wanted to return to Shalem. She had reminded them of the lions and men who would come looking for plunder. The young women of Shalem would not become wives of those men. They would use the girls as harlots as Shechem had used Dinah.

Dinah would soon need a maidservant. I would choose one of the young women. When I asked her if she had a preference, I thought she would choose Ismet, the friend to whose home she had gone to visit the day that changed us from neighbors to enemies.

Dinah would have nothing to do with Ismet. "She gave me to Shechem. She never was my friend. She only pretended."

Instead, she chose a girl who had not been among those who pretended to befriend her, one who stood apart from them, Freeda.

Oh the third day, I came to Ismet to determine where to assign her. "Do you think we welcomed Dinah because we wanted her?" Ismet had spat. "No. Shechem was to be my husband until you came. Shechem wanted to meet her, to use her. He said if I helped, he would take me as his bride when he cast her aside. I wanted to be his wife. I did not desire to share my husband with her, or with anyone." She fought back the tears in her eyes, refusing to allow them to fall. "Shechem betrayed me as I betrayed Dinah. But she will never be my friend. I cannot forgive her."

"For needing a friend? For wanting another young woman to share her life with?" I asked.

"No. Dinah has an exotic beauty I could never compete with. Shechem would never have married me, even after he shared Dinah with his friends. He would still want her."

I swallowed the bile that filled my throat. *Were there more men who used her besides Shechem? She did not tell me of others.*

I fought to keep a smile on my face. Ismet did not need to know how much her words hurt. *Did she say them just to break my heart?*

I could not trust Ismet, nor any of the others who had professed to be Dinah's friends. Like Ismet, they received assignments to help wash pots and pans or clothing. Some would help in the weaving tent eventually, but not yet. They had too much hatred in them. I asked our guards to maintain a watch over them.

It might have been better to leave them behind as they wanted. We kept them with us because Noora requested it. I prayed their hearts would soften. I prayed my heart would soften.

I found assignments for everyone, many below the status they held when they lived in Shalem. Even Noora received an assignment. She would not allow us to leave her out. "I served as the healer for our people, delivering most of the babies. I should help Bilhah. We will stay busy with these extra people."

"I will talk with Bilhah, but I am certain she will welcome you."

Bilhah was grateful to have Noora's help. She trusted Noora. I did not. I could not.

On the second day on the road, Rachel slumped over her camel.

"Are you well?" I asked. I had come forward after speaking with more of the women from Shalem.

Her face was pale. It had lost all color, but still she grinned. "It is nothing. The child is active. All is well."

"Well? When you are too ill to sit up?" I leaned across the space between our camels and touched her forehead. It burned. What illness did she have? I knew of no woman who burned because she carried a child.

"Yes. I have no strength to sit up. Jacob tied me into the saddle so I would not fall off my camel."

"Will you make it to Bethel?" I feared the child would come before our arrival.

"I will make it. I pray to regain my stamina. My Benoni needs his mother."

"Benoni? A strong name." *Son of my sorrow? Does she expect to die?* "Yes, he will need his mother. Stay strong."

She struggled to sit taller. "I will live, Jehovah willing."

I sent my prayer to Jehovah in her behalf.

"You can rest on the Sabbath. Jacob will not travel then. Did he tell you how long it will take us to reach Bethel?" I babbled, unwilling to consider that her weakness could lead to her end.

"He says we should be there before the Sabbath. I hope Bilhah can help me."

"She will." I touched her arm. "I will pray for you."

Rachel smiled and stared at her hands.

How had I allowed her to go among the women of Shalem, searching for their leader? She had little strength before then. Now she had almost none.

For the next three evenings, men put Rachel's tent up first, before any other. She went to her sleeping pallet, staying there until hers was the only tent left to pack onto the camels before riding onward. Bilhah, Noora, and I took turns riding near her, ready to offer help.

On the fourth afternoon, Jacob signaled for us to stop and set up our tents. "We have arrived," he said.

I stared around. I saw no village, no buildings, few trees. Only a well and a pile of rocks.

"Here?"

Jacob ordered his camel to sink to its knees and stepped off its back. "Yes. Here. This is where Jehovah came to me and promised the blessings of Abraham when I fled Esau's anger."

The menservants set up Rachel's tent, and Jacob helped Rachel to lie down once more. While the menservants set up the other tents, Jacob took Reuben and his other sons to gather stones to build an altar.

Zilpah had dinner cooking quickly and brought Rachel a bowl of soup before others were ready. "You need to eat."

We helped her sit and eat. Then she lay back to sleep.

I feared Jacob would insist on performing his sacrifice that evening, but he spent time in preparation, only stepping into the tent to see that Rachel and her child were resting.

Early the next morning, we rose, prepared for a sacrifice. Dinah and I sat beside Rachel, waiting for Jacob to call us to the rite. The morning had almost passed before we received the call.

Joseph and Reuben carried Rachel to the altar, helping her to lie on a blanket to observe the sacrifice. Dinah and I sat next to her, ready with cool water and anything else she might need.

I kept Dinah close, uncertain of her reaction to the women of Shalem who sat with respect behind us. Dinah's shell had cracked when her father took her to speak of her ordeal alone. But her moods rose and fell, sometimes raging, other times sagging in a puddle of tears.

Jacob offered a sacrifice to Jehovah, saving our portion to share. Zilpah and the cooks she supervised prepared a meal to share with the portion of the sacrificial lamb.

Rachel insisted on sitting with us to eat. However, she ate little and soon asked to be helped back to her sleeping pallet. Joseph and Naphtali carried her. I feared for her health.

Dinah feared for her Mother Rachel, as much as me. She joined me in prayer before going to her sleeping pallet. Still, during the night her cries woke me. I hurried to her part of the tent and found her thrashing on her pallet.

I touched her, and she screamed, "No! No! Not again."

I shook her gently. "Dinah. Dinah. This is Mother. You are safe."

Dinah's eyes popped open and she threw her arms around me. "Mother. I dreamed he came for me again. It hurt me. Oh, Mother." She sobbed on my shoulder for almost an hour.

"He cannot hurt you again. He is gone," I said as soothingly as I could.

"I know." She leaned back. "I am happy Simeon killed him. He should not have killed all those other men, but Shechem and Hamor deserved it. Shechem could not have kept me so long without Hamor's help."

"And Noora? Did she help?"

Dinah shrugged. "I do not know. I never saw her. She sent food for me, but I do not know what she thought about her son keeping a woman hostage."

"I do not know, either. Noora helps Bilhah heal. She appears to be an honorable woman."

Dinah wiped away the last of her tears. "She may be. I do not know her."

I hoped she knew what she claimed to know. Bilhah trusted her. I needed to do the same. Rachel would require her help soon.

I would not ask Noora to help me with Dinah. I needed to trust Jehovah to heal my daughter.

Birth and Death

Noora had delivered many babies while in Shalem, including some who struggled. We prayed she could save Rachel.

When Jacob had returned from his prayers after his sacrifice, Noora insisted Rachel needed to sleep another day.

"Tomorrow is the Sabbath," Jacob agreed. "We will rest one more day. Then, we must move on to Ephrath, where we will find people to help us. It is but a day's ride away. Then we will travel on to Mamre to live with my father."

He posted extra guards each night, still fearing the men of the surrounding lands. Both Levi and Simeon received the assignment to take the middle of the night duty to join the guards. All the other sons took their turns as well, but those two received the worst duty hours.

On the afternoon of the Sabbath, men stood on the hills above us. They stood staring at us for almost an hour before slipping away. Our men kept their weapons near as we worshipped that day.

After resting through the Sabbath, we were on the trail once more.

Before we traveled far, Rachel cried out.

"What is the problem?" I asked as I rode close to her.

"Benoni comes," she moaned, her hands grasping her enlarged stomach. "The pains are harsh."

I turned to signal to Noora and Bilhah, but they had heard Rachel's cry and were there to help. I rode up to where Jacob led our caravan.

"Jacob," I cried. "We need to stop. Rachel is giving birth."

"Now? Here?" He pulled his camel to a stop and gazed around us. "This is not the best place to stop, but it will have to do." He signaled the caravan to stop. He called Tzevi, his head manservant, forward.

"We need to put Rachel's tent up as fast as possible," he called as he signaled to his camel and leapt off it.

"Rachel's tent? Is there a problem?" Tzevi asked.

"Yes." Jacob glanced at the file of riders coming to a stop. "Rachel cannot wait. She is giving birth to our son."

Tzevi brought a fist to his chest, then rushed away to find the tent and get it set up as fast as possible. Jacob dismounted from his camel and hurried to Rachel's side, ordered her camel to kneel, and lifted her from her saddle.

I stood back, waiting for the tent to be prepared. I found her sleeping pallet and blankets, and a few other pieces of furniture. When the sides were up and it was safe to enter, I asked the men to carry the furniture into the tent.

Jacob carried her into the tent, followed by Bilhah and Noora.

Then I waited, praying for Rachel.

I paced in front of the tent door, fearing we would lose both the babe and his mother. One of the young women, Aqeela, who had joined Bilhah and Noora to learn to heal, stepped through the tent door, scooting to retrieve hot water from over the fire Zilpah had started.

As she returned, I stopped her. "Will Rachel live?"

"I do not know," she murmured. "Noora fears for the mother, though she believes we can save the child." She rushed past me into the tent.

I allowed the tent door to close before I buried my face in my hands, sobbing. *How can I live without my sister? How can her son live without a mother? Oh, Jehovah, bless us all, but bless Rachel and Jacob now.*

After a time, my sobbing slowed, and I dried my eyes. Jehovah would do what was best, as always.

I paced the length of the tent and turned to pace toward the other end. A babe's cry reached me through the tent wall.

I ran toward the door, only to hear Jacob scream, "Rachel! No, Rachel!" My heart leapt to my throat. What happened?

I raced into the tent to find Jacob kneeling beside Rachel, sobbing. Bilhah cut the cord connecting the little boy to his mother, wrapped him in a blanket, and handed him to his father. Jacob took him and bowed over Rachel, sobbing into the babe's blanket.

"No, Rachel," he cried. "Do not leave me. How will we get along without you? How do I raise our son alone? Do not go."

His sobbing broke my heart. I knelt beside him and rubbed his back. "What happened?"

Jacob raised his head. "They said they could save the babe, but not the mother." His voice broke, and he buried his face again in the baby's blanket.

"She was too weak to deliver the child," Noora whispered. "She had no strength to survive his birth."

"Oh, baby. What will we do with you? How do we feed you?" Jacob wailed, fighting to swallow his tears.

"Rachel called him Benoni," I said.

Jacob lifted his head and turned to me. "Son of my sorrow?" He shook his head. "No, I will not remember the sorrow of his birth with that name. His name is Benjamin, son of my right hand." He drew the babe into a close embrace.

Benjamin squalled, seeking food as many newborns do.

"How will we feed him?" I asked.

"Haala gave birth a month ago," Noona said. "She has an abundance of milk. I will ask her to share with this poor motherless child."

She left the tent, returning sooner than I expected with a young woman. She must have stood with the others near the tent.

The woman, Haala, knelt next to Jacob. "Your son is hungry. I will feed him for you, in place of his lost mother. He will live to honor her. May I take him?"

Jacob resisted, but Benjamin's wail increased. He dried his tears on the blanket, then handed Benjamin to Haala. "Bring him to me after he eats, please."

She nodded, tucked the child close to her breast, and carried him from the tent.

The near silence hurt. Jacob continued to weep softly. I sniffed. *How can I go on without Rachel? We have been together since her birth. We shared Jacob through all these years, and she finally softened enough we could be friends once more. And now Jehovah takes her from me?*

I swallowed my tears and wiped my eyes on my sleeves. "She is at rest with Jehovah," I said, taking Jacob's arm. He turned and took me into his arms, weeping on my shoulder.

Bilhah joined us, her tears joining ours. Noora nudged us away. "I have much to do to prepare her body. Go mourn together."

"I will stay," Bilhah said. "She was my mistress. I have a responsibility to her." She turned and touched Rachel's body. "I loved her."

We took Rachel's body back to Beth-el and found a cave on a lonely hill to bury her in. Jacob, Joseph, and his brothers closed the cave so no robber nor animal could open or desecrate her final resting place. Jacob called the place Bethlehem. Bilhah, Zilpah, and I stood together for a time with Jacob, hugging and weeping for our lost sister. How would I live without her? How would Jacob?

Israel

Jacob came to my sleeping pallet the night after we buried Rachel. Together, we shared our grief at her loss.

"She waited so long for this child," I wept onto his shoulder.

"She had years with Joseph, years to be a mother to him," Jacob said through his tears.

"Why could not she raise Benjamin?" I lifted my head from his shoulder and stared into his eyes. "He and Joseph deserve to have their mother here to love them."

"I do not know. Joseph and Benjamin have you," he smiled through his tears, "and Bilhah and Zilpah. They will not lack a mother's love."

"Did you know?" I asked. "Did you know she would not survive?"

Jacob sat back and wiped his face with his huge palms. "I suspected. She was ill for so long. She became fragile and thin when she should have become rounder with Benjamin."

I nodded. I had similar fears for the same reason. "But did Jehovah tell you?"

"No. I did not know until Noora said she could save the child, but not the mother. I feared as I watched them work to bring him into the world." He gave his head a little shake. "But when she spoke those words, I knew. I knew Jehovah would take her home to Him. She had suffered enough." He closed his eyes, fighting back the tears.

I nodded. Her life had not been as easy as mine. I brushed my fingers across the scars on my face. "And now you are stuck with me, your ugly, scarred wife."

Jacob pulled me close into his arms and embraced me, love spreading from him to me in ways I had never felt before. "Leah, my dear, dear love," he whispered. "You have never been ugly. Your beauty is incomparable."

"Even to Rachel?"

"Rachel was my first love, a bright star with a temper and an intensity difficult to ignore. You, Leah, have had the quiet strength keeping me whole. I thank Laban every night for insisting I marry you."

I pushed away from him. "But you spent your nights with Rachel unless we tricked her or you."

"Rachel's temper ..."

"And your love for her was blind. We knew. We accepted it."

Jacob pulled me into his arms and kissed me as he had that first night so long ago when he thought I was Rachel. Fire burned in my blood.

"Oh, Jacob. What could have been?" I moaned.

"We had what was right for us, then and now." He leaned back once more. "I must share with you, for if not, I will burst." He sat on my sleeping pallet.

"Share? What do you have to share?" I settled next to him.

He sat back a little. "After the last sacrifice, I spent the night alone, communing with Jehovah."

"Oh? I thought you went in to Rachel." I could have bitten my tongue off at the hurtful thought.

His head swayed a bit. "Yes, for a short time, I knelt beside her and prayed for her and the babe. But I left, needing to be alone with Jehovah."

"I am sorry for my jealousy," I said.

"No need. I understand." He rolled his lips inward and breathed until he could speak again. "Jehovah called to me. As always, I listened."

"What did He say?" I whispered.

"He blessed me as he did so many years ago. Then he said I am no longer Jacob. My name is Israel. As He changed my grandfather's name from Abram, He changed mine to Israel. I have found worthiness in His eyes."

I gazed at Jacob. His soft smile and the way he glowed caused me to set my hand in my lap. I dared not touch him.

"He promised me more, commanding me once more to be fruitful, and multiply, as if twelve sons are not a multiplication. Abraham had sons, but sent them away. Father had two, Esau and me. And I have twelve sons. These will be faithful to Jehovah and multiply into a nation."

My eyes widened with each word. I held my breath, waiting for more.

"'A nation and a company of nations shall come from you,' Jehovah said. Kings shall come from my loins, even the King of Kings. And the land He gave to Abraham and Isaac, my father, will be mine, the land of my family. We are to stay together as one family, not separate from each other as Abraham sent away his other sons."

I allowed my breath to escape. My sons were worthy, even in their lack. They would become great.

"He said other things before He left me, but this is what I am allowed to share with you. I am now Israel, and our sons will continue, owning the land given to my father and grandfather as the children of Israel."

Jacob, or Israel, leaned forward and kissed me. "I feared I would be forced to divide my sons, send them away as Abraham did. I see the problems it caused. I did not know my uncles. We were alone. My sons do not have to fear that loss. We are a family who will bless the earth."

My smile, tentative at first, grew broader. "You will not cast me away?"

"I never would. Nor will I cast away your maidservants given to me in yours and Rachel's need. Bilhah and Zilpah and their sons are my family. They inherit the land together." He pulled me into a close embrace.

"Will it cause problems?"

"Not if they remember their God. Jehovah is a jealous God and will not bless them when they bow down to others. But He will remember and bless the sons of Israel."

"That sounds special," I murmured and lifted my lips, daring once more to kiss him.

"It is special."

We took our time preparing to leave the next day. None of us wanted to leave Rachel alone in that cave.

"Rachel is safe with Jehovah," Jacob told us as we prepared to mount our camels. "And I have been given a new name from Jehovah. I am no longer Jacob. I am Israel. You are the children of Israel."

A murmur spread through the camp, most repeating Jacob's words.

"Israel?" Reuben asked. "What does that mean?"

"One who struggles with Jehovah. In my struggles, He changed my name."

"How will it affect us?" Judah asked.

"Not much. For now, it means we return to introduce you to my father, Isaac."

Israel gave the signal, and we mounted our camels, prepared for another journey.

I turned to stare at the place on the hill, almost indistinguishable from any other spot. Our sons had covered it well. We did not want wild animals or robbers to despoil her resting spot. "Until we meet again, my dear sister."

Isaac

We three mothers, Bilhah, Zilpah, and I, shared in caring for little Benjamin as we traveled on toward Mamre and Isaac. We wrapped him next to our bodies, holding him safe and close to us, allowing him to sleep as newborns did.

Haala stayed back, keeping her own son wrapped close to her on the ride, until near time for Benjamin to wake. Then she gave her son, Safar, to her mother and rode forward, offering to feed Benjamin. I remembered knowing when my child needed to eat. My breasts would prickle and threaten to let the milk soak into my clothing if I did not find the child and feed him.

I wondered how Haala knew Benjamin would waken, for she also fed Safar. But she always knew and rode forward in time.

At night, Benjamin slept with Zilpah, for she had invited Haala and Safar to share her tent. When little Benjamin woke, Haala was there to feed him, as Rachel would have been.

I rode near the front of the caravan now, taking Rachel's place as honored wife. Since leaving Shalem, men rode in front and around us, watching for others who would try to destroy us or take our animals. We saw no more men.

Some women of Shalem complained of the drab, brown desolate landscape, knowing only their homes. But I did not complain.

We traveled over rough hills along the way. I loved the desert and watched for the smallest flowers gracing the earth. Some grew close to the ground, but intricate, tiny flowers decorated the plants.

The salt cedar trees scattered over the mountains. Their pink blooms brightened the view. The scattered red and pink desert roses, my favorite, brightened my mood. Bilhah had us all searching for the desert thyme she needed in her herbal remedies.

At the top of a hill, I glimpsed the blue sea in the distance to the west. In the east, another sea glittered.

"What are they?" I asked Israel.

"The sea to the west is a great sea, filled with fish and salty water. It extends farther than we know. The long, glittering sea you see to the east is the Salt Sea. As a child, my family sometimes traveled to the Salt Sea to gather salt. So much salt gathers along its shores, there is no need to distill away the water. We can gather salt from either sea. It is a blessing to the people of this area."

I turned and gazed at the great sea. "Will we ever go there?"

"It is but a two-day ride there. Perhaps we will go."

I sighed. "I have always wanted to go to the sea."

"Perhaps we will travel there."

Jacob, or Israel, I struggled to remember to call him by that name, glanced along the trail. "We will arrive soon. I remember this place. We will camp up ahead, and enter Mamre in the morning."

He rode forward, warning the lead men of his plans, and then back along the caravan, giving directions.

Tomorrow we would meet Isaac. Would he welcome us? Esau said he would. But Isaac is an old man, and Jacob, or Israel, had not brought his family to meet him.

When we stopped, I went among the women, warning them to clean and prepare themselves. "We are going into the presence of Israel's father, Isaac, tomorrow. We must go as honored women who support his son. We must make a favorable impression."

I found my sons and warned them as well to prepare to meet their grandfather. Israel had warned them already. Everyone brushed their clothing and cleaned themselves to prepare for the next morning.

Israel insisted we would enter Isaac's home village as a people joyfully returning home, not slinking in as an unwelcome son who had run away. When we lined up, prepared to enter Mamre, every person had cleaned themself.

I expected to see a city, perhaps smaller than Harran, but a neat, organized city. What I saw disappointed me somewhat. No one lived in a settled house. Everyone lived in colorful tents.

Flower and vegetable gardens edged their neat tents. Wide, rocked paths extended between each tent to the next and on around the place. Date palms, terebinth, and acacia trees shaded many tents. I did not expect to see this beautiful tent city.

I could not decide whether to call this a city or a village. But many more tents lined the paths than the tents we brought with us. Together we would become a small city, a small tent city — *if* Isaac allowed us to stay.

My stomach clenched at the thought of moving on. Where would we go? Who would protect us from the anger of the men in the lands surrounding Shalem? None had attacked us during our flight, but I continued to fear they would come.

Israel — it was becoming easier to use that name — patted my hand. "Do not fear my father. He is an old man, but he loves me. Remember, I returned often to meet with him during our days in Succoth."

I swallowed my fears and stared ahead, forcing a smile to sit on my face. I did not fear Isaac. I feared what we would do if he did not allow us to stay.

Israel led us into the settlement and had us dismount at the edge. "Set up our tents here," he told Tzevi. "We will move them to a permanent place later."

While men set up our tents and unpacked our possessions, Israel took my hand and called his concubines and children to join him. We strode down the wide lane leading to Isaac's tent.

An old man sat beneath a terebinth tree on a colorful blanket. Israel led us forward to greet him.

I rearranged Benjamin in his wrapping against me and waited for my six sons and Dinah to arrange themselves around me. Bilhah's Dan and Naphtali stood beside her, while Gad and Asher found places with Zilpah. Joseph stood beside his father.

A servant assisted the ancient man to stand as Israel led us toward him. When we came near, Israel fell to his knees, and we, his family, followed his example, falling to our knees before this ancient man.

His wizened face, wrinkled with age, with his white hair hanging past his shoulders, gazed at us. His piercing blue eyes, much like Israel's, shone with intelligence, welcoming us.

"Jacob. Jacob, my son," he cried in a voice stronger than I expected. "I heard you were coming. It is past time you brought your family to meet me."

He kissed his son's cheeks, and Israel stood. "Father, may I introduce my family?"

He beckoned me forward. "This is my first wife, Leah."

"Oh, ho. The one Laban insisted you marry first?" His merry voice induced me to smile.

"I am the ugly sister. Jacob desired my beautiful younger sister. Father could not entice another man to marry me, so he disguised me as Rachel and married me to your son. I expected to be turned out, but Jacob has always been kind to me."

Isaac kissed my cheek. "You were never ugly. I see your beauty. I see my Rebekah in you, beautiful and kind. Would that Esau had waited for you as Jacob waited for Rachel."

He lifted his head and looked around. "Where is your Rachel? I do not see her."

Israel swallowed. "Jehovah took her home. She could not survive the birth of her second son, Benjamin."

Isaac threw his stringy, thin arms around his son, and together they wept. After a long while, they separated, wiping their eyes.

"And the babe?" Isaac asked. "Did he live?"

I unwrapped Benjamin and held him close for his grandfather to see. "This is Benjamin, your youngest grandson, born two days ago."

Isaac touched his tiny face. "He will be a blessing to your family."

Israel insisted his father retake his seat before introducing his sons and concubines, though Reuben and some of the older sons had met their grandfather earlier.

Jacob seated me beside his father and sat beside me. He then called the others forward and introduced them, beginning with my sons and Dinah. Each bent to kiss his cheek and spoke soft words to him. After Dinah, Jacob introduced Joseph, then Bilhah and her sons, and Zilpah and her sons.

Isaac called to a servant and told him to prepare a feast for us. The man ran off to pass on the order to slaughter a steer and a ram.

We sat in a loose circle around Isaac and visited until Benjamin fussed. I stood to take him to Haala, but she was there, reaching for him.

Before long, the sons excused themselves to settle their animals. Bilhah and Zilpah, too, excused themselves. Bilhah went to examine our injured. Zilpah returned to supervise the preparation of the midday meal and food to offer to the women of Isaac's camp for the feast.

I stayed with Israel and Isaac, wondering when my sweet husband would share with his father the change in his name. He cleared his throat to speak when a shout rose from down the wide lane. We looked up to see Esau racing toward us. He slid to a stop, his stallion scattering stones as he reared back.

"At last," Esau cried as he leapt off his horse and ran to embrace my husband. "You brought your family. I heard you left Shalem."

Israel shrugged. "I was forced to leave. My sons ..."

"I heard. The men from all around Shalem —"

"Are they marching here for revenge?" Israel asked.

Esau shook his head. "They hide in their homes, fearing you and your sons will enter their homes and destroy them as you destroyed the men of Shalem."

"What?" Israel cried. "They fear me and my sons? Twelve men?"

"Destroyed all the men of Shalem," Esau said.

"After they deluded the men of Shalem, saying our daughter could not marry their man unless they all were circumcised like us. The son of their leader desired Dinah so deeply he convinced the men of his village he could have Dinah, and we would take their daughters, and trade with them if they all accepted circumcision. They expected exceeding wealth from us. Two of my sons went in three days after the rite, when all the men still lay on their sleeping pallets from pain, and slaughtered them. It was no honor." Israel bowed his head and held it in his hands.

Esau tipped his head back and roared with laughter. "Two men ... after circumcision..."

"It is not funny. It is a sin," Israel said, raising his voice as he seldom did.

"But it saved your little band," Esau said after hiccupping and swallowing his guffaws. "The men of the other cities do not know and now fear you."

"Have you gone before Jehovah in repentance?" Isaac asked.

"I did when I learned the actions of my sons, and again after offering sacrifice in Bethel," Israel said. "I was forgiven. Jehovah came to me and confirmed the promises given when I left Mamre so many years ago."

Esau gasped.

Isaac lifted his head. "Those were?"

"I received the promises you and Grandfather Abraham received. My family will become a company of nations, kings will come from me, and the land promised to Abraham and you, my father, will belong to our family."

Isaac nodded. "I have received the same word. Is there more?"

Israel swallowed. "Yes, there is more."

"Share with us," Esau said.

"My name was changed." Israel said, taking his time to speak the words. "I am no longer to be known as Jacob. I am now Israel."

"You struggled with Jehovah?" Esau asked.

Israel ducked his head. "Yes, when I left you so many years ago, I stopped at Bethel. I spent the night wrestling with Jehovah, seeking a blessing. Before He left me, He gave me the blessing I wanted."

"The blessing I gave you before you left us," Isaac said.

"Yes, He repeated your blessing. This time, when I stopped on the return here, He changed my name."

"Israel," Isaac whispered the name with reverence. "Jehovah never changed my name as he did for my father and now for you."

"Perhaps your name was right all along and did not need changing," Esau said.

"We know Jehovah loves you," Israel said.

"Yes, Jehovah loves me. I have been blessed, although I would have preferred to have my two sons with me through these past many years. Since your mother..." His voice broke, and he cleared away the tears clogging his throat. "Since Rebekah left me alone, I waited only to see you and your sons before welcoming a return home to Jehovah. I miss Rebekah, my mother, and my father. I am ready to go home."

"How many years have you lived?" I asked.

"I near my one hundred eightieth year, many more than I thought I would live, many more than I desired."

"I am happy you waited for me to bring my family home. I wish you could have met Rachel." Israel glanced at me and squeezed my hand. "She was a bright star with a temper and an intensity difficult to forget. Almost the opposite of my gentle, kind Leah. Jehovah blessed me with two beautiful, amazing women." He lifted my hand and kissed my fingers.

I smiled. "Two sisters in opposition to each other. Loving you kept us together."

"I know," Israel whispered. "I know."

"You have been blessed," Isaac said. "Thank you for returning to me. Your family will enlarge and strengthen our community."

"You will have us stay here with you?" Israel asked.

"My end will be soon. My people need a new leader." He waved at Esau. "You have a land and people you lead. Your people will be known throughout the world."

Esau nodded. "I do not need to return to Mamre. Jacob, er Israel, is welcome to it and to the lands around it. We are strong and happy in our own land."

Israel ducked his head. "I thank you. We will join your people. You are our leader."

"Until Jehovah takes me home," Isaac said.

A maidservant came and whispered in his ear.

Isaac shook his head.

She whispered more insistently.

"It seems I must rest. All I do is rest anymore. It is time to return to Jehovah." He paused and shook his head before speaking again. "I will return soon to enjoy the feast. Esau, will you stay?"

"I will. My sons accompanied me. It is time for my sons to know your sons, my brother. Let us help you to your sleeping pallet, then we will acquaint our sons with each other."

Israel and Esau helped their father to his tent to rest, then we walked to our tents and Israel called to his children to meet their uncle and cousins.

I left them and returned to my tent. The men needed time to themselves.

Goodbye

Isaac's feast, filled with lots of food and laughter, helped us get to know the people of Mamre and Esau, his wives, and sons. Rebekah's maidservants came to me to tell me about her and offer their services.

I had no need for more maidservants, since I had assigned five or six young women to each of the three women who looked to Israel as our husband. He had warned me of the attitudes of those with whom we would come in contact. Many from other lands based their understanding of a man's wealth on the number of maidservants his wives had. I agreed to consider them to help our family.

Early the next morning, a messenger came to wake us. Isaac was on his sleeping pallet, ill, and asked Israel to come to him.

"Do you want me to go with you?" I asked.

"Not now. Perhaps later. Father thought he was dying before."

I rose and dressed, wearing my blue dress and a blue shawl around my shoulders. On my head, I wore a matching tichel. I went out to sit in front of the tent to watch the sunrise. The eastern sky changed from black to purple to deep maroon, pinks, and blues until the sun lifted above the hills. It was a beautiful morning. The sky matched the blue of my dress and tichel.

A messenger ran toward Bilhah's tent. She soon appeared, tying her dress and tucking her tichel over her hair, then hurried toward Noora's tent. I watched, wondering why Bilhah would be called and why she would go for Noora. It must have something to do with Isaac's sickness.

Soon, the two women raced across our camp into the old camp of Mamre. Isaac must be sicker than Israel thought.

A young boy ran across the open space in the center of our camp, calling to me. "Leah! Leah!"

I stood. "Here I am."

"Israel sent me for you. He would like you to go to Isaac's tent."

"Did he call for his sons?"

"Another messenger has gone to get them. Come quickly, please."

I remembered the way to Isaac's tent, but followed the boy at a trot, hurrying past slow-moving women, many stretching as they stepped from their tents. My mind raced ahead. Was the kind old man who compared me to Israel's mother returning to Jehovah as my beautiful sister had? What would Israel do? He had not returned to stay since he had fled Esau, and now his father was dying.

The boy held the tent door open for me. I nodded to him, then saw Israel and Esau kneeling beside the low pallet. Beside each son ranged their kneeling sons. Esau's wives knelt beside him.

With a cry, I rushed to kneel next to Israel. "Isaac," I cried.

He opened his eyes and peered up at me. "Ah, Leah, my Rebekah's image. You have come."

I took his wrinkled, bony hand in mine. "You cannot leave us yet. I have not had time to get to know you."

In a weak, scratchy voice, Isaac answered. "But we have met, and I see my love in you. Care for my son, Israel. He will need your love and support in the coming years."

I turned to glance at Israel, then bowed over Isaac's hand and allowed my tears to spill.

"Do not weep, dear Leah." Isaac's voice strengthened. "You know me through my son. I will be with you and him in the coming days and years. Jehovah bless you." He gasped and lay back, unable to say more.

I knelt beside Israel's beloved father, his cool hand warmed by mine. Israel set his hand on my shoulder. We knelt like that for a long time. Zilpah joined us, kneeling on Israel's other side. Bilhah and Noora stood at Isaac's feet.

We finally sat back on our heels, waiting and watching, praying for him. "Bilhah told us he has little time left," Israel murmured in my ear.

The old man's chest sank in. his breathing slowed. We stared. Did it stop? I tried to breathe for him.

He gasped and sucked in a deep breath.

I breathed again.

Rough, ragged breaths escaped from Isaac's lips. It hurt to listen to him breathe.

I silently prayed for his release.

Israel set his hands on his father's head and prayed, calling on Jehovah to take his father home to live with his beloved wife and parents.

I tried to silence my stuttering, gasping breath and looked around at the others sitting near the ancient, beloved patriarch. Their surprised expressions softened, accepting Israel's prayer.

Isaac's breath stopped. I gazed at him. Not stopped, but so shallow I could not see nor hear it.

Noora slipped between Israel and Zilpah and set her fingers on his neck, searching for his lifeblood beating.

Isaac's chest stopped moving. I turned my gaze toward Noora. After a long, aching silence, Noora shook her head and dropped her hand. "He is gone," she whispered.

A lump filled my throat, but no more tears fell. I had spent them all during our vigil.

"Jehovah has taken our father home," Israel said.

"May Jehovah bless him and us," Esau said.

A woman I did not know pushed forward and set her fingers on Isaac's neck. "He is gone," she murmured. "I will prepare him."

"No," Israel said as he stood. "Esau and I will complete that task. We are his sons. It is our right."

"There is a cave in the hills," Esau said, joining Israel on his feet.

The rest of us moved from our knees to our feet, our sons moving easier than me.

"No," Israel said. "We will take him to Machpelah and bury him with Mother, Abraham, and Sarah."

"Eliphaz," Esau looked at his son on his right, "take Reuben and his brothers to prepare."

"Gather horses, a bull, and a wagon to carry our sacrifice," Israel said. "Prepare to go to Machpelah."

Eliphaz nodded and led his two brothers and our eleven sons out of the tent. I wrapped my arms around Israel's waist, squeezed him, and nodded to the other women.

We filed out of the tent, leaving Esau and Israel with their father. Zilpah, Bilhah, and I sat beneath the tall terebinth tree to wait. Esau's wives, Adah, Aholibamah, and Bashemath, joined us. We sat in muted conversation, learning more about the life of our husband's twin brother. It surprised me to see the sun pass the zenith, moving toward evening.

Maidservants brought us food left over from the previous evening's feast. We nibbled on it, our hunger depressed by our grief.

People from both our camp and Isaac's gathered, finding seats around the terebinth tree, while giving the six of us wives space.

Before the sun set, Reuben and the others returned with news they had everything prepared. They sat near us, speaking in low voices. The crowd grew, but the noise did not.

Not long after Reuben and his brothers returned, Israel and Esau stepped through the tent door, the blanket carrying Isaac's body between them.

The crowd silenced and stood to honor the patriarch who had led them for so many years. Tears flowed unheeded down the faces of men and women. I brushed my cheeks, expecting tears, but my face remained dry.

Israel and Esau took turns speaking about their beloved father and his love for Jehovah. Israel reminded us we would all return home to Jehovah's arms if we lived a righteous life as Isaac had.

After sharing with the crowd, Esau and Israel carried Isaac between them on a litter through the night to Machpelah. Our sons carried torches ahead and behind us, lighting our feet and the horses pulling the wagon with the sacrifice, and those following behind for us to ride home.

We arrived as the sun's first rays lifted above the eastern hills, shining on the stones covering the mouth of the cave. We women dozed waiting as Israel, Esau, and their sons uncovered the sacred burial cave.

Esau and Ishmael lifted Isaac's body from the red earth where they had laid him while uncovering the cave. They carried him inside and set him on a shelf near Rebekah. I stood beside Israel as he and Esau waited near the entrance for those who came with us to pass by Isaac, bending to speak their love to him.

Then, the family filed past, each one bending to speak in his ear. The sons came next, then Esau and Israel's wives.

"Thank you for your love and kind words," I whispered to him when it was my turn.

Israel caught my hand, keeping me with him as he bent to speak his last words to his father. A tear slipped from his nose onto the blanket. When he stood, he grasped my hand and led me out of the cave.

We stood waiting at the cave's mouth for Esau, who soon followed us out.

We each set a stone in the doorway, then our sons finished, raising the stones to cover the entrance, protecting Isaac, Rebekah, and the others from both wild animals and men.

We rested while Israel rebuilt the altar and prepared the sacrifice. I felt Jehovah's love as we thanked him for Isaac's life. I felt his presence and knew of His love for the family patriarch.

We eschewed the traveling tents, for on the horses we were not far from Mamre. We rode home to the waiting feast.

Isaac's people had prepared a funeral feast for all to share. This feast, only a night after the joyful feast Isaac had prepared to welcome us to Mamre, began as a somber event. But before it ended, people were swapping stories about Isaac.

The feast lasted long into the night. I stayed beside Israel most of the night. Men and women made their way to where we sat, offering their support and allegiance to Israel.

New Home

Israel and Esau met for hours the next day. We, their women, cleaned and aired the tent Isaac had used.

"This is not the tent he shared with Rebekah," Bashemath said. "He could not bear to sleep where they had spent their lives together."

I glanced around the small, dark tent. "This is smaller than I expected a leader of such a large clan would live."

"It is. He took a travel tent and claimed it as his own."

When we finished cleaning the small tent, Bashemath led me to a large, colorful tent. Someone had opened the door and rolled up the windows to allow fresh air inside.

"This is the tent Isaac and Rebekah shared." She led me inside.

A large open space for gatherings filled the front. In back, past a curtained door, a large pallet covered with beautiful blankets sat in the middle. Along the edges were baskets and trunks. Tables between the baskets held beautiful bowls and books.

I peeked into a basket and found pens, paper, sand, and other writing needs. "Rachel wrote her story," I whispered.

"So did Rebekah. She wanted others to know about her life."

"Have you seen it?" I asked.

Bashemath grinned and walked to a table and picked up a book. "Here it is."

"Have you read it?"

"Yes. She was gracious to me, and to Esau's other wives. You will want to read it." She handed it to me.

I flipped through the pages. "This will be interesting to read."

"You will have time," she said, running her finger along the table. She glanced at her finger. "The maidservants have kept this tent free of dust."

"Why will I have time?" I stepped to stand next to her.

"This will be your tent. Jacob, er Israel, will take this tent. It is the tent of the leader of these people. They will expect you to move in."

"I have a tent." I walked to a trunk and opened it.

"As nice as this one?"

I turned. "No. This is nicer than even the house I grew up in back in Harran." I looked through the contents of the trunk.

"It is no wonder our people live in tents. When we must move, we can take our homes with us."

"I have learned that in the last year. It is easier to keep things in baskets and trunks, ready to go." I set the lid down. Rebekah had beautiful lace table covers.

"You will learn to appreciate this tent," Bashemath said.

We walked out of the tent into the heat of the day. "How is it cooler inside?" I asked.

"The windows. Breezes blow across to cool it. The camel and goat hair and wool used to weave the fabric help keep it cool."

"It is so colorful and beautiful," I said. "Abraham had the best and most beautiful tent made for Sarah."

"Sarah?"

"This was Sarah's tent. Israel told me about it."

Bashemath nodded.

Warmth filled me. I never expected to see the tent Sarah lived in. "And you think they expect me to live here?"

She shrugged. "You and Ja — Israel will have to decide."

We returned to my tent, and Dida brought us tea and cakes. We sat in the front, under the awning, visiting and sharing stories of our lives. Adah and Aholibamah, Esau's other wives, and Zilpah and Bilhah, Israel's concubines, came to sit with us, sharing stories.

Evening came, and our husbands joined us. Dida and other maidservants brought us a small meal left from the previous two nights of feasting.

"Will you take the tent Father and Mother lived in?" Esau asked.

"Their tent? Is it still livable?"

"We went in it today," Bashemath said. "It looks like a maidservant has kept it clean in the years since her death."

"Perhaps," Israel said, glancing at me. "We shall see."

I nodded.

"We will leave you tomorrow," Esau said later, as we neared the end of the meal. "It has been wonderful to spend this time with you."

"Visit often," Israel said. "Father stayed here for many years. I hope I can do as he did."

"I will know where to find you now that you have returned to Canaan."

"I do not plan to leave Canaan again."

"We will be happier if I go home to the other side of the land. Our land is rich, but there is not space for both of us and our flocks here." Esau wiped his hands on a cloth. "I will miss your face, but it is best for us to separate our men and our flocks. Your sons will be kings of their lands, as mine will be kings of our lands."

"I look forward to your visit again soon," Israel said.

The brothers stood and embraced. Esau's wives and Israel's hugged.

As I hugged Bashemath, I murmured, "Come with Esau when he comes again."

"And you, when Israel comes to visit, come with him. We need to get together more often."

We rose early the next morning to wave goodbye.

Before the dust from their horses had settled, Sachia, the lead maidservant of Mamre, hurried to get Israel's attention. "Will you need help to move your possessions into the big tent?"

"The big tent?" Israel asked.

"The big tent your grandmother gave to your mother. It belongs to your wife now." She turned to me. "Will you need our help?"

I swallowed and gazed at Israel. He shrugged. "It is a woman's tent."

My tent? Do I need another tent? One that belonged to Rebekah and Sarah? It is beautiful. I could move in alone. My women can do it, but it will bring me closer to the women of this village if I accept help. If Israel is to be the leader of this community, I must do my part. They do not know Rachel, only me. I must do what I can for him.

"Yes, Sachia. I would appreciate your help. I have six maidservants. If you brought a few more, we could empty my tent faster."

And I can give my tent to Noora. She deserves a tent.

"I will return with some help," Sachia said, turning and walking away.

"You will live in that tent?" Zilpah asked.

"Have you been in it?" I asked. "It is nicer than my mother's home. If I am to help Israel lead the people of Mamre, I must accept the gift of that tent."

"I grew up in that tent," Israel said with a laugh. "Yes, I have been in it. We will move your tents close to that tent," Israel said, nodding to Zilpah and Bilhah. "You two need to be part of our family community."

"And our sons?" I asked.

"They will not want to live too close to us. Some will find women to marry."

"Joseph and Benjamin will need to stay closer for a time," Zilpah said, rocking baby Benjamin. "I will keep Benjamin with me."

"Joseph can —" I said.

"No, Joseph is too old to be living in a mother's tent," Israel said. "He will be given Isaac's tent. I saw you cleaned it. It is the right size for a young man."

"But he is too young to be alone with his brothers!" Bilhah argued.

"He will have a tent of his own, but it will be close to ours. He is not ready to join the young men."

We separated to pack our belongings yet again.

Woman's Leader

We settled into our new life in Mamre with few problems. The people who had looked to Isaac for leadership accepted Israel as their new leader. Since Rebekah had died before Isaac, the women had learned to seek guidance from Sachia. I did not insist that they come to me, but she often turned their questions my way.

I had not experienced having the leadership of so many women. Until the event at Shalem more than tripled our population of women, I had limited my leadership to the women servants who had worked for us in Harran. Even in Succoth, we did not increase the number of women servants. In Mamre, the number of women tripled again, for the guards, hunters, and herders who served Isaac had wives and daughters who had not served Isaac and Rebekah.

Sachia came to me in private, warning me of the questions and problems she had directed my way. She listened to me as I worked through their issues and encouraged me. Soon the women came to me before asking Sachia, trusting my judgment.

I spent many sleepless nights praying for understanding and wisdom. Israel noticed my concerns. "What keeps you awake, my love?" he asked one night after I had bounced on our pallet until he could no longer ignore me.

I sat up and turned to him. "The women of Mamre look to me to solve their disagreements. I fear I have not the wisdom to offer advice or judgment." I buried my face in my hands.

He set a gentle hand on my shoulder. "You have always acted fairly with the women in our household. Why do you worry?"

"The women were few then, and I knew them all intimately. These women are near strangers."

"Yet their problems are the problems of women, which you understand." I dropped my hands and gazed into his eyes. "How do you do it? Answering all those problems the men bring to you?"

He took my hands in his. "I often turn the question back to them. I ask what they think the answer would be, or what the other person would do. I let them resolve most of their problems."

"And when that does not work? What do you do?" I stared into his eyes, searching for the answer.

He inhaled and breathed out slowly. "I pray. If I can, I give them time to consider the solutions. I use the sense Jehovah gave me. You have more sense than any woman I know. Think what you would have done to you or for you. Most of the time, that will be the right answer."

I chewed on my lip and considered the problem brought to me that evening. "I know what I would do, and what each of the others wants done. No solution is the same."

He ran his hands through my hair, comforting me. "Is there common ground? Something common to all?"

I let his stroking of my hair soothe me as I considered his question. "Yes. And it will be the best solution. Now, if the women will accept it."

He patted my back. "I knew you would figure it out." He kissed me. "We have a long day tomorrow. Shall we sleep now?"

He pulled me into the comfort of his arms, and I soon slept.

When I presented the solution to the disagreeing women the next morning, they fell at my feet. I bent to help them stand.

"I am but a woman, like you are women. Do not worship me. We worship only Jehovah."

"But you gave us the answer we need."

"You could have done it yourself. I took it to Jehovah. You could have done the same."

"We do not receive answers from Him," one woman said, staring at her feet.

"We are not worthy," the other agreed, lifting her head long enough to speak, then ducking it again.

"How are you not worthy? You obey the commandments. I have seen it. What more do you need?" I could not believe they did not trust Jehovah.

"We have always depended on Isaac or Rebekah to speak to Jehovah for us," the first woman said, flicking her eyes up to me.

"Do you not pray for yourselves?" I said, trying to keep my surprise from my face.

"We join the prayers when Isaac, and now Isreal lead us in prayers."

"But never pray for yourselves? Never cry to Jehovah for individual needed blessings? Not even in your deepest despair?"

The women did not lift their heads. After a moment's hesitant thought, one lifted her head. "In my deepest despair, yes."

"And did you not discover an answer to your concerns?"

She rolled her eyes upward, thinking. "I did. Jehovah answers my private prayers, but He does not speak to me."

"Perhaps not in words, but as you offer prayers, personal, private prayers, Jehovah answers. You hear his words in the warmth of your heart, the love you feel, the surety of the answer. Is it not so?" I lifted an eyebrow in question.

The women thought on my words and nodded. "It is so," the first said. "But I did not recognize Jehovah's word in it."

I smiled. "It was there."

I met with other women, teaching them to recognize the answers coming from Jehovah. We met in groups, and the women worked together to make their lives happier and better.

Israel took me to visit Esau and Bashemath. Her tent home was lovely and comfortable, though not as big as the tent I received from Rebekah.

We enjoyed our time together. I loved having another sister.

Dreams

In those early years that we lived in Mamre and our sons spent more time with the animals, Israel kept Joseph home more than he sent him to work in the fields or herd the flocks. The other sons began to believe their father preferred the younger son over them.

I remembered Issachar's complaints before we left Succoth. Rachel made it more difficult for her son to fit in with the men.

One morning, Zebulon came to visit me before taking the sheep to a new pasture. "Mother, you need to speak to Father."

"Oh? What is the problem?"

"My brothers complain about Father's keeping Joseph home when he should go into the hills with us. He prefers Joseph to us."

"Your father loved his mother."

Zebulon huffed out a breath. "We know, but it is time Joseph became a man. He is sixteen now. He cannot be held back like Benjamin."

"Benjamin is a little child."

"But Joseph is not. He is a man and should be treated as one." Zebulon shrugged. "Father should know better. Joseph should want the ability to be a man."

I nodded. "I will speak to your father."

Perhaps Zebulon spoke the truth. Israel held Joseph back because of his love for Rachel. He tried to protect his younger son, born of her. Although he loved me, Israel continued to hold his great love for her in his heart and sought to keep her sons safe.

When I brought the problem up to Israel, he shook his head. "I cannot send Joseph where he might be hurt. What would his mother think?"

"What does Joseph want?"

"He asks to go with his brothers."

"And?"

Israel set his head in his hands. "I cannot do it. Not yet. I cannot lose her son."

Other sons came to me asking for my help. I tried, but Israel struggled to let Joseph leave Mamre with his brothers or alone.

I started waking many times at night, needing to relieve myself. I worried about it and struggled with exhaustion from it.

But other things drew my attention. Our sons became angry and hateful at the perceived preferences Israel gave to Joseph.

Levi and Simeon came to me one afternoon.

"Why does Father prefer Joseph?" Levi asked.

"Does he?" I asked.

"He keeps him close to Mamre, rather than sending him out to distant lands to feed the flocks," Simeon added.

"He is but seventeen years," I argued, knowing Rachel would have prevented him from going as far as Simeon or his other brothers went.

"We went into the wilderness at that age. We were out guarding our flocks among strangers in Succoth when we were younger than Joseph."

"And your brothers were with you," I said.

"And we would be there to protect Joseph," Simeon cried.

"Joseph is Rachel's oldest son. Israel remembers how she desired his protection." I grimaced in memory of her protective care.

"It is time to allow him to be a man." Simeon set his fists on his hips.

"He is yet a lad." I narrowed my eyes.

"Because Father does not allow him the space to become a man." Levi's hands moved with his words, ending with a heavy sigh.

"Give him time. He will give him space to grow." I forced a smile.

"Perhaps," Simeon said with a frown.

They were not convinced. I would have to speak to Israel about it once more.

Before I could, Israel confirmed Joseph as his birthright son. We knew Reuben had lost that privilege, as had Simeon and Levi, but I had hoped he would give it to Judah.

He did not. Joseph received a long coat to cover his clothing, an outward symbol of Israel's promise that Joseph would have the birthright.

After that, I lost all hope that Joseph's older brothers would remember their love for Rachel and treat their brother well. What was once gentle teasing became hostility. At every opportunity, they tripped him, striving to make him feel and look clumsy. Their frustration with their brother intensified.

I struggled with my health and had no strength to remind them to treat their brother with grace.

Then, it became worse when Joseph dreamed dreams.

One evening, Joseph came to his father seeking understanding.

"I have dreamed a dream," Joseph said. "I shared it with my brothers, but they hate me for it."

"Sit," Israel said. "Share your dream with me."

I handed Joseph a cushion to sit on. "Be comfortable while you share."

I returned to my cushion next to Israel.

"I dreamed a dream I do not understand. Perhaps you can help me interpret the dream," Joseph said.

"And the dream was?"

"We were binding sheaves of grain in the field. Each of us had a sheaf. And my sheaf arose and stood upright, while the sheaves of my brothers bowed down to my sheaf."

I stared at Israel. "Is Joseph to rule over our sons?"

"That is what my brothers asked. They asked if I should rule them or have authority over them. They do not like my dream, and hate me for it."

Israel nodded. "It would cause problems among your brothers. They are older. They have protected you in your youth, and now you tell them you will be their ruler and have authority over their lives."

Joseph ducked his head. "I know. What should I do? Is this a dream or did it come from Jehovah?"

"It came from Jehovah. To stay safe, you should not remind your brothers of the dream."

Joseph nodded. "I can do that."

But the hostility from his brothers increased. When I saw Judah tripping Joseph, I called him to me.

"Yes, Mother?" Judah said. "Are you well? You look unwell."

"I am Judah," I said, and coughed. "But when you trip your brother, you make me more unwell. Joseph does not deserve your cruelty."

"Did you hear what he dreamed? He acts as if Jehovah Himself sent him the dream. He thinks all his brothers will bow down before him."

I nodded. "Has he not stopped talking about it?"

"Yes, but we see it in his eyes. He thinks about it all the time."

"If it is to be, do not give him reason to mistreat you."

Judah opened his mouth to argue, then shut it again. "Yes, Mother. I will stop teasing him. Will that help you get well?"

"It will help."

Judah bent to kiss my forehead. "I will do my best." He turned to leave.

"Tell your brothers to stop as well."

He waved. "I will tell them, but I cannot promise they will listen."

The cruelty slowed for a time.

Then Joseph returned to talk to Israel.

When he settled on his cushion, Joseph chewed on the inside of his mouth and ran his hands through his hair.

"Did you dream again?" Israel asked.

"If it were the only dream, I would say nothing. I want to believe it was a dream, my imagination. But it was not."

"You dreamed another dream, my son?" Israel asked. "Tell it to me."

"Last night, I dreamed another dream. I dreamed of the sun, the moon, and eleven stars, all bowed down to me. I did not ask for it. I do not desire such a thing to happen."

I gasped.

Israel's face went red. His nostrils flared, and his breathing became heavy. "What is this dream you have dreamed? Not only do you dream your brothers will bow down to you and obey your commands, but you dream that your mother and I will also bow down to you? It is not right for a father and mother to bow down to their son, especially their younger son."

"Can I control my dreams? They come from Jehovah," Joseph cried.

"Take your dreams to your tent and discuss them with Jehovah," Israel commanded.

Joseph rose and left.

Israel raged. "How can he expect me, his father, to kneel to him? It is not right."

"Can you argue with the visions of Jehovah?" I asked. "Perhaps they are true and came from Him."

"Perhaps," Israel replied and sat back down with his chin in his hand.

Torn Coat

Joseph's older brothers learned of his second dream. I suspect he told them, for he struggled to keep things to himself. He did not speak of his dream to his father again, but his brothers' cruelty increased. He must have shared it.

Israel saw the problems between his sons and used that as a reason to keep Joseph apart from his older brothers. One day, four years after coming to Mamre, months after Joseph's dreams, he sent our sons and their herders to take their flocks to Shechem, where sweet grass grew. He hoped the time and separation would help quell their anger toward Joseph.

Then, about two weeks later, hoping it would help them renew their love for their brother, Israel sent Joseph to take supplies to his brothers and ensure all was well. He expected Joseph to return within a week with news.

But Joseph did not return that week. Nor the next.

Israel feared for his younger son and spent many nights in prayer.

At last, Reuben and the others returned, leaving their flocks with herders. They found us sitting beneath the terebinth tree, in prayer for Joseph.

"Have you seen Joseph?" Israel asked. "Have you seen your brother?"

"We left Shechem and went on to Dotham. We did not see Joseph. But we heard he was looking for us and returned with our flocks back to Shechem." Reuben stopped to take a deep breath. "We found this."

He unwrapped a bloody, torn coat that looked much like the one Israel had given Joseph. "We found this along the way. It looks like ... Is this Joseph's coat? It looks like a lion attacked him."

Israel stretched his hand out and jerked it back.

I sat still, holding my breath.

Israel reached forward once more, touching the coat, pulling his hand back as if it burned him.

I expelled my breath but said nothing. I feared the coat was Joseph's. What would Rachel say if she were there?

One last time, Israel leaned toward the coat and took it from the ground where Reuben had left it.

We knew it was the coat Israel had given to Joseph. Torn and bloody as it was, its distinctive color identified it as Joseph's. But where was Joseph?

Israel held the coat up, then clutched it to his chest.

"Joseph! O Joseph!" he wept. "Why did I not believe you? Why did I send you alone to find your brothers? What happened to your sling, your staff? How did a lion take you? I trusted Jehovah to protect you. Oh, Joseph." He fell to the ground, weeping.

We all tried to comfort him, but Israel would not allow it.

"I shall go to my grave mourning my son as my father mourned me," he cried.

He stumbled into our tent and fell on the pallet, weeping.

Oh, Joseph. What will I tell your mother?

Illness

My sons married. Simeon married Najeeb, who loved him even after he had destroyed the men of Shalem. Reuben and the others also found wives. Some from among the young women of Mamre, some from among the young women of Shalem. I breathed a sigh of relief when none showed an interest in Ismet.

"We do not trust Ismet," Judah told me when I mentioned her.

My heart rested at the thought. But my body did not. I was always thirsty and ran often to the latrine to relieve myself. I lost weight, even though I ate my usual food.

I could not rest, for the women continued to turn to me to resolve their problems. I knew Bilhah worried about my health, but I was only tired because I could not sleep.

Zilpah brought me special tidbits, hoping to help me gain weight. It did not help. I continued to lose, becoming thin and fragile. I needed to increase the seams in my clothing and tie the sashes tighter to keep my dresses on me.

Fatigue set in. I struggled to have sufficient strength to bounce my grandsons on my knee. I could only hold them for a short time before setting them back on the floor to play. I slumped in exhaustion as I watched them, dreaming of the days when my sons crawled on my lap and ran with me in the meadows outside our home in Harran.

No longer.

I had little strength to play for long with my grandsons.

Israel prayed for me at night, begging Jehovah to help me heal.

"He will heal me in his time," I told him.

"I cannot lose you too," he whispered. "I love you, my Leah."

I kept a cup of water or tea near me, drinking more than ever. But I continued to thirst. Nothing would quench my thirst. The women still brought their problems to me.

I dreamed of Joseph as the lion attacked him. Later, I dreamed of him locked in a prison. Each time, Rachel stood beside me, asking me why I had not taken better care of her son. How was he gone from us?

Bilhah brought Noora and Lael to help care for me. They gave me potions and draughts. Some helped, but none did for long. I knew Jehovah would take me home before the others were ready for me to go.

Then, Zilpah struggled to help in the cooking tent, giving the chore to her assistants. She complained of dizziness and difficulty breathing. I feared and prayed for her.

When Israel came to see me, I begged him to bring me a stack of vellum and extra ink.

"Why do you need a stack of vellum?" he asked.

"I will not live much longer. I need to do as Rachel did and write my life story for my children. Dinah and our sons and their children need to have something to read to remember me."

He bowed his head. When he lifted it, tears filled his eyes. "I remember when Rachel asked for vellum. I did not expect her to leave me so soon. Do not leave me. I need you."

"I will stay as long as Jehovah allows it," I promised.

He gave me a stack of vellum and extra ink, carrying it to my tent. "Writing will help you rest. But do not leave me."

"I will try to stay with you," I said, caressing his face.

Zilpah disappeared from the cooking tent. Bilhah told me she worked to write the story of her life as well.

"I fear she is ill, more than she admits," Israel murmured.

"She will heal," I said.

"She, like you, is in Jehovah's hands. I must trust him to bless you." He leaned forward and kissed me. "I do not know what I will do if Jehovah takes you two home."

"He will sometime. I plan to stay with you until the end." I smiled up at him from my seat on my sleeping pallet.

He smiled, but grief filled his eyes.

Bilhah visited me often, seeking to keep me healthy. But I had infections that would not heal.

One day I heard Bilhah's keening cry. Too sick to rise from my sleeping pallet, I lay in fear, waiting to learn what had happened.

Eventually, she came to my tent with tears streaming down her face.

"Zilpah said it was only a stomach problem, and she suffered from the heat."

"But the day is not hot," I said.

"No, but she suffered as she did in the heat of summer. I helped her to her pallet and hurried away for a bowl of cool water." She caught her lip between her teeth. "But when I returned, she was gone. She had no one to hold her hand, no one to tell her of their love. She went home to Jehovah alone."

"She is gone?" I gasped.

Bilhah bowed her head. "Yes. Jehovah took her home. You must do all you can to stay with me and Israel. He will be lost without you."

I struggled to sit. "Take me to her."

"You are too weak."

"No. She must know I loved her. She and I have been together since we were ten. I must go see her."

Bilhah called Benjamin to help.

At fourteen, Benjamin had grown tall and strong. He lifted me in his arms and carried me to Zilpah's tent, a tent he had vacated for a tent of his own only two months earlier.

He ducked to enter the door, then set me next to Zilpah, who lay on her pallet. Her face had lost the worry lines. I expected to see her face filled with pain. Instead, a small smile graced her face. The pain of her last years was gone.

"Zilpah!" I cried. "No! I was to go home first."

Benjamin knelt next to me and laid his head next to her and sobbed. "Mother Zilpah. Do not leave me."

We knelt like that until Israel found us. "She has gone home to Jehovah. She has no more pain. Do not weep."

He lifted Benjamin from his knees and hugged him. "Tell Bilhah it is time to prepare her body. We will take her to the cave in the hills to the north. Can you go prepare it for her?"

Benjamin nodded and left.

Israel lifted me into his arms. "You cannot leave me too. Promise me you will stay with me." He bent to duck out the door.

"I will stay with you as long as Jehovah allows me. I would not leave you unless Jehovah wills it."

"I love you, Leah. You know that?"

"I do, Israel. I thank my father for his deceit every day."

"As do I, dear Leah. As do I."

He set me back on my sleeping pallet and kissed me. "Do not forget."

Gad and Asher did not want their mother to be buried at Machpelah. It was too far away for them. Instead, they took her to a cave near Mamre that Joseph had found.

Bilhah came in the next day to tell me about Zilpah's burial. "Israel wept as he did when Rachel died," she said. "He is losing his women."

"When I go, he will have only you to bless him. Treat him well. He will need your love."

"You will not leave us, too!" she cried.

"Not soon, I pray. But Jehovah will call me home."

"I pray it is not for a long time. Israel needs and loves you.

After Zilpah's death, the women stopped bringing their problems to me. I missed them. They came to visit, but shared problems with another, probably Bilhah.

My health continued to decline. I knew Jehovah would take me before I was ready and worked as often as I could on my story between my bouts of illness. Bilhah, Noora, and Leal gave me different tinctures and teas. None helped for long. I no longer had the strength to leave my pallet. I will leave my husband, and my sons and their families with Bilhah.

That night, Israel came to see me as he did every evening.

"Are you better?" he asked, pulling me onto his lap.

I clung to him, too weak to sit on my own, and shook my head. "I fear I am near the end."

"No!" he cried. "What will I do without you? You have been my strength through all these years."

"Since you lost Rachel?" I asked.

"No, since Laban forced me to marry you. Will you forgive me?"

"Forgive you? Forgive you for what?" I leaned back in his arms to gaze into his face. He cradled me in his arms, holding me so I would not fall.

"I allowed Rachel to decide where I spent my time." He kissed me.

"You loved her more than you loved me." I kissed him.

"I loved you as well. I should not have allowed her such control." A tear slipped from his eye. "Will you forgive me?"

"I forgave you long ago, while we lived in Harran. I knew my sister's temper and your love of her. When you told me you loved me as well, I no longer minded her jealousy."

"You are an amazing woman, Leah. Why can you not stay with me?"

I set my head on his shoulder. "I do not know. Perhaps I must report to my sister and explain what I have done with her family since she left."

He kissed me on the cheek. "You have cared for us well, as you did before she left us." He sucked in a deep breath. "Oh, Leah. What will I do without you?"

"You will bring Bilhah to this tent and love her as you always have. Treat her well. She deserves the same love you have given me."

"You want me to bring her here?" He tilted his head back to stare into my eyes.

"Why not? It is the tent belonging to the wife of the leader. You are the leader. She will be the only wife you have left."

"If you insist."

I set my head on his shoulder, too weak to hold it up.

I do not know how much longer I have. Writing this weakens me.

I pray Jehovah blesses my beloved Israel and our sons.

For women and sisters
who share more than they expected.

Book Club Questions

1. Leah suffered from an illness when Rachel was born. How did this affect their relationship? Do you think it would have been different if the disease had not scarred her face? Have you or someone you know changed a relationship because of a tragedy? How could it have been resolved differently?
2. Leah, along with all the maids, dreamed of Jacob. Several times in the book it is suggested that things may have been different if Esau had come to marry one of the girls. How would things have been different if Esau had come with Jacob? What if they had come earlier?
3. Laban insisted he find a husband for his older daughter, Leah, first. Beyond law or custom, why would he have insisted on having Leah married first? He appears to his daughters as selfish. What other reasons could he have had? Have you experienced times when someone seemed to be greedy when the motives were different?
4. Leah feared Jacob would go to the judges of Harran and demand an invalidation of the marriage. Why did Jacob choose not to go to the judges? How would it have changed Leah's life? Have you given or received compassion similar to the compassion Jacob showed Leah? How did it change lives?
5. Leah conceived in the first week of her marriage, while Rachel could not have children for many years. They wondered if this was a pattern with the women in the family. Sarah and Rebekah were also required to wait. Why

would Jehovah bless Leah and not Rachel? What could they have gained from the requirement to wait longer than other women to have children? Did Leah's children show she was less loved by Jehovah? Why or why not?

6. Leah received a commandment to offer Zilpah to Jacob to be his concubine. She knew it would cause even greater challenges for her and Rachel. Why did she use the excuse of her empty womb and not share the actual reason? How did this help or hurt Leah's relationship with Rachel?
7. Jacob took his sons to work with the animals earlier than the usual eight years. Why would he decide this would be necessary? How did Leah come to terms with having her little boys become men so early? Would you struggle to allow a son to work with their father earlier than you expected? What would help you agree?
8. Leah considered Dinah's friendship with the girls in Shalem a good thing for her daughter. Three people suggested reasons for Shechem taking Dinah. Which purpose seems most likely, Shechem, Dinah, or Ismet's description? Could there be another actual cause?
9. Leah became a leader of the women in Mamre after Isaac's death. She struggled to feel prepared. What had she done in the years since her marriage to Jacob to prepare her for the new responsibility? How did she grow into it? Have you or someone you know received assignments they were not ready to assume? How did you get the help and confidence to continue?

Acknowledgements

Another book written and published, and you read it! Thank you.

I give thanks to the readers who asked me to write this series. These last four books took me much longer than I expected, more than a year. I have learned much about the lives and characters of Jacob's wives and concubines. It has been good for me.

I thank my patient sweetheart, Jack. He has always supported me as I write and ignore him. He helps me get my books written.

I am grateful to my family, who continue to support me. My parents are old. Dad can no longer read my books, but he always encourages me. My children continue to support me as well. I am blessed with a wonderful family.

Without the help and encouragement of ANWA (American Night Writers Association) this would have taken much longer to prepare for your reading pleasure. Thanks go especially to my friend and supporter, Carol Malone.

As always, I thank my wonderful editor, Marsha Ward. Her careful editing makes this book better for you to read. Once more, Dar Albert has created a beautiful cover. I give both talented women my profound gratitude.

I thank my AngelCAST team for a read of the final version, finding the last typos and mistakes. Any they missed are my responsibility.

Last, and most important, I give gratitude to you, my reader, for choosing to read this book of fiction. Thank you for reading. I would love to hear whether you liked it.

Did You Enjoy This Book?

If you did, will you do something for me?

I'm an independent author, publishing my books without the backing of a major publisher. That means no six-figure advances and no advertising budget. This makes it difficult to promote my novels and put them in places new readers can find them. But you can help me.

Honest reviews and genuine "word-of-mouth" advertising make all the difference. I'm not asking for one of those awful book reports I used to try not to sleep through, that you did in school. What will help me is if you would leave an honest star rating and a couple of sentences on the bookseller's site where you purchased this book. Or a brief review on your blog. Or tell your friends about it on your favorite social media sites.

Let people know what you liked about this book, and why they might like it, too. And if there was something you didn't like, you can say that, as well. Constructive criticism helps me write a better book next time.

But please. No spoilers!

Would You Like a Free Book?

If you have not yet agreed to receive my weekly newsletter, Angelique's Historical Fiction Reader, maybe now would be a great time to join. If you would like a short story about Eve assisting Adam, click here[1] to receive *Avenging Angel.*

If you want to read the short story about Shamgar, the healer who helped Ziva and Crites, click here[2] to receive *Damaged Healer.*

If you currently receive my weekly newsletter and did not receive one of these free books, let me know. I'll be happy to forward you a link for either book.

Angelique@AngeliqueCongerAuthor.com

Happy Reading,

Angelique

---

1. https://dl.bookfunnel.com/to6h2blg9y
2. https://dl.bookfunnel.com/ldg1thkpcj

Books by Angelique Conger

Ancient Matriarchs

Eve, First Matriarch

Into the Storms: Ganet, Wife of Seth

Finding Peace: Rebecca, Wife of Enos

Moving into Light: Zehira, Wife of Enoch

Out of Darkness: Imma, Wife of Noah

We Stood Beside Them: Other Wives of the Patriarchs

Lost Children of the Prophet

Lost Children of the Prophet

Captured Freedom

Abandoned Hope

Brotherly Havoc

Betrayed Trust

Convicted Deliverance

Trouble Escaped

Contrary Devotion

Impassioned Grief

Love Defied

Hidden Purpose

Concealed Innocence

Struggle for Limhah

Combating Cults

Fighting Foreign Armies

Defending Faith

Into Egypt

Out of Egypt

Discovery

About the Author

Many would consider Angelique Conger's books Christian-focused, and they are, because they tell stories of women and events in the Bible. She writes of people who believe in Jehovah. However, though she's read the Bible and searched for more about these stories, not finding much to help, her imagination fills in the missing information, creating fascinating stories that keep readers wanting more..

Angelique Conger discovered the wonders of writing books later in her life. Books, however, have always been important to her. As a little girl in a small town, she received a library card of her own at the tender age of five, unusual in those days. She made good use of it.

Angelique reads a book, or three at once, much of the time. She reads most genres of books and, until a few years ago, only toyed with writing them. Since beginning her creative journey, she has spent hours each day learning the craft of writing and editing.

Angelique lives in Southern Nevada with her husband and two cats, who show love by sharing her pillow and sleeping at her feet. She enjoys visits from her grandchildren and their parents.

Don't miss out!

Visit the website below and you can sign up to receive emails whenever Angelique Conger publishes a new book. There's no charge and no obligation.

https://books2read.com/r/B-A-NFPH-ACZWI

www.ingramcontent.com/pod-product-compliance
Lightning Source LLC
LaVergne TN
LVHW041113080826
845145LV00007B/1802

* 9 7 8 1 9 4 6 5 5 0 8 4 2 *